X·MEN®

SHADOWS OF THE PAST

COMING SOON

The Science of the X-Men
by Link Yaco and Karen Haber

X-Men: The Chaos Engine Trilogy
by Steven A. Roman and Stan Timmons

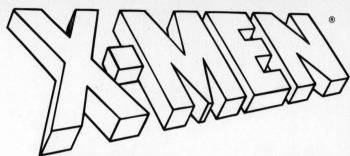

SHADOWS OF THE PAST

MICHAEL JAN FRIEDMAN

INTERIOR ILLUSTRATIONS BY

JOSÉ LADRÓNN

bp books inc
New York

DISTRIBUTED BY SIMON & SCHUSTER, INC

Special thanks to Mike Thomas, Mike Stewart and Lili Malkin.

X-MEN: SHADOWS OF THE PAST

A BP Books, Inc. Book

PRINTING HISTORY
BP Books, Inc. hardcover edition / June 2000

The BP Books World Wide Website is
http://www.ibooksinc.com

ISBN 0-7434-0018-6
PRINTED IN THE UNITED STATES OF AMERICA
10 9 8 7 6 5 4 3 2 1

To Gil Kane—*MJF*

To Francisco Ruiz, Studio F—*JL*

CHAPTER ONE

rofessor Charles Xavier adjusted the plaid woolen blanket that covered his legs and looked out over the rolling, green hills of the Westchester Hills Cemetery. There were gravestones as far as the eye could see under the crisp, blue autumn sky.

Xavier gazed at the nearest of them, a simple rounded marker that stood at the head of an empty, rectangular grave. He inspected the words carved into it, studied the texture of the stone, and sighed.

Not that he was any stranger to death. Xavier had lost his parents to it, many years earlier. He had lost one of his most promising students to it. He had even lost his son. But he had never quite gotten used to the finality of it.

After all, he was a man of considerable resources, assets and abilities, which far outweighed the liability of his crippled legs. He found it difficult to accept defeat of any kind, even when his opponent was the most implacable adversary of all.

So as Xavier sat in his wheelchair by the open grave of an

old friend, autumn sunlight filtering through the branches of a tall old hemlock, he couldn't help feeling he should have done something to *rescue* Jeremiah Saunders. He couldn't help feeling that the man's death was somehow his fault.

"Looks like we're early," said a voice behind him.

Xavier looked back over his shoulder at Bobby Drake, the baby-faced young man who had been one of the very first students at his Xavier Institute for Higher Learning. "So it would seem," he replied.

They were silent for a moment. The professor heard the wind rustling brittle autumn leaves.

"Is this good?" asked Bobby.

"Good?" Xavier echoed. It took him a moment to divine his companion's meaning, but he finally understood what Bobby meant. "You mean am I close enough to the grave?"

It was only after he had said it that he realized the question could have been taken two ways. The thought gave him a bit of a chill.

"Are you?" asked Bobby, apparently oblivious to the double entendre the professor had uttered.

"Yes," said Xavier. "I am fine, Bobby, thank you."

"You're welcome," said the young man. "Let me know if you change your mind, all right?"

"I will," Xavier assured him, as grateful for Bobby's company as he was for his assistance.

They waited for another couple of minutes, during which time the professor adjusted his blanket twice more. He wasn't pleased with the wait, but he was used to it. It was the price of punctuality.

Finally, others began to approach the gravesite in twos and threes—perhaps a couple dozen people in all, each one dressed in an appropriately dark suit or dress. Next came the long, black hearse, backing up to the empty grave so the

4

cemetery workers could haul the mahogany coffin out and lay it on the hard, cold ground.

Finally, a silver-haired, walrus-moustached man in a gray corduroy sports jacket made his bowlegged way through the gathering. Xavier recognized the fellow as Tristam Carter, the dean of Empire College and one of the deceased's longtime colleagues.

"Thank you for coming," said Carter in a gravelly voice. He looked around at the assembled mourners. "All of you." He took a folded piece of paper out of his pocket. "I'll try not to be too long-winded."

A breeze came up, ruffling the leaves again. This time, it had the smell of distant hearth fires about it.

"Jeremiah Saunders had a good, long run," the dean began. "He did what he wanted to do with his time on Earth, and he did it better than anyone else I know. Certainly, Jeremiah's Nobel Prize is ample proof of that. After Watson and Crick, I can't think of anyone who contributed more to the understanding of human genetics."

It was no exaggeration, thought Xavier. Even he had a long way to go before he could eclipse Saunders' efforts.

"Jeremiah wasn't a religious man," Carter said. "He made mention of that several times in the seventeen years in which we worked together. He didn't believe in empty rituals, he would often say.

"And yet," the dean continued, "Jeremiah believed very strongly in the existence of a divine plan. How else, he would ask me, could everything in nature fit together so perfectly? How could it all work, despite the complexity of the challenge? And he believed that nowhere was this plan manifested more splendidly than in his chosen field . . . genetics."

Xavier recalled the first time he had attended one of Saunders' classes. Barely in his forties, the dark, intense-looking Saunders was already one of the country's leading experts on genetically-linked diseases.

By that time, the teenaged Xavier had come to realize he was no normal human being—and that his differences lay somewhere in his genetic makeup. As a result, he was far and away the most attentive student in the entire cavernous lecture hall.

By the end of the hour, the younger man knew he had found his calling. And Professor Saunders was the one he had to thank for it.

"Jeremiah wasn't very outgoing," Dean Carter noted. "He didn't make many friends in his lifetime. But the friendships he made were genuine. They were true and lasting. And as you know—or you wouldn't be here today, mourning Jeremiah's passing—he prized the people closest to him as if they were chests of precious treasure."

With that, the dean turned to a tall, handsome young man with dark, wavy hair, who had a stocky, red-haired woman at his side. The fellow was standing in stunned silence by Saunders' coffin, his eyes lowered as if unable to look at the polished surface of the mahogany box.

His name was Jeffrey. He was the genetics professor's grandson, whom Saunders had raised from the age of three and a half.

Certainly, the death of his only caregiver would have been reason enough for the youngster to seem dazed and confused. But the problem went deeper than that, Xavier knew.

It wasn't just grief and shock that muddled Jeffrey's thoughts as he stood in the autumn light. The young man suffered from what his grandfather had sometimes called "a condition."

Saunders had always employed the same words, the same euphemism for Jeffrey's problem. It was as though his grandson were afflicted with something too horrible to speak of out loud, or else something too insignificant to even bother naming.

Strange, Xavier thought, that a man of science—a man whose expertise was in genetics—would be so circumspect in his description of mental retardation. And yet, that was the way in which Jeremiah Saunders had chosen to deal with his grandson's situation.

Why? Xavier asked himself. He had never pressed the matter, so he didn't know the answer.

But now, with his friend gone, he was inclined to guess. Was it the knowledge that, with Jeffrey's parents deceased, the professor's brilliance would never be passed on? Or did it hurt too much to look at such an undeniably handsome boy and be forced to accept his limitations? Xavier sat back in his wheelchair and wished that he asked. He should have imposed on their friendship at least that much, if only to understand his friend a little better.

"I don't know how much of this you can understand," Carter told Jeffrey, "but we all thought a great deal of your grandfather. He was as kind to each of us as he was to you. And though you were the apple of his eye, we like to think we were planted somewhere in that orchard as well."

That drew a few chuckles from the other mourners. But not from Jeffrey. He didn't even seem to know the dean was addressing him.

Xavier pressed his lips together. The last time he had seen Jeffrey, just a few months earlier, the boy was playing basketball in Saunders' yard. His tee shirt was on backwards and his shorts were a couple of sizes too small, but his grace and athleticism had been nothing short of startling.

"Jeffrey's become quite the basketball player," Xavier had observed between sips of lemonade.

Saunders had nodded his head, an unmistakably proud and loving gleam in his otherwise filmy, bespectacled eyes. "Yes," he had responded. "Quite the basketball player indeed."

But that was all that he had said.

And even now, as the young man stood beside his grandfather's grave, a stranger would never have suspected his deficiency. A casual observer would have said that Jeffrey was a lucky fellow, one who was likely popular with the opposite sex.

Xavier sighed. *How wrong that observer would be*, he thought. *How hopelessly, tragically wrong.*

As learned as he was, as learned as Jeremiah Saunders had been, there was so much about the science of genetics that they didn't understand. Which minute twisted strand of genetic material caused one child to be born with a deadly hole in his heart, another with Downs Syndrome, and still a third with spina bifida?

Or the ability to fly at great speeds and great altitudes, or cloud the minds of others with illusions, or turn his flesh into a substance as hard as titanium? How did that all work?

To find the answer was to unlock a future where a thousand deadly or heartbreaking conditions could be prevented. It had been Jeremiah Saunders' dream to provide the key to that future.

After all, he had seen the way his son and daughter-in-law, Richard and Jamie, had suffered when they learned of Jeffrey's condition. The way they had looked at their perfectly formed little baby and tried to accept the profound imperfections inside him.

An imperfect mind in a superior body, Xavier reflected.

He shook his head. He had an inkling of how the boy felt. After all, his was a superior mind trapped inside a decidedly imperfect body.

And what made his mind so superior? Not just his capacity for reason, though he compared favorably in that regard with anyone on the planet. Not just his insatiable thirst for knowledge.

Charles Xavier could do things with his brain that other people couldn't even imagine.

He could read minds and control the actions of others. He could project his consciousness beyond his body to the four corners of the Earth. When necessary, he could launch mental assaults or guard against the assaults of others.

In short, he was a *mutant*—a being whom nature had randomly separated from the crowd, designating him as the next step in human evolution.

It more than made up for the loss of Xavier's ability to walk and the pain his damaged spine cost him. It even made up for the stares and whispers of pity that seemed to accompany him wherever he went.

Even now, he saw, a middle-aged woman was gazing at him out of the corner of her eye, wondering how he had been laid low. She was sympathizing with his disability, trying to imagine how he felt. Xavier didn't want or need the woman's pity.

With all the possibilities his mutant mind made available to him, his confinement to a wheelchair wasn't really a handicap at all. It was simply a challenge—one of many that he faced every day, and not the greatest of them by a long shot.

Dean Carter looked around at the mourners. "As you may

know," he went on, "Jeremiah was partial to the poetess Emily Dickinson, who said, 'Dying is a wild night and a new road.' " He glanced at the coffin. "If that's so, we wish our friend a good trip."

Saunders' friends began to disperse, some of them holding tissues or handkerchiefs to their eyes. A few gathered around the dean to congratulate him on his speech. And still others lingered near Jeffrey, not certain if it was wise or proper to express their condolences to the young man.

But Xavier was certain. Beckoning for Bobby to follow him, he rolled his wheelchair towards Jeffrey. The boy—

No, the professor thought, correcting himself. *Jeffrey isn't a boy at all.* It was easy to fall into the trap of thinking of him as a child because of his demeanor, because of the innocence that shone in his bright blue eyes. But he was an adult, a man of nearly twenty.

The *man*, then, stood with his back to the grave, looking at no one and nothing in particular. He looked displaced, disoriented . . . and more than a little frightened.

It wasn't difficult to understand. Jeffrey's grandfather, the man with whom he had lived nearly all his life, was gone. From his point of view, there was no telling what might come next.

His life had changed—and changed radically. That was enough to make anyone afraid, much less a retarded man.

Xavier stopped his wheelchair in front of Jeffrey Saunders, but the youth didn't appear to notice him. The professor looked up at his face. "Jeffrey?" he said softly.

The fellow blinked. Then he turned to Xavier with a look that tore at the older man's heart—a look that told the professor he knew something more than people gave him credit for. He may not have understood death completely, but he had an inkling of what had happened to him.

He knew that he had lost something—something precious—and that it could never be replaced.

"Jeffrey," Xavier said, reaching out to take the young man's hand. Despite the magnitude of his intellect, he found it difficult to find the right words. "I'm sorry," he said.

Jeffrey blinked once again, and the professor saw that his eyes were wet with tears. His fingers closed on the older man's, gripping them tight with surprising strength.

Again, Xavier groped for words . . . and failed. Even if he had succeeded, words seemed to hold little meaning for Jeffrey. Fortunately, the professor had other options.

With the simplest of efforts, he cast an emotion out to Jeffrey Saunders, a pure feeling free of the trappings of artifice and intent. *I feel sad too,* his feeling said. *Like you, I have lost a friend.*

The professor's mind and that of the retarded man came together for the briefest of instants, but the effect was clearly visible. Jeffrey stiffened, almost as if someone had struck him a physical blow. Then he blinked rapidly, confusion clouding his face.

Jeffrey didn't know what had just happened. Xavier was certain of that. But he had felt the link, received the emotional message.

And in its wake, he smiled.

Xavier smiled back at him. Then he released the retarded man's hand. The professor would miss his friend Jeremiah Saunders for as long as he lived, and nothing would ever change that. But at least he had connected with the person Saunders loved most in the world.

It wasn't all that much in the scheme of things, Xavier reflected. But it was something. And in times of grief, any gesture, no matter how small, could be of immense comfort. He knew that from experience.

Abruptly, Xavier felt a drop of rain on his hand. Then another, on the skin of his bald head. He looked up and saw a couple of dark clouds sliding over to blot out the sun.

The redheaded woman came forward. "Hello," she told Xavier. "I'm Maryellen Stoyanovich. I'll be looking after Jeffrey at Westminster House." She smiled at the young man. "That's where his grandfather wanted him to stay when he passed away."

The professor nodded. Saunders hadn't had any blood relatives besides Jeffrey. It made sense that he would have made arrangements with an institution for extended care.

"Is there a basketball court there?" Xavier asked.

The woman's brow wrinkled. No doubt, she hadn't expected such a question. "Yes, there is, actually. Why?"

"As you will find," the professor explained, recalling his conversation with his friend, "Jeffrey has become quite the basketball player."

Mrs. Stoyanovich smiled again. "I'll remember that."

She would, too. Xavier could tell. He reached into his sport jacket and fished out a business card. "You can reach me at this number," he told the woman. "I would appreciate it if you would keep me appraised of Jeffrey's progress."

"I will," Mrs. Stoyanovich promised. She read the information on the card. "You run a school?"

"I do," Xavier answered.

"My sister is looking for a private school for my nephew. He's quite bright, you know. Is your place very . . . exclusive?"

"Very," the professor replied truthfully.

Mrs. Stoyanovich shrugged. "You should meet him. You might find he's just what you're looking for."

"I might at that," Xavier allowed.

But he doubted it quite strongly—unless the redheaded woman's nephew was a budding mutant.

The rain began to come down harder and their conversation was necessarily ended. As Mrs. Stoyanovich guided Jeffrey toward an automobile waiting in the distance, the professor watched them go.

He knew it wouldn't be easy for the retarded man to become accustomed to new surroundings. He just hoped that, over time, Jeffrey would grow to like Westminster House.

Of course, only time would tell. No one's future was assured, Xavier reflected—least of all, his own.

Finally, he glanced over his shoulder at Bobby, who had demonstrated admirable patience, and pointed to his own vehicle. "It appears it's time to go," said the professor.

"Sure thing," his student told him, and wheeled him in the direction of their specially outfitted van.

It took a few minutes for Bobby to raise Xavier's chair into the vehicle with a built-in hydraulic lift and secure it to customized metal foundations in the passenger compartment. But by the time the rain began coming down with real force, the professor was safely inside.

Looking out the water-streaked window, he could see that the gravediggers were lowering Jeremiah Saunders' coffin into the ground. Xavier was sorry that they had to work in the rain, though they seemed dressed for it.

"Back to Salem Center?" Bobby asked as he swung into the driver's seat and pulled his door closed.

"I believe so, yes," said the professor. He smiled at his protégé. "Thank you for accompanying me, Bobby. One should never be required to attend a funeral service alone."

The younger man laughed. "Are you kidding? There's no way I would have let you go without me. Besides," he chuckled as he started the van and pulled out onto the cemetery's main road, "I wanted to see what some of my old professors look like these days."

Bobby was joking, of course. He had graduated from Empire University not too long ago. His instructors couldn't have changed much in a short period of time.

Xavier remembered visiting the university for the first time just a few days after Jeremiah Saunders had moved there from the city to teach. He remembered how much he had liked the rolling, tree-lined grounds and the quiet location.

He wouldn't have minded the prospect of staying there and teaching genetics alongside his friend, in a place where the only threat to one's existence was the law of "publish or perish," and "cut-throat" meant only that one had to safeguard one's ideas from one's rivals.

In a better, less violent universe, he might have entered that world and remained in it the rest of his life. He might have devoted his life to study and contemplation. Unfortunately, that wasn't what fate had had in store for Charles Xavier.

He was born unlike normal human beings. And because of that, he had been compelled to follow a much more dangerous and difficult path than that of even the most determined academician.

For a time, Xavier watched the scenery move past him. He found it soothing in a way, perhaps even therapeutic. But then, he so seldom allowed himself the luxury of doing nothing.

"You okay, professor?" asked Bobby.

Xavier realized he had been dozing with his eyes open. He turned to his companion. "I'm fine."

It was beginning to get dark, the professor noticed. In the west, beyond the sparsely dressed trees, the sun's light was contracting into the promise of a particularly beautiful sunset.

"Pity about your friend," Bobby said. "He was a heck of a teacher . . . even if I didn't understand half of what he was talking about."

Xavier was surprised. "You attended Professor Saunders' lectures?"

The younger man nodded. "A few."

The professor grunted. "I wasn't aware that you had an interest in the sciences, Bobby."

His companion shrugged. "Well, you know, considering my . . . special circumstances, I guess you could say, I figured it wouldn't hurt to know something about genetics."

Xavier nodded. "Yes. Yes, of course."

He was so wrapped up in the intricate, the global and the impersonal that he sometimes missed simple logical connections between one mundane item and another. But now that he thought about it, it made perfect sense that Bobby Drake would want to learn about genetics.

Like Xavier himself, Bobby was a mutant, a human born with a twist to his DNA. That twist gave him the power to turn into a human icicle—a literal Iceman—capable of drawing ambient moisture out of the air, freezing it and using it in a variety of applications.

But then, all those who had been students at Xavier's school were mutants, a subspecies sorely in need of training and direction if it was to survive the hostility that had lately been directed toward it.

It was this need that had drawn Xavier to the life he led. It was the knowledge that people like him, left to their own devices, might be destroyed by the hatred and paranoia of others—or worse, that they might turn their talents against mankind, justifying that paranoia.

Too many, with names like Magneto and The Toad and

Unus, had done just that. They had seen in their mutant abilities a superiority that was both unfounded and dangerous. Mutants, Xavier believed, had to co-exist with the rest of mankind, using their special powers to build a peaceful and enlightened future for everyone.

"Um, if you don't mind my asking . . ." said Bobby, drawing the professor out of his reverie.

"Yes?" Xavier responded.

"That tall, darkhaired guy who didn't say anything . . . that's Professor Saunders' grandson, right?"

"It is," Xavier confirmed.

"What's wrong with him, exactly?" Bobby asked.

The professor frowned and leaned back in his chair. "He was born with a brain defect—one that has cropped up from time to time in the Saunders bloodline. As a result, Jeffrey is incapable of processing information the way you and I do."

"And his parents?" asked the younger man.

"They died when the boy was three and a half," Xavier explained. "In a collision with a man who had had too much to drink. Fortunately, Jeffrey was at home with a babysitter at the time."

Bobby looked at him. "That's a pretty sad story."

The professor nodded. "I wish there were something I could do for Jeffrey. However, even with all my resources, there's nothing I can do. For now, his problem is untreatable."

He recalled again the emotion he had seen in his friend's eyes the day they watched Jeffrey playing basketball. He remembered the pride Jeremiah Saunders had taken in his grandson's accomplishments.

Now that he thought about it, Xavier had experienced that emotion himself on occasion.

He had not raised any children of his own, but he taken

in a great many students over the years—and he had come to love them as if he were their father. What's more, the majority of them understood the depth of his affection for them. He didn't need to articulate it. It was simply understood.

Perhaps it was the same way with Jeffrey and Jeremiah. He had never seen his friend display a great deal of affection for anyone, his grandson included. But Xavier was quite certain that that affection had existed.

At any rate, Jeffrey seemed to think so. The professor had gleaned that insight during his brief contact with the young man's mind. Despite all that had gone wrong in his life, Jeffrey felt well-loved.

Xavier glanced at a sign on the side of the road. It told him that Salem Center was only eight miles away. Closing his eyes, he massaged the bridge of his thin, patrician nose with a forefinger.

In fifteen or twenty minutes, he estimated, he and Bobby would be back at the professor's school. He would return to his study and take a moment to put the loss of his friend from his mind.

Then he would check his worldwide information network for appearances of previously unknown mutants. If he found such appearances, he would take steps to bring the mutants into his circle. If there weren't any appearances, he might actually get some sleep that night.

If so, it would be a welcome rest indeed. And in the morning, Jeremiah Saunders' funeral behind him, Xavier would resume his normal life. That is, he reflected, as normal as life could ever get for the leader of the mutant team known as the X-Men.

"Hey!" Bobby exclaimed suddenly.

The professor opened his eyes and saw the look on his companion's face. It was unquestionably an expression of trepidation, caused by something Bobby had seen on the road ahead.

Xavier turned and saw the cause of the younger man's surprise, caught in the van's high-beam headlights: two large, muscular figures clad head to toe in skintight silver costumes, standing right in the path of the professor's speeding vehicle.

They didn't seem the least bit perturbed by the prospect of an impending collision. Far from it. It seemed they were expecting it—even looking forward to it.

"Bobby!" Xavier cried out.

But the youth was already swerving to get around the figures. Though their garb and their attitude suggested they might be enemies, he couldn't take a chance that it was just a fraternity prank.

However, as soon as Bobby pulled the wheel to the left, the pair on the road moved as well. They blocked the van's way all over again, inviting it to plow into them or smash into a tree alongside the road.

Bobby Drake had driven his share of fast cars. However, even an Indy 500 winner would have been running out of options at that point.

Bobby muttered something beneath his breath and swerved again—this time to the right. But to the professor's chagrin, it didn't matter. The silver figures darted back to the other side of the road, obstructing their path every bit as effectively as before.

By then, it was clear to Xavier that these weren't innocents. Using his power of telepathy, he communicated the observation to Bobby with lightning speed. *It's time for a change of tactics,* he advised.

"Hold tight, sir!" the younger man exclaimed through clenched teeth. "We're going through them!"

His fingers tightened on the steering wheel and his foot slammed down on the accelerator. A fraction of a second later, the van leapt forward like a wild beast prodded by an electrical charge.

Like the professor and Bobby themselves, their vehicle—discreetly marked with the name Xavier Institute for Higher Learning—was not at all what it appeared to be.

Beneath its hood was a customized V-8, fuel-injected engine that could outrun almost anything on the road—even though it carried the extra weight of bullet-resistant glass in all of its windows and heavy-gauge steel plating on its specially reinforced body.

With their silver garb, the figures in front of them reflected the van's high beams back into the professor's face. He flinched. Then the van was on top of the unmoving strangers, slamming into them at more than a hundred miles an hour.

It was like plowing into the unyielding rock of a mountain. Xavier felt himself being thrown forward, only to be restrained by his shoulder harness and the passenger's side airbag that exploded from the compartment in front of him.

A moment later, he felt the air around him turn frigid, as if a blast of arctic wind had invaded the van. Turning his head, he saw that Bobby had gone from normal-looking flesh and blood to the faceted, crystalline appearance of the mutant operative called Iceman.

The plastic skin of the driver's side airbag froze solid on contact with Bobby's icy hide and shattered like rice paper under pressure from his hand. Then Bobby did the same thing to Xavier's airbag.

The professor couldn't find the men in silver. The crash had transformed the windshield into a maze of fractured glass, almost impossible to see through. But it wasn't hard to imagine that they were still in the vicinity, taking up positions outside the van.

Bobby glanced at Xavier, his eyes a glacial blue. "Are you all right?" he asked, icy vapors issuing from his mouth.

"I'm uninjured," the professor told him.

"And I'm going after those bozos," Bobby announced, a note of undisguised anger in his voice.

Xavier didn't try to dissuade him, anger or no anger. Every one of his students had worked hard to prepare for situations like this one. Bobby Drake could handle himself as well as any of them.

Unfortunately, the impact of the collision had jammed the driver's side door shut. But that was no obstacle for Iceman. Bobby simply covered the crack between door and jamb with a frigid hand and wedged increasing amounts of ice into the narrow opening.

After a moment, the professor heard a high-pitched sound—the shriek of twisting metal—as the door began to open. Planting the heel of his foot against it, Bobby shoved it open the rest of the way and vaulted out of the van.

Xavier unlatched his seat belt. Then he dragged himself through the doorway his X-Man had opened.

It was only then, in the wan light of the moon and stars, that he got a decent look at his adversaries. They were a good deal bigger and more muscular than he had imagined at first glance, and their eyes blazed with a fierce white flame.

But as powerful as their bodies were, their minds would likely be another story—and no one was as adept at breaking down a brain's defenses as the professor was. Laying himself down on a patch of grass, he cast a mental bolt at the nearer of his two enemies.

To his surprise, nothing happened.

Strange, he thought. Frowning, he turned to the other silver suit and tried the same thing.

Still nothing.

His mental assaults had felled some of the most determined and powerful minds on Earth. And yet, Xavier reflected, they seemed to have no effect on these two.

He decided to change tacks—and launch a mental probe instead of a bolt. After all, he required information more than anything else right now. He needed to know what kind of being he was dealing with and how he had mustered the strength to resist a point-blank mental assault.

That's when the professor received his second surprise in as many moments—because try as he might, he couldn't find an intelligence driving his adversary's actions. He couldn't even find a *hint* of an intelligence.

Xavier wouldn't have been so shocked if an independent mind were there and it had been shielded from him. But that wasn't the case at all. The silver-suited figure was completely and utterly vacant. He was a puppet, a shell, propelled by someone else's will.

But whose? That was the question, the professor asked himself. Meanwhile, Bobby Drake was hardly standing idle. As Xavier watched, he sent a blast of half-frozen slush at one of the silver-suited figures.

"Try this on for size," Bobby announced rakishly. "It ought to make an ice cube like you feel right at home!"

Their antagonist said nothing in response. He just stood there as Bobby's slush flowed around him and then hardened, enveloping him in its blisteringly cold embrace.

Bobby didn't wait long to admire the results of his strategy. After all, the ice surrounding the silver-suit was thick enough to hold a fair-sized tank in check.

Instead, he turned his attention to their other opponent,

who had begun advancing on him with purposeful but unhurried strides. Creating an arsenal of big, rock-solid ice balls, the mutant sent them hurtling at the second silver-suit. They struck him hard, battering him, forcing him to pause in his progress . . . but ultimately failing to incapacitate him.

Suddenly, Xavier heard a sound like thunder crackling nearby. He turned and saw an aura of blue energy blazing about the silver-suit that Bobby had already immobilized. Hairline cracks began to appear in their assailant's thick, icy shell. Then there was a flash of light and fragments of ice went hissing in every direction.

The professor frowned in combined anger and concern. The first silver-suit was free. And like his partner, he was advancing on Bobby.

Xavier didn't like the way the conflict was proceeding. He also didn't like the fact that the mastermind behind their opponents was unknown to him. It meant that he and his protégé would have to do battle without knowing whom they were fighting—always a dangerous proposition.

Bobby? he called out telepathically, using his preferred method of communication in combat situations.

His student cast a glance in his direction. *Right here, Professor. You see the way that guy shrugged off my ice shell?*

I did indeed, thought Xavier. *Quite possibly, he has an invisible force field at his disposal. If so, your ice never touched him.*

Bobby shook his head. *Looks like these dudes have got more going for them than nifty costumes and big muscles.*

They also seem impervious to my mental bolts, the professor told him. *As far as I can ascertain, they have no minds of their own. They are being directed by an unseen intelligence.*

Bobby frowned. *Not good. Not good at all.*

Then he stopped communicating and started battling again. Xavier took some small comfort in the knowledge that there were few who could fight as hard as Bobby could—few who could match his recklessness and his intensity.

Unfortunately, the silver-suits proved to be more than Bobby could handle. When he hit them with a barrage of sliver-thin ice darts, the missiles bounced right off them. When he tried to root their feet to the ground in massive blocks of ice, it took them only a moment to shatter the blocks and resume their progress. And when he made the ground beneath them too slick to walk on, they still found traction.

Bobby backed off until he was standing right in front of the professor. *We've got a problem here, sir.*

Keep fighting, Xavier told him.

He wished he could give his X-Man some assurance, some insight he could follow to victory. But he had nothing to give him. He could master and befuddle any human con-sciousness on Earth—but in the silver-suits, there was noth-ing for him to master.

To that point, their enemies had seemed content to let the mutants take the offensive. Abruptly, that all changed.

One of the silver-suits raised his hand, clenched it into a fist and pointed it at Bobby. Before either Xavier or his X-Man could do anything about it, a sun-bright energy burst exploded from their opponent's fist.

Professor . . . ? came Bobby's thought.

Then he was flung backwards like a rag doll. He hit the

side of the van hard and slid to the ground. A moment later, his icy exterior began to melt like snowflakes on a warm window pane, exposing the very human-looking being beneath it.

Xavier bit his lip. *Bobby?* he called out telepathically.

There was no answer. Fortunately, Professor X's power allowed him to ascertain that the young man wasn't dead, just unconscious. But for all intents and purposes, he had been removed from the battle.

And all the professor had been able to do was sit there in the moonlight and watch. As much as it galled him to acknowledge it, he was helpless against this kind of adversary.

No doubt, the one behind this attack had anticipated that. In fact, he had counted on it.

As Xavier entertained this thought, the silver-suit who had leveled Bobby swiveled his hand like a cannon on a hydraulically-operated turret. This time, he pointed his fist directly at Professor X.

Helpless, Xavier thought again. Then came the blinding flash and the impact.

The biggest surprise in Bobby Drake's mind when he came to was the fact that he was coming to at all.

The mutant had felt certain, in that impossible-to-measure instant of time between his recognition of the energy burst and his being struck by it, that he was a dead man; a bona fide, deep-fried corpse with all the trimmings.

And if he did by some trick of fate live to see the world again, he would never have predicted that he would do so unimprisoned and unrestrained.

Yet that was what happened.

Bobby was lying on the grass beside the van where he had fallen, the stars blazing brightly in the dark open sky above him, his hands and feet unfettered. And even more miraculously, his super-powered attackers were gone without a trace.

Then a possible explanation floated to the surface of his consciousness—one he wasn't at all thrilled about thinking. *What if they had only been interested in Professor Xavier?*

He bolted to his feet and looked around. To his chagrin, he didn't see his mentor anywhere. "Professor X!" he shouted into the night.

Then it hit Bobby that he had gotten to his feet too quickly. Still dazed from the impact of the energy blast, his knees wobbled like jello in an earthquake.

Fighting the vertigo, he staggered around the van. He expected to find the worst on the other side.

Instead, he found Professor X sitting calmly in the driver's side doorway of the vehicle. The older man looked up at him, his temple bruised slightly but otherwise in good shape.

"I'm fine, Bobby," Xavier reassured him, answering his unspoken question. "You, however," he said with concern in his voice, "are looking somewhat the worse for wear."

The younger man touched a forefinger to the point of his brow, where a throbbing pain had developed. His fingertip came away wet with blood. "I guess I am," he conceded.

"No internal injuries, I trust?" asked the professor.

"Just some bruises, I think."

"I'm relieved to hear that."

Bobby eyed his mentor with relief. "I thought for sure I was going to find you gone, sir . . . or worse." He looked up and down the moonlit ribbon of asphalt highway. "What happened? Where did they go?"

Xavier shook his head. "I regret to say I don't know. I was

rendered unconscious by a force blast a few seconds after you were. When I awoke, I was still here ... and our assailants had disappeared."

The younger man puzzled over it for a moment, but couldn't come up with a plausible explanation. "It's just weird," he said at last. "It seems like a lot of trouble for someone to go to just to trash our van and give us a couple of headaches."

"I am compelled to agree," the professor replied. "Unfortunately, I was unable to pick up any thoughts or clues from them telepathically, so I cannot answer as to their motive. Unless they return and reveal it to us, we may never know what it was."

Bobby smiled humorlessly. "No thanks, sir," he said. "I'd rather live with the mystery than have to deal with those guys again."

"Indeed," said Xavier. "Let's hope we have seen the last of those two." He craned his neck to get a look at the crumpled front end of the van. "I must assume," he said dryly, "that our vehicle is no longer roadworthy."

The younger man found himself chuckling at the comment despite his injury. "You can say that again, sir."

He leaned inside past the professor and rooted around on the floor until he found his suit jacket. Then he pulled his cell phone from an inside pocket and flipped it open.

"Don't worry, sir," Bobby said as he dialed the number of the Xavier Institute for Higher Learning. "I'll just call home and one of the guys will come pick us up."

"Thank you," the professor said with a nod. Suddenly, he looked very weary. "Truthfully, I would like nothing better than to put this day behind me."

The younger man grunted. "That makes two of us."

Abruptly, he heard a voice on the other end of the phone. "Hello?"

Bobby Drake smiled ruefully at the sound of his team-mate's voice. "Hank? It's me."

"Bobby?" came the cultured reply. "I was starting to get worried. Is everything all right?"

The mutant glanced at the van. "That all depends."

"On what?" asked Hank.

"On how you like rental cars," Bobby told him.

CHAPTER TWO

"Bobby . . . ?"

Professor X heard the name spoken out loud. The voice behind it was thin and weak but strangely familiar. It took him a moment to realize that the voice was his own.

With an effort, he opened his eyes—but he didn't see anything. He was lying in darkness on a hard, flat surface, a series of confining metal bands stretched taut across his chest, his arms and his legs.

"Bobby?" Xavier whispered again.

This time, he sent out telepathic signals in search of the younger man's consciousness. However, Bobby was nowhere to be found. That meant he was either still unconscious, outside the range of the professor's summons or—

No, he thought forcefully. *I won't contemplate that last possibility. At least, not yet.*

Clearly, something was wrong. And just as clearly, it had something to do with the silver-suited, super-powered figures who had attacked Xavier and his young companion.

He remembered that he had been unable to draw a telepathic bead on either of their assailants. He remembered how helpless he had felt, how utterly, gallingly inept. And he remembered the brilliant, bone-rattling impact of his adversary's energy attack.

More than likely, it was that enemy who had brought him here—wherever here was. The professor expanded his telepathic senses to see if he could find a clue as to his surroundings. It was no use.

The place was devoid of sound as well as light. There was no hint of movement, no stray thought that Xavier could sift from his environment. Just the cold, hard reality of his bonds and the sharp tang of metal on the chill, climate controlled air.

Obviously, he was a prisoner. But *whose* prisoner? Who was the guiding force behind the silver-suits?

Surely, a voice hissed softly in the professor's mind, *you've not forgotten your old friend.*

Xavier's heart began to beat faster beneath his metal restraints. *A telepath*, he thought. It made sense, given that the silver-clad supermen who had attacked him had no volition of their own. A telepath could have directed them without the use of any mind-enhancing technology.

But such a feat would have taken an adept of considerable skill and experience. And any foe that powerful could easily read the professor's thoughts if he left them unshielded.

Quickly, Xavier put up screens against the intrusion. He envisioned a massive stone wall surrounding his mind to keep his mysterious adversary from gaining further access to it.

A moment later, he could feel the ticklish brush of a mental probe testing his barrier. *Really*, the voice slithered chillingly through his brain, *if I have power enough to make a prisoner of you, your little mental wall will hardly prove an obstacle.*

The only emotion the professor sensed in his enemy was amusement. As a result, he was unprepared for the mind-splintering agony that smashed at his head, pounding his mental barrier like a sledgehammer.

Xavier writhed in pain, forced to bite his lip to keep from screaming. Clearly, he realized, he was still debilitated from the beating he had taken on the road. Rather than endure another assault, he dropped his barrier for the moment.

There, the voice said. *That's much better. I do so prefer unrestricted access to your mind.* A soft chuckle whispered through the throbbing ache in the mutant's brain. *Especially here and now. Your confusion, your discomfort . . . they're quite delicious, you know.*

"Who—?" Xavier croaked through parched, swollen lips. "Who are you? What do you want?"

I told you, came the reply. *I am an old friend.*

"That's a relief," the professor said dryly, speaking out loud so as to minimize his enemy's access to his mind. "Imagine the trouble I would be in if you were an enemy."

Laughter rumbled through his head. *Yes, please do imagine that,* the voice told him. *Ponder the implications of being physically and psychically helpless in the clutches of one who hates you. Think what such an individual might do to you . . . the pain he might inflict. The damage he might do to you and those close to you.*

Xavier had already entertained such thoughts, but he quickly tamped them down into the deepest recesses of his subconscious. The last thing he could afford now was to give his enemy, whoever he might be, ammunition to use against him. And at the moment, fear was the greatest weapon his tormentor had in his arsenal.

He couldn't erect another telepathic firewall—his adversary would only detect it and attempt to batter it down again. Still, the professor had to maintain some control over his thoughts and emotions. And he had to do this without the one who had invaded his brain realizing he was holding something in reserve.

"Then let's get on with it," Xavier retorted with feigned impatience. "If you know me as well as you claim, you know also that I have no patience for mind games."

Ah, but it is all mind games between us, the voice said with growing heat. *It always has been and it always will be.*

The professor felt something revealing then—a telepathic twitch, a tiny flare of anger. It was the slip he had been waiting for, the stray emotion that marked the intruder as surely as if he had signed his name on the darkness in phosphorescent characters.

Xavier smiled grimly to himself. So *that* was who it was.

I thought by now you would have given up on the idea of revenge, he shot at his captor. *After all, you haven't proven very adept at it.*

Another flare of anger, bigger than the one before it. *Very good*, the voice snapped harshly in the professor's head, sending pinpoint needles of pain through his forebrain. *I forgot that I must never underestimate you, Terran, not even for the briefest of moments.*

Suddenly, the room was awash with light. Xavier squeezed his eyes shut and turned his head from the source of it. Then he opened his eyes slowly, allowing them to adjust to the brightness.

He was in a large room, filled from floor to ceiling with dark, oily-looking, angular machines whose purpose and function he could only guess at. However, the mutant knew one thing with absolute certainty, even before his vision cleared enough to inspect the devices more closely . . . they were not of earthly origin.

Rather, they were from a distant world called Quistalium. But that came as no surprise, because so did the professor's captor . . . the malevolent arch-schemer known on Earth as *Lucifer*.

Xavier caught a flash of movement out of the corner of his eye. Craning his neck, he got a better view of it. A moment later, a tall, powerful-looking figure loomed beside the mutant and gazed down at him.

Lucifer wore a crimson tunic and loose-fitting pants of the same color, cinched at the waist by a purple sash. His gloves, boots and cloak were purple as well, as was the helmet that covered most of his face. Only his eyes, pale blue and cold as ice, and his mouth, twisted into a snarl over a black slash of goatee, were visible.

But how could he be standing there? Professor X wondered. Hadn't his own people killed him, disappointed in his failures?

"I thought you were dead," he said.

Lucifer's mouth quirked into a sneer. "As one of you Terrans once said, news of my death was greatly exaggerated."

Suddenly, Xavier realized that something else had been exaggerated. After all, his enemy's footsteps hadn't made any sound when he approached. "You're a simulacrum," he concluded. "A hologram."

Lucifer's eyes glinted cruelly. "Right again," he responded. "But then, you have always been a difficult man to deceive."

Many years earlier, when Xavier was a young man in search of his destiny, he had discovered Lucifer's handiwork in a remote walled village in Tibet. An advance agent for his species of space conquerors, the Quistalian had brought the local populace under his control and was using the town as his base of operations.

Xavier led a revolt against Lucifer, throwing a wrench into the alien's plans. However, he paid for his presumptuousness when Lucifer dropped an immense stone slab on him—crushing his spine and crippling him from the waist down.

Even now, the professor could feel the terrible, sudden weight of the stone, heavier by far than anything he might have imagined. And he could feel the even greater weight of pain and sorrow as he was struck by the magnitude of his loss . . . .

"Yes," said Lucifer—a voice in his head again. "I remember it vividly. You should have seen the look on your face, Xavier . . . the comical, wide-eyed expression of shock . . . of horror . . . ."

The professor had to quell his own rising storm of anger. "Then you remember also," he said evenly, "that what happened to my legs didn't stop me. If anything, it made me more determined to stop you."

Lucifer's simulacrum scowled. "You and your X-Men, you mean."

Xavier nodded. "My X-Men."

In fact, one of the reasons he had brought his group of young mutants together was to thwart the Quistalian's next move. But he had to wait for a number of years.

Then Lucifer brought a terrifying array of alien technology against Xavier's original task force—five young mutants code-named Cyclops, Marvel Girl, Beast, Angel and Iceman. However, the teenagers proved themselves more than a match for the Quistalian. Like their mentor before them, they defused his plans to enslave the human race.

In punishment for his failure, Lucifer was banished by his masters to the Nameless Dimension, where neither time nor space existed in any recognizable form. But even then, he tried to get his revenge on Xavier—using his alien powers to manipulate various Earthmen and sometimes even imbuing them with ionic energy powers.

Fortunately, he was beaten each time. And when the Quistalians got wind of his ill-fated efforts, they terminated him for attracting too much attention. Or so the professor had been given to believe.

It seemed now that Lucifer had survived after all. But if he was compelled to speak through a hologram . . .

Yes, the villain told him. His voice was a bitter, hissing response in Xavier's head. *You're correct, of course. I'm still a prisoner here in the Nameless Dimension.*

Abruptly, another piece of the puzzle fell into place. "And those brutish figures in the silver suits . . ." said the professor, "they were powered by ionic energy, weren't they? Just like all the other pawns you've manipulated over the years."

Lucifer shook his head. "No," he replied out loud, "not like the other pawns. Those two were made *entirely* of ionic energy. That made them a good deal more dangerous—not to mention a lot easier to control."

Xavier understood now why the silver-suited drones hadn't evinced any detectable thoughts. Their master hadn't bothered to program them with minds of their own.

"As you can see," Lucifer breathed, his eyes narrowed to slits, "I've learned a few new tricks since we last saw each other. But then, I've had nothing but time on my hands."

The professor saw the simulacrum's eyes blaze with shame and indignation. He knew why, too. Quistalians were conquerors by nature. The impulse to dominate was in their blood. It was difficult for one of them to accept defeat at the hands of an apparently inferior species.

"It was you who brought me to this pass," Lucifer snarled. "My suffering and humiliation . . . they are all your doing."

Xavier shook his head from side to side. "All I did was act to save my planet," he said reasonably. "It was no more than you would have done if our positions had been reversed."

"No!" the simulacrum roared suddenly, its deep voice echoing from one bank of alien machines to another. Its gloved fingers coiled into fists. "Your place was not to resist, Terran! Your place was to submit—as the inhabitants of a thousand worlds submitted before you!"

The professor sighed. He might as well have tried to teach a scorpion the philosophy of peaceful co-existence. Lucifer simply wasn't capable of embracing a non-Quistalian view of the universe.

Unfortunately, this wasn't merely an academic exercise. In the present case, the very deadly, very hostile scorpion in question held Xavier's fate in the palm of his hand.

"I am Lucifer," the hologram rasped, shaking with accumulated fury. "I am a Quistalian, an initiate of the great and terrible Arcana. I lived to bring honor to myself and my people—until you made a fool of me."

He lowered his face closer to his prisoner's, his lips pulled back from his teeth like a wolf's, his eyes cold and merciless. "I can still win honor, Xavier. I can still serve Quistalium. But first, I must escape my confinement and destroy the source of my humiliation."

The muscles writhed in Lucifer's jaw. It looked to Xavier as if he were in real, physical pain.

"Only then," the hologram insisted raggedly, "can I prostrate myself before the Supreme One and beg his mercy! Only then," he thundered, shaking his fists at the machine-studded ceiling, "can my name be restored to the list of his most trusted agents!"

It was at that moment that the professor realized the full extent of what he was dealing with. Lucifer was no longer just a powerful adversary, no longer just a tool bred to conquer other species and crush them beneath his heel. He was in the process of becoming something else now, something infinitely more treacherous.

He was in the process of going insane.

Nor was it difficult for Xavier to understand how it had begun. After all, the Quistalian had spent years in a place where time and space had no meaning. Was it any wonder that his grip on reality had started to slip?

Lucifer's simulacrum straightened, walked over to a bank of machines and inspected its control panel. Then he cast a glance back over his shoulder at his captive.

"Do me a favor," he said.

The professor looked at him. "A favor?" he echoed warily.

"Yes." The hologram's eyes narrowed in the oval slits of his helmet. "Remember each of my defeats at your hands. Savor each detail for me. Turn it over again and again in your mind. That way, I won't have to look far to fuel the flames of my hatred."

Xavier met Lucifer's gaze, but he didn't say anything. He was too busy trying to think of a way to escape his confinement—because he knew now that he wouldn't survive any other way.

"And above all else," said the hologram, considering the machine again, "keep hope alive in your heart. After all, you beat me before. You must feel some confidence that you can do so again."

Suddenly, he pounded his fist on the control panel, but there was no contact. After all, he was immaterial.

"Then," Lucifer continued, his voice taut and guttural, "I can strangle that hope, little by little. I can have the pleasure of watching it die . . . before I destroy you as well."

The professor tried not to think about such things. "I'm pleased that you don't harbor a grudge," he said as evenly as he could.

Lucifer whirled—only to smile at him like a predator picking at a corpse. "I do harbor one, yes," the alien admitted. "Indeed, it's all that has sustained me since I was sent to the Nameless Dimension."

Xavier decided that he needed to distract his captor. He needed to keep the alien talking until he could learn more about this place, until he could find some breach in its defenses.

"I had heard of the Nameless Dimension," Lucifer told him, "but I never dreamed how stark and featureless it could be. How empty of stimulation. Someone could go . . . quite mad there."

Unexpectedly, he laughed. It was a short, ugly sound that originated deep in his throat.

"That is why I needed to find something on which to focus—something on which to obsess. A grudge, for instance. Or the plotting of vengeance against my enemies."

The professor decided to change the subject. "And the reason I'm not already being tortured to death?"

The Quistalian grunted disdainfully. "Truly, Xavier, you exhibit greater curiosity than common sense. But then, you have always been an intellectual first and foremost. It is a pity I need to destroy you. I could use someone of your talents."

The mutant scowled at his captor. "I think you know the likelihood of my working for *you*, Lucifer."

"I do," said the hologram. "But imagine," he whispered fiercely, closing his fingers around an imaginary planet, "imagine how it might feel to be lord of your entire world."

"A lord obliged to serve a Quistalian master," Xavier noted. "In that case, it would not feel very good at all."

Would Lucifer have even suggested such an alliance years earlier? The professor sincerely doubted it. Clearly, the Nameless Dimension had taken its toll on him.

Abruptly, the villain smiled. *You forget, I am in your mind, Xavier. You think perhaps my time in the Nameless Dimension has changed me . . . driven me over the brink to madness?*

The mutant cursed himself. *Careful*, he thought, at a level Lucifer couldn't reach. *You musn't slip that way again.*

"What do *you* think?" Xavier asked.

The hologram shrugged, as if it weren't very important. "Perhaps I have gone a little mad after all. And perhaps I am unable to recognize it because the madness prevents me from seeing clearly." He shrugged again. "An intriguing philosophical question for another time—but one with which we need not concern ourselves at the moment. You see, the time has come to effect my redemption in the eyes of my masters."

He pointed a thick, gloved forefinger at his captive. "And you, Terran . . . you are the key to that redemption."

I'd rather die first, Xavier reflected, letting the thought appear to slip from behind carefully laid mental blocks.

At that precise moment, as though it were the result of a single synapse firing in the professor's brain, he released his astral image—a projection of himself controlled by his mind but unfettered by the boundaries of the physical world. His astral self was utterly invisible to the naked eye and, if Xavier had accomplished all he intended, invisible as well to Lucifer's telepathic scrutiny.

"You'd rather die?" the Quistalian repeated. "I assure you . . . that can and will be arranged."

Xavier kept the tiny portion of his mind that was linked to his astral projection buried as deeply as he could. That way, his mental doppelganger would have an opportunity to pinpoint his whereabouts without Lucifer knowing about it. And once the professor possessed that information, he could arrange an escape.

After all, his astral projection could travel at the speed of thought. It could contact his X-Men and alert them to his predicament. And even if Lucifer somehow became aware of the message, he would be powerless to keep it from going through.

Then something occurred to Xavier. What if he wasn't on Earth anymore? What if the Quistalian had taken him to some orbital facility, shielded by force fields from the prying eyes and instruments of Earthmen?

It was a disturbing thought. If he was no longer earthbound, his task became infinitely more complicated. It would be harder not only to reach his team, but also for *them* to reach *him*.

"Your X-Men?" Lucifer sniggered as he caught the stray thought from Xavier's mind. "They won't even know you're in danger before they're struck down themselves."

The professor didn't like the sound of the remark. He cared less about his own welfare than that of his students. "Would you care to explain what you mean by that?"

"Why not?" said the simulacrum. "As we speak, the ones

you call Bobby Drake and Henry McCoy are returning to your facility in Salem Center. And neither of them has any inkling that you're my prisoner, since you're sitting in the same vehicle they are."

Xavier's brow furrowed with consternation. "Am I? And how am I managing to accomplish such a feat?"

Lucifer tapped his forehead with his finger. "I told you, Terran . . . I have labored long and hard to reach this moment. You remember the two who accosted you on the road?"

"The silver-suits," the mutant offered.

"Exactly. And you remember that I said they were made entirely of ionic energy?" He lifted his bearded chin with unmistakable pride. "Well, they aren't the only ones."

Xavier could feel his teeth grind together. "You made a duplicate of me? Out of *energy?*"

The alien grinned. "I did. And he has taken your place."

The professor absorbed the information, mulled it over. "But it can't be long before my X-Men see him for what he is."

"I would not bet on that," Lucifer told him. "Your duplicate possesses all your memories, all your thought patterns, gathered by Quistalian sensor devices during our previous encounters. Your young friends will be hard pressed to see through the deception."

Xavier contained his trepidation. "And if I may ask . . . what specific purpose does this ruse serve?"

The projected image of the alien wagged a warning finger at his captive. "No," he said, "that would ruin the surprise. Let us take this one slow step at a time."

He had barely finished when the professor caught another flash of movement out of the corner of his eye. Turning his head, he saw the two silver-clad super beings who had attacked him and Bobby. They moved toward him mechanically, their expressions vacant and their eyes ablaze with white fire.

"It's time for you to leave now," Lucifer told him. "But don't worry. We'll see each other again before you know it."

Xavier didn't understand. He said so.

"It's quite simple, actually," his captor remarked casually. "You see, this facility contains an intriguing little device for transporting an individual into the Nameless Dimension."

The mutant's mouth went dry as he realized for the first time why he had been brought here. *No*, he thought fiercely.

"My assistants," Lucifer went on in the same casual voice, "will use this device to transport *you* here."

No, Xavier thought again.

"I look forward to the company," the alien said as if he were confiding in him. "And also, for you to have a taste of the hell I have endured since I was sent here."

The professor swore under his breath. It was too soon. His astral projection hadn't yet completed its probe of the area.

It had taken Lucifer years to discover what he believed was a means of escape from the Nameless Dimension. Xavier didn't have years. He didn't even have days—not with his enemy's doppelganger running loose among his X-Men, planting the seeds for Lucifer's triumph.

"Unfortunately," the Quistalian went on, "we won't be companions for long. After all, your duplicate's first priority is to see to it that I'm liberated from my dimensional prison—and that you're abandoned here for the rest of your pitiful life."

As he spoke, his silver-clad puppets lifted the table on which the professor was bound. Then they began to walk it back the way they had come, toward a semicircular portal at the far end of the room.

Lucifer's simulacrum followed, smiling broadly beneath

the forward edge of his helmet. Clearly, the Quistalian was deriving sadistic amusement from the professor's plight.

Xavier struggled against his metal bonds, refusing to go down without a fight. His world was far from perfect, but he couldn't let it fall prey to a pack of alien slavemasters.

In desperation, he directed a stream of mental energy blasts at the silver suits, but they didn't so much as flinch. Then he assaulted Lucifer's simulacrum, with the same results.

Poor, pitiful fool, the alien hissed in his brain. *You've lost! Try to accept it with some grace!*

The professor bit his lip. Grace was the least of his concerns right now. He wanted only to warn his students before Lucifer could put his scheme into effect—whatever it might be.

He watched as the drones maneuvered him through the portal into a considerably smaller and more poorly lit enclosure. The walls there were covered with dark, serpentine tubes and glowing amber nodes.

The only furniture in the room was a set of metal supports, located immediately below a large fixture that resembled nothing so much as an oversized heat lamp. The silver-suits laid his table on the supports, locked it into place and backed away from it.

Lucifer stood off to the side, gloating. "I will say goodbye, Xavier. But only for a moment, you understand. Then we will be reunited in a significantly more exotic environment."

One of the drones moved to the wall on the professor's right and manipulated a control switch. Abruptly, the fixture above Xavier began to glow with a seething crimson light.

The mutant turned his head and shut his eyes against the awful glare. But soon, he had other forms of discomfort with which to concern himself.

Bathed in the Quistalian device's lurid illumination, the muscles in his arms and legs knotted painfully. Then his skin began to crack and blister. And a moment later, it felt as if a white-hot poker had been plunged into his belly.

Lucifer! he bellowed in his mind.

At the same time, Xavier felt his astral projection returning to him. It had managed to determine his location, a place deep underground in the northwestern part of the United States. It could go now and find his X-Men, let them know . . .

But even as he began the thought, he realized it was too late. The Quistalian device had begun its work in earnest. And as it shuttled him off this plane of existence, his astral image went with him, drawn inexorably back into his mind . . .

Dragged forcibly with Professor X into the roiling, eternal nothingness of the Nameless Dimension.

CHAPTER THREE

P rofessor Xavier was drowning in the depths of a cold, viscous sea. Or rather, he felt he would be . . . as soon as he
tried to pull his first breath into his lungs.

Fortunately, he had sucked in some air as Lucifer's ray
washed over him. It wasn't that he'd had any idea that his
destination would be like this—a bizarre environment of thick,
oily liquid. It was just a reaction to the pain the ray had
inflicted on him.

Had the professor been prepared for such a place, had he
had any idea of what he would have to face, he would have
fortified himself even more. He would have taken in as much
oxygen as his lungs could hold.

But he hadn't.

And now he was caught in a nightmare, a horrible death
pressing in on him from all sides. With no way of knowing
which way was up, he began to thrash about with his arms,
turning his head this way and that . . . seeking something—
anything—that might give him a chance to orient himself.

A feeling of panic surged through him. But that, he

knew, could be the death of him. Bringing all his considerable willpower to bear, he forced himself to relax, to examine his predicament coldly and logically in the small amount of time left to him.

If he remained calm, he had a chance to prevail—a chance to survive. He would give himself that chance. Then even if he failed, even if he lost his final battle, he would at least know he had first tried everything he could think of.

Experience told the professor that he had perhaps fifty seconds left before the breath in his lungs needed to be released. Then he would be compelled to suck in that first and last liquid breath. *Fifty seconds,* he reflected, consulting his wristwatch. It didn't seem like a lot of time for him to figure out where the surface was and reach it.

But it was all he had.

Normally, the light would have been a clue. The surface would have been wherever the illumination was the brightest. However, it seemed to be of equal intensity in all directions. *No help there,* Xavier thought.

On the other hand, he couldn't be too distant from the oxygen he craved, since a liquid this thick would start to block light at a relatively shallow depth. So if he could figure out in which direction to swim, he probably wouldn't have to go far.

Abruptly, the professor recalled a trick he had learned from a scuba diver. Expelling a tiny bit of the air stored in his lungs, he watched the bubbles it made. Since air was lighter than water, they would eventually rise in the direction of the surface.

But as he waited, it became plain to him that the bubbles weren't going anywhere. They were just hanging there in front of him, as if the thickness of the stuff around him was preventing them from making any headway.

Inwardly, Xavier cursed. How much time did he have left? He looked at his watch again. Thirty-five seconds.

The surface, he told himself. *Find the* surface.

Unfortunately, he had no other ideas, no other strategies for orienting himself. With all the survival training he had undergone, all the mental exercises, he was unprepared for something like this. So he seized the only option open to him.

He guessed.

It's the lady or the tiger, Professor X told himself.

Flip a coin, pick a door, and hope, with the odds dead even, that a ferocious bundle of orange-furred feline didn't come springing out at him. Except there were a great many directions from which to choose. Many doors. And only one of them contained his salvation.

Xavier began to swim toward what seemed like "up" to him, sweeping his arms through the heavy liquid in long, powerful strokes. He wished he could go faster, but his paralyzed legs were useless to him, as much a burden here as on dry land. As usual, the professor would have to work with what he had and hope for the best.

His chest tightening with the need to exhale, he glanced at his watch. Twenty-five seconds to go. And Xavier still had no idea where he was . . . or whether he was headed towards or away from the surface.

He considered the insanity of the situation. Why had Lucifer bothered to transport him here just to drown him? If it was the professor's death the Quistalian desired, why didn't he just kill Xavier while he lay there in front of his simulacrum? It made no sense.

Twenty seconds.

He could feel his face flushing, his fingers going numb from lack of oxygen. And still he pulled himself along.

What was it the mental projection of Lucifer had said? *I*

look forward to the company—and also, for you to have a taste of the hell I've endured since I was sent here.

Clearly, the alien had meant for Xavier to end up in the Nameless Dimension. Then why had he sent the mutant here instead? Was it a mistake? Had he miscalculated somehow—or given his drones the wrong instructions?

Fifteen seconds.

His strength was ebbing. The compulsion to exhale was becoming too powerful to resist.

Think, Xavier told himself as he continued to pull at the liquid with powerful strokes, more and more certain that the answer was floating right in front of him. *Why are you here?*

Ten seconds . . .

The professor was in agony. Darkness encroached on the edges of his vision, threatening to claim him.

And suddenly, it came to him.

A smile crossed his tightly clamped lips and he stopped swimming. *Of course,* he thought, his lungs near to bursting. Lucifer hadn't meant to kill him. And he hadn't made a mistake either.

He had sent Xavier here on purpose . . . to the Nameless Dimension, the same realm the Quistalian himself had inhabited for the past decade. And Lucifer would have drowned here long ago if this environment weren't somehow capable of sustaining an oxygen-breathing being.

Five seconds.

His lungs near to exploding, the professor knew he had nothing to lose by acting on his guess. So against his every instinct, he opened his mouth and released the last of his breath.

It bubbled eerily from his nose and mouth. Then, again

fighting his animal instincts, reasoning that he would either survive or end his life then and there, Xavier inhaled a deep draught of the oily liquid.

For a moment, it seemed to him that he had made a mistake. The stuff filled his throat, threatening to asphyxiate him. But when it reached the professor's lungs, he found it strangely satisfying—strangely invigorating. In fact, he realized with relief, it was every bit as nourishing as the oxygen he had been breathing all his life.

Whatever this stuff was, he thought, pulling in some more of it, it wasn't a liquid as liquids were constituted on Earth. Xavier couldn't begin to understand how or why it worked as it did—and while it would be interesting to subject it to analysis some day, he could live for now without knowing its precise nature.

All that was important was that he was sustained by it. He was alive. And if he was alive, he could still win out over his enemy.

Keep telling yourself that, Xavier!

The words slammed through the professor's mind like hammer blows. It was Lucifer, he realized, but the villain's telepathic voice was far louder and far more immediate than it had been on Earth. It made sense, now that he thought about it. After, all, they were no longer on opposite sides of the dimensional barrier.

Xavier tried reaching out with his mind to pinpoint the exact location of the voice. But he found, to his deep concern, that he had trouble focusing his thoughts. Something was wrong, he told himself. Some element of this dimension was affecting his telepathic powers, making it difficult for him to utilize even a fraction of his abilities.

It was like a sighted man losing ninety percent of his

vision. Once again, the professor felt helpless, unable to maneuver. Panic gripped him. And once again, he managed to submerge the feeling.

He had to maintain control, he told himself, as he had done before Lucifer transported him from Earth. He had to minimize the villain's ability to invade and read his thoughts. No matter what happened, no matter how bad the situation got, he couldn't let himself surrender.

Oh, yes, Xavier, the voice thundered painfully in his skull. *Fight me. Cling to your thin, sickly hopes . . . so I can crush your soul the way I intend to crush your feeble body.*

Sensing a movement behind him, the professor used his arms to turn himself around. His eyes narrowed as he saw what was speeding towards him. Standing upright, propelled by his ionic-energy powers, came the crimson-garbed figure of Lucifer.

It wasn't the simulacrum, either—not this time. It was the Quistalian himself. Even from a distance, Xavier could see the hatred blazing in his enemy's eyes, the rage twisting his thin, cruel lips.

Lucifer wasn't coming to talk. Of that much, the professor was certain. He knew as sure as he was breathing liquid that there would be considerable misery in his immediate future.

Xavier couldn't deflect the Quistalian's attack—not with his telepathic abilities muted by the Nameless Dimension. However, he could still erect a shell around the deepest part of his consciousness and try to hide his psyche inside it.

His body would take a beating. There was nothing he could do about that. But he could protect his sanity and that was more important. Even in a diminished state, the mutant's mind was his greatest asset. To lose that would be to lose everything.

Lucifer slowed as he came nearer, his purple cape billowing majestically about him, his posture that of the hunter that has cornered his prey. Finally, the alien stopped altogether and hovered in front of Xavier.

You don't look happy to see me, Lucifer told him. *I was hoping for a warmer greeting from such an old friend.*

The Quistalian wasted no more of his strength on telepathic communication. Instead, he unleashed a barrage of brilliant, white energy bolts. They struck Xavier with triphammer force, sending him tumbling end over end through the thick liquid atmosphere.

Then, before the professor could catch his breath, his adversary hit him again. And again.

Lucifer toyed with him as a cat might toy with a mouse, swatting at him and sending him pinwheeling away so he could pursue him and catch him all over again. And while the alien blasted his body, his psionic attacks pounded Xavier's mental defenses.

All the professor could do was roll with the blows, trying his best to disassociate himself from the pain and the suffering and the humiliation. He continued to focus his energies on one goal and one goal only—to maintain the shell that kept his mind from serious harm.

Of course, complete non-resistance would have made it clear to the Quistalian that Xavier was up to something. So every so often, the professor lashed out with his fists or launched a halfhearted psionic counterattack, making it appear that he was concentrating all his power on the struggle—and that it just wasn't enough to make a difference.

Xavier hoped fervently that Lucifer would eventually have his fill of revenge or simply grow tired of battering him. After all, as tough as he had made himself, even he couldn't endure such punishment indefinitely.

But to his chagrin, the alien wasn't done with him—not

by a long shot. Though Lucifer stopped walloping him with his ionic energy bolts, he continued to assault the mutant with his fists.

Through his pain-clouded vision, Xavier could see the sadistic glint of pleasure in the eyes of his helmeted tormentor. With every cruel, damaging blow that he brought down on the professor, the Quistalian's face beamed with evil delight.

The thick liquid environment did little to diminish the speed and impact of Lucifer's blows. His fists flew at the professor with bone-crushing force, bloodying the mutant's mouth and nose, raising bruise after bruise and welt after welt.

Finally, panting from his exertions, his eyes shining with the knowledge that he had brought Xavier to the brink of unconsciousness, the alien ended his attack. With a sigh, he allowed himself to float back a little and observe the results of his handiwork.

"You cannot imagine how long I have dreamed of this," Lucifer rasped, his cape undulating behind him. "To see you flail helplessly, to hear your mind scream in pain . . . it is like a symphony to me."

The professor didn't say anything. He couldn't. He was too close to unconsciousness to come up with anything intelligible.

Lucifer smiled at his silence. "You cannot appreciate what I'm saying, can you? But you will learn, Xavier. Oh, how you will learn! And the time I spent imprisoned here will be as the smallest fraction of the eternity I have planned for you. But that is not all . . ."

As he spoke, the alien began to construct a cage of ionic energy around the professor. Having allowed himself to be battered so soundly, Xavier was only dimly aware of the glittering strands of force that wrapped themselves around him, binding his arms to his sides, encircling his torso and tightening around his neck. Before they were done, they had forced his chin to tilt up at an awkward and uncomfortable angle.

"Unlike me," Lucifer went on, "you won't even have freedom of movement. You'll remain immobilized by my force fields, your arms every bit as helpless as your legs. While I was free to search for a means of escape, you will be denied that luxury." He sneered in triumph. "You are mine, Terran . . . finally and irrevocably mine!"

With that, the Quistalian began to laugh—an hysterical laughter that chilled Xavier to his soul. The professor was more certain now than ever that the Quistalian's long imprisonment in this realm of nothingness had indeed driven him mad.

"Alas," said Lucifer, "I will not be sharing this ocean of hell with you much longer. You see, the transportation device I used to bring you here can reverse its effects. It can also transport someone out again—though not as it is presently put together."

Of course, Xavier thought. Otherwise, the alien would already have had his ionic-powered agents return him to his original reality.

"The device needs to undergo a significant alteration," Lucifer explained. "A retrofit, if you will. Fortunately, all the requisite components are already present on Earth, stored in three different abandoned but still functional Quistalian facilities."

The professor had always suspected that some of the aliens' sites had remained hidden. Now his suspicions were confirmed.

"On the other hand," said Lucifer, "my drones aren't up to

the task of retrieving these parts. They have tried, of course, but they are primitive beings without independent thought or intelligence, useful only for the simplest tasks . . . accosting motorists on the highway, for instance. But you already know that, don't you?"

Xavier didn't utter a word in response. He kept his mind blank, his eyes unfocused. He would let the alien believe he was still reeling from the beating he had absorbed.

"However," Lucifer noted, pointing a gloved finger at his prisoner, "your doppelganger is another matter entirely. As I told you, it has been programmed with your thoughts, your memories. It is therefore capable of independent thought and action . . . the kind of thought and action that can obtain for me the components I need."

He pantomimed the action of a puppeteer with his hand. "I pull the doppelganger's strings, like so . . . and it, in turn, pulls the strings of your precious, fawning X-Men!"

His willpower at an ebb, Xavier couldn't help but respond to that bit of news. His eyes widened . . . and his enemy barked out a laugh.

"Yes," he observed, "you understand now . . . don't you, my friend? Your X-Men are as much to blame for my fate as you are. Surely I cannot leave them out of my plans!"

Indeed, the professor was beginning to see where Lucifer was going with his scheme. Still, he allowed the alien to articulate it.

"And what could be sweeter," Lucifer asked, "than to make my old enemies the means by which I free myself? What could be more fitting than to have *them* obtain the components I require? Just one thing, Xavier . . . the knowledge that you will be looking on all the while, gazing through the dimensional barrier but helpless to interfere with my plan."

The mutant bit back a curse. *No*, he told himself, *don't. Don't give your enemy the satisfaction.*

"I can see you've already begun dwelling on what I've told you," the Quistalian observed gleefully. "Good. That is just as I had hoped. After all, watching your X-Men risk their lives to liberate me . . . only to see me destroy them as soon as I leave this place . . . should be even more of a torment than anything I have inflicted so far.

"But as a bonus," he said, "as an added pleasure, they will be acting under the direction of a being they believe to be their beloved leader—a being with your countenance."

Lucifer moved closer to Xavier, so they were almost face to face. "And that," he noted in a honey-sweet voice, "is an irony you will no doubt remember the rest of your days."

The alien patted the professor's swollen cheek with mock affection. "Enjoy the show, my old friend. I know I will. I go now to a place where I can concentrate, focus my mental energies—so I can destroy everything you hold dear."

Then he turned and moved away, leaving a gossamer trail of ionic energy in his wake. Little by little, he was swallowed by distance until Xavier lost sight of him altogether.

Taking a breath of his liquid environment, the professor sagged against his shimmering bonds. He was exhausted, even more from the effort of maintaining his psychic shields than from the physical abuse he had suffered.

He needed a moment, just a moment, to drop his guard and rest. A second or two to gather his strength. Then he would try to break the restraints in which Lucifer had left him.

But to have a chance of success, Xavier had to concentrate all his strength on the task. That meant he had to drop the protective barriers he had erected around his psyche minutes earlier, forcing his innermost self to relive everything he had suffered at Lucifer's hands.

He didn't hesitate. After all, what choice did he have?

Suddenly, the pain overwhelmed him. It was like a poisonous, red wave, crushing him, making his nerve endings quiver with accumulated trauma. Under that piercing, wrenching onslaught, one of the most disciplined individuals born on Earth moaned in agony.

But that wasn't the worst of it—because in the professor's dazed and weakened state, he accidentally let down one barrier too many. He dropped the barricade he had put up around the worst suffering he had ever known, the torment he lived with every day . . .

The pain of his crushed and ruined spine.

For years, he had held that agony at bay through sheer force of will. But now, clumsily, he exposed himself to it, and the electric fury of it nearly caused him to spiral into darkness.

Somehow, Xavier managed to fight it back. Somehow, using reserves of strength he didn't know he possessed, he forced the mind-numbing misery back down into the depths of his subconscious.

Then, gasping, he applied every bit of his flagging concentration in an effort to rebuild his defenses. Make them high and strong, he told himself. Seal the pain where it can no longer hurt you. Take back your body and your mind from the unspeakable agony.

Slowly, little by little, the tides of suffering ebbed and receded, until at last all that was left was a dull residual ache. Only then could the professor turn his thoughts back to Lucifer, to attempting to break the bonds the alien had created.

Applying all the strength in his arms, he tried to push out—to stretch the ionic energy bands beyond their breaking point. But they wouldn't budge.

A second time, he pushed out with his elbows, straining his physical capabilities to the limit. And a second time, the bonds resisted him.

Xavier sighed with frustration. Clearly, he would have to find another way to free himself. But that could wait. For now, he had to focus all his energies on sabotaging Lucifer's scheme.

It wouldn't be easy. He knew that. His adversary had had a long time to plan his escape . . . to plot out his vengeance in exacting detail. The professor had a good deal less time at his disposal—a day, maybe two at the outside, depending on how quickly Lucifer's doppelganger worked.

But defeat was never something Charles Xavier had embraced eagerly. He wouldn't begin to do so now.

CHAPTER FOUR

The duplicate Professor Xavier—who all too recently had been an ambient cloud of ionic particles—sat comfortably in his large, handsome study, and reflected on everything he knew about the Xavier Institute for Higher Learning.

The real Professor X had created the institution in New York's Westchester County, in the town of Salem Center, years earlier. To the casual observer, the hoary gray compound appeared to be nothing more than a private academy dedicated to children with exceptional abilities. Indeed, it was a school; but what made the students exceptional was something other than their intelligence.

For this unassuming mansion, set on several acres of rolling, wooded hills, was also the haven and headquarters of the uncanny X-Men, Earth's first team of mutant Super Heroes.

Years before, Xavier had initiated the work of seeking out and training certain youngsters—men and women born with extraordinary powers as a result of unexpected quirks in their genetic codes.

In short, *mutants.*

The professor had known from the beginning that he wouldn't be able to identify them all. However, he had vowed to find and work with as many of them as he possibly could. His goal was to sequester young mutants and protect them from the rest of humanity, whose fear of their kind was inexorably turning into a conflagration.

The professor had already encountered mutants who had come of age under a shadow of fear and suspicion—a shadow that had cast a permanent darkness over their lives, embittering them beyond redemption. These individuals felt that their unique powers and abilities placed them a level above humanity, even though that same humanity loathed them and held them in contempt.

Rather than try to prove themselves worthy of respect and acceptance, they turned to evil and the conquest of their fellow human beings. Xavier couldn't do anything for them any longer. But for those still coming to grips with the world, he had much to offer.

He gave them a direction. He held out the promise of camaraderie and acceptance ... of accomplishment. But most of all, he gave these frightened, young mutants peace of mind.

Over the years, Professor X had schooled a great many of them. In time, they became members of his X-Men. They formed teams, split and reunited in new configurations. However, no group would ever be as close to his heart as the first one he had assembled.

Their names still struck a remarkably powerful chord in Xavier's consciousness, both individually and together. Scott Summers. Jean Grey. Warren Worthington III. Hank McCoy. Bobby Drake. But he thought of them by other designations as well—the names to which they referred when they were in combat . . .

Cyclops.

Marvel Girl.

Angel.

Beast.

Iceman.

Xavier and his five original charges had been together, off and on, for several years. It was a long enough time for the older man to consider the quintet his family.

And the stately old mansion that housed the X-Men? It was as deceiving as the people who lived inside it.

After inheriting the building and the land on which it sat, the professor had seen the entire structure gutted and refurbished to his own specifications. It had been trans-formed into a high-tech fortress equipped with state of the art reconnaissance and defensive systems, with several of its rooms dedicated to highly specialized purposes.

Of course, a casual visitor to the Institute would see nothing but ordinary classrooms and living quarters. It was only by looking beyond the carefully constructed facade that one might discover such places as the subterranean Danger Room—a training facility capable of generating an almost unlimited array of holographic environments, each with its own unique collection of computer-programmed obstacles and challenges.

Of most interest to the ionic-energy doppelganger was the sophisticated device known as Cerebro, a highly intelli-gent network capable of detecting the psychic emanations of other mutants. But he was also intrigued by the mansion's extraterrestrial energy battery—the gift of a distant species known as the Shi'ar—which had been installed some time ago to guarantee Xavier an uninterrupted supply of power.

Naturally, few people were ever allowed to see beyond the facade. Only those mutants who lived and worked there were privy to the school's secrets. Bobby Drake, for instance. And Hank McCoy. And of course, Professor Charles Xavier himself.

Or in this case, his duplicate.

Henry McCoy, known to the civilized world as Beast, pushed aside his dangling laser beam projector, removed his protective goggles and took a closer look at his handiwork.

The mutant was pleased—and justifiably so. The centimeter-long titanium component lying on the dark, stonetopped table in front of him appeared to be precisely in line with his design specifications.

"And they said nothing?" he asked, his furry blue brow bunched in concentration on the component.

"Not a word," Bobby said, removing his goggles as well. He was sitting on the opposite side of the table, peering at his friend over a landscape of miniaturized power-transfer parts.

"You're certain?" Hank pressed, still hunkered over the component and inspecting it for flaws.

"It's just the way I told you," said Bobby. "They showed up out of nowhere and trashed the van. Then they whipped our butts but good. And while we were unconscious, they disappeared."

Satisfied that the component was all it needed to be, Hank glanced at his companion and pushed his glasses up his nose. "Without taking a thing? Not even a stick of chewing gum?"

"That's right," Bobby confirmed.

Hank grunted. "Sorry to make you repeat this all over again. The problem is it makes no sense."

"Tell me about it," said Bobby. He took a sip from his cobalt-blue coffee cup—a touch of the mundane in the midst of a bristling array of shining, otherworldly technology.

"And Professor X wasn't able to get a telepathic insight into either one of them?"

"He told you himself, didn't he? It was as if their minds were total blanks."

Hank shook his head. "Mysteriouser and mysteriouser."

Bobby sighed. "You know, you're the only one I've ever met who speaks that way. I mean . . . 'mysteriouser'? Is that even a word?"

"It is now," Hank replied. He indicated his blue-pelted, lab-coated anatomy with a hairy, long-fingered hand. "I may look like the offspring of a blueberry and an orangutan, but I'm every bit as qualified a lexicographer as Noah Webster."

"What you are," said Bobby, "is weird."

"Says the man who turns into a popsicle at the drop of a degree," Hank countered deftly.

Still, he had to admit that his friend had a point. Even in as unusual a group as the X-Men, he cut a rather bizarre figure.

But then, Hank reflected, he had been that way from birth. Far from being a typical bundle of joy, he had resembled a strange cross between human and simian, with a squat, powerful body and unusually large hands and feet.

As he grew, he exhibited a strength and agility that was anything but normal. He could climb and swing on playground equipment the way a monkey might negotiate a stand of jungle trees, clinging by long, dexterous toes that were more agile than a normal person's fingers.

Shortly after he left the X-Men for the first time, he was transformed into something even more like his namesake. Now covered head to toe in shaggy blue fur, he was indeed more beast than man—at least in appearance. But in a final irony, his inhuman appearance housed a scientific mind as brilliant as any found on Earth.

"Might they have been robots?" Hank speculated, picking up his own coffee cup and taking a sip. "Or androids, perhaps?"

Bobby shrugged. "They might have been anything, pal. Neither of us got close enough to find out."

Frowning, Hank considered the collection of devices hanging over the table from a suspended Shi'ar power node. They included, in addition to the laser projector he had been using, a microwave emitter, an electromagnetic field generator and an x-ray gun.

"It sounds to me," he said slowly, "as if this was an effort at reconnaissance. In other words, Bobby, someone was attempting to gauge the extent of your combat capabilities."

"But why?" Bobby asked. "And who were they working for? And considering what pushovers we turned out to be, why didn't they just finish us off then and there? If somebody's planning to come after us, all the attack did was serve to put us on alert."

Hank smiled at his friend. "Against . . . ?"

Bobby thought about it for a moment, then made a sound of disgust. "All I know is if I see any guys wearing tinfoil suits coming at me, I'm going to hit first and ask questions later."

Hank chuckled, exposing his sharp, white canines. "A wise approach in our line of work. But I should remind you, the outcome of your conflict could have been a good deal worse. After all, neither you nor the professor suffered any real damage."

Bobby sighed. "You mean other than the embarrassment of having my head handed to me? Nope. No damage."

"Well," Hank said, "as you point out, at least we've been alerted to a potential danger. However, barring a return engagement with your men in silver, it appears your encounter will remain a mystery."

"I suppose." Bobby drained the last of his coffee and looked at his wristwatch. "Anyway, I better get back to work. I've got the computers running a check on the Shi'ar energy generator."

Hank tilted his furry head and looked at him askance. "I've known you since the first days of the X-Men, Bobby Drake and I can tell when you've got something on your mind besides work."

His friend blushed. "Okay, so maybe I've got something planned for *after* I've checked the generator."

"And that would be?"

"Well," said Bobby, "I just installed our new oversized, state of the art, ultra-high-resolution video screen, and it's been a while since I've had a chance to enjoy my favorite trilogy . . ."

Hank rolled his eyes. "*Lethal Weapon 1, 2* and . . . be still, my beating heart . . . *3*? I thought you had gotten over that juvenile fare when you received your degree."

"Hey," said Bobby, rising to the challenge, "it's not juvenile at all. It's just . . . I don't know. Action-packed."

"One would think," Hank replied wistfully, "that a fellow who battles Magneto and his intractable entourage on a regular basis would spend his free time on more staid pursuits."

"Don't you get it?" Bobby asked him. "That's the point. Magneto is real. The Juggernaut is real. *Lethal Weapon* is just a movie."

"So's *Dr. Zhivago,*" said Hank. "Now there's a cinematic work eminently worthy of an afternoon's—"

Behind them, the door to the laboratory hissed open and Professor Xavier glided in on his golden antigrav unit. "Good morning," Xavier said. He turned his eyes on Bobby. "How are you feeling?"

"Great," the X-Man replied. "Nothing like a good night's sleep to make a guy forget a bad beating. How about you?"

The professor nodded. "Much the same," he said in his deep, untroubled voice. "Though I am still puzzled by the assault, I did not seem to sustain any lasting injuries." He turned to Hank. "I trust you've reset the mansion's security system?"

"To priority one," the blue-furred X-Man assured him. "Just as you requested, sir. No one will be able to approach the grounds without setting off an alarm."

Xavier nodded. "Excellent. Thank you, Hank." He turned his attention to the array of power-transfer components on the laboratory worktable. "Still working on the accelerator, I see?"

"That's correct," Hank confirmed, picking up a cylindrical piece of titanium about two feet long. "Actually, miniaturizing a particle accelerator is proving to be more of a challenge than I expected."

"I'm not surprised," said the professor, "considering you're attempting to do in twenty-five inches what has previously only been done in devices the length of a city block."

Hank regarded the piece of titanium. "The difficulty lies

in generating a sufficiently strong magnetic field. Without it, I can't propel the particles at the requisite speed."

"Is our Shi'ar technology not helpful in this regard?" asked Xavier.

"It is," Hank told him. "Infinitely so." He put the cylinder back on the lab table. "It's just a matter of time before I find a way around the magnetic field problem."

Xavier nodded approvingly. "The boon to physics research facilities around the world would be immeasurable."

"And Hank promises that he won't be using Shi'ar parts in the final product," Bobby piped up. "That way, he can make it available without having to worry about alien technology falling into the wrong hands." He jerked a thumb at his friend. "At least, that's what he told me."

"And it's all true," Hank said. "I intend to use Shi'ar parts only to prove that my theory is valid. Once that's been accomplished, I can dedicate myself to finding an alternative power source."

"That may prove to be the most difficult task of all," the professor said in sympathy.

Hank picked through the pile of parts scattered across the table's stone surface. "No doubt," he conceded. "However, as a wise man once recommended, one step at a time."

Xavier seemed tempted to smile. "Touché," he replied.

After all, it was the professor who had given Hank that advice a long time ago, shortly after he had arrived at the Xavier Institute for Higher Learning. And the mutant known as Beast had never forgotten it.

Apparently, neither had Xavier.

"Well," said Bobby, getting up from the table, "I'd love to stay and hear about Hank's ground-breaking efforts to expand the frontiers of science, but I've got to make sure our generator is still humming. It's a mundane job, I know . . . but someone's got to do it."

Hank grinned, unable to resist taking advantage of the straight line. "You said it, not me."

Xavier didn't intervene. He didn't even crack a frown. Nor was Hank surprised. After all, he and his fellow X-Man carried on this kind of banter all the time.

Flashing a lop-sided smile at the professor, Bobby left the lab.

Hank picked up his protective goggles and slipped them back over his eyes. "Care to lend a hand, sir?"

Xavier shook his head. "No, thank you. Perhaps some other time." He looked around at the laboratory, its walls lined with alien technology. "The Shi'ar have been quite generous," he observed, as if he was only noticing their contributions for the first time.

At bit of a loss, Hank nodded. "So they have, sir."

Without another word, the professor glided out of the room. The apelike X-Man watched him go and saw the door slide closed behind him. Then he reached for the laser again and returned to his work.

What's more, Hank McCoy didn't give his mentor's comment a second thought. After all, he was the same Charles Xavier whom the mutant had known since he was a raw teenager . . .

The one steady rock in an ever-changing flood of uncertainties.

The real Charles Xavier chafed with mounting frustration as he mentally watched the interaction between Hank McCoy, Bobby Drake, and the being they believed was him.

As Lucifer had promised, he could see the events unfolding in Salem Center. The dimensional barrier was strangely penetrable in that regard, if one put one's mind to it. But though the professor could see his X-Men, even hear them, he seemed incapable of connecting with them—incapable of sending them a warning about the grave and immediate danger they faced.

To Xavier's dismay, the doppelganger appeared to be a flawless recreation of the genuine article. It seemed likely that Hank, Bobby and their teammates would follow its orders without question, even if those orders led them to their deaths.

No, thought the professor. *I can't allow it. I've got to try harder to break through to them.*

He cleared his mind as thoroughly as he could. Then he concentrated on his task as he had never concentrated before, expending every last iota of psionic energy at his disposal. And for the briefest of moments, no more than a fraction of a second, he felt himself make a feathery connection with the world of his origin.

Hank, he thought, seeking out his protégé's mind. *Listen to me, please. It's Professor Xavier . . .*

But despite the effort behind his overture, it didn't penetrate deeply enough into the X-Man's consciousness. It remained tangential, superficial. Something was stopping Xavier—and he knew what it was.

Hank's mind was too complex, too crammed with competing thoughts to hear a small voice crying out from another dimension. *No doubt,* the professor thought, *I would run into the same problem if I tried to establish a link with Bobby.* As fully-realized intellects, his X-Men simply weren't receptive to what he was transmitting.

Then, as quickly as it had come, the connection was gone.

Xavier went limp, exhausted and disappointed. After all, he had failed to obtain the results he desired. Still, he told himself, his undertaking had gone for something. He had proven to himself that he could punch through the interdimensional barrier, if only briefly.

It was the most modest of accomplishments, to be sure. In some eyes, it might not have been an accomplishment at all. But to Xavier, it was the first sign of hope that he had managed to glean from his situation, and he resolved to cling to it as tightly as possible.

Closing his eyes and concentrating again, the mutant tried to strengthen his link with Hank. But his efforts were distracted by a new vision in his head—that of the doppelganger entering Xavier's private office ensconced in Xavier's antigrav unit.

Without hesitation, as if he had spent every day of the past several years in this room, the energy construct went straight to the professor's desk. But then, this being was, for all intents and purposes, Charles Xavier. It knew all that he knew, responded as he might respond. Indeed, the only real difference between man and duplicate was the latter's slavish obedience to its Quistalian master.

Settling itself behind the desk and placing its fingers on the professor's computer keyboard, the doppelganger keyed Xavier's access code into his computer terminal. A menu flashed on the screen before it and it purposefully selected an item.

The real Xavier wasn't able to divine the duplicate's thoughts, but he *was* able to peer over the imposter's shoulder and see the monitor screen. He was able to make out the item that the duplicate had selected: a database of alarm systems connected to a variety of sites around the world.

In the Nameless Dimension, the professor frowned. After all, he knew that database all too well.

Some time ago, he had listed the bases of operations

used most often by his various adversaries. Of course, these facilities were deserted, abandoned long before. However, knowing there was a chance that his enemies would return to them, Xavier and his team had deactivated their offensive and defensive capabilities and left them standing.

Then they had hardwired miniaturized sensors into them and linked the sensors to the X-Men's security system through wireless modems. That way, if any of their vanquished foes happened to return to an old haunt, an alarm would sound in the mansion—alerting the X-Men and giving them advance warning of trouble.

The professor had established this kind of precaution in Lucifer's Quistalian base in the Balkans—the site of the alien's second defeat at the hands of Xavier's fledgling X-Men. It was that site that the energy duplicate was accessing now.

And not *just* accessing. As the real Professor X looked on, the doppelganger tampered with the site's sensor reports.

Lucifer, through the actions of his Xavier-puppet, was wasting no time putting his revenge scheme into motion. He was planting a seed that he could harvest at a later time.

And all the true Charles Xavier could do was bear witness to it as he floated helplessly in the Nameless Dimension.

CHAPTER FIVE

B*obby?* said a voice.

Bobby Drake turned over and swiped sleepily at his ear. Maybe he could make it go away, he thought.

Bobby? the voice said again.

He burrowed his head deeper into the pillow. But he had a sinking feeling that the voice wasn't going anywhere.

Bobby? it demanded.

He sighed. *I'll get up in a second, Mom.*

I am not your mother, Bobby, said the voice.

Not his mother? Then who . . .

Grudgingly, Bobby opened his tired eyes and saw that he was in his bedroom at the Xavier Institute for Higher Learning. And with that realization came a second one.

"Professor?" he said out loud.

Yes. And I require your presence in my study.

Heaving a sigh, Bobby tossed his covers off, threw his legs over the side of his bed and raked his fingers through his sleep-tousled hair. Then he glanced at the digital alarm clock on his nightstand and saw that it was barely six in the morning.

He groaned. "I hope the fate of the world depends on this, sir."

It may indeed, Xavier replied telepathically. *Please dress quickly, Bobby. I await your arrival.*

The mutant stretched and yawned. "I hear you loud and clear, Professor. On my way."

Padding across the cold wooden floor on bare feet, he went into his private bathroom and splashed some water on his face. Then he brushed his teeth, threw on a pair of well-worn jeans and a longsleeved white tee shirt and made his way to the stairs.

Bobby knew, of course, that Professor Xavier wouldn't have summoned him at this hour if it weren't a matter of importance. But even though he was a working super hero, part of a team that had, time after time, battled to save the world from death and destruction, a guy needed his sleep.

Bobby had barely completed the thought when he saw a flash of blue and almost collided with his friend Hank. Clad in oversized red gym shorts and a black tank top, the furred mutant was also hurrying out of his room in response to the professor's summons.

"Sounded urgent," Hank muttered, latching onto the rounded post at the top of the banister and swinging around it.

"It always does," Bobby replied. Then, giving in to a sudden, antic impulse, he added, "Race you!"

With that, he shot a spray of super-cooled moisture at the stairs, creating an ice slide beneath his feet. Then he slid down the chute like a snowboarder on a wintry hillside.

Not to be outdone, Hank twisted through the air beside him and landed on the floor below. But before he could change direction, Iceman had zipped by on a high bank of his ever-extending slide.

"Really, Bobby," his furry friend called out as he bounded after him, "you're not a callow youth anymore. I don't see why you still feel compelled to engage in these childish contests."

"You're just afraid you'll lose!" Bobby tossed back as he negotiated an icy path through the living room.

"Afraid?" Hank growled incredulously.

Suddenly, Bobby heard a quick series of thuds. Before he knew it, his friend had somersaulted over his head and was surfing the ice slide ahead of him. Unfortunately, the thing wasn't quite sturdy enough to hold someone of Hank's considerable weight.

As it began to crack, Hank sprang forward onto his hands and vaulted off the slide again. However, Bobby didn't have that option. Instead, he had to lay down an icy detour—one that threatened to smash him into a wall full of original Currier and Ives prints.

With no other recourse, he curled the end of his slide back and executed a tight loop-the-loop. However, he couldn't slow himself down as much as he would have liked. The next thing he knew he was sitting on the floor, his head spinning wildly.

Abruptly, a big, blue paw materialized in front of him. "Need a hand?" asked Hank McCoy, exposing long, sharp canines as he grinned from ear to pointed ear.

Bobby gave him a dirty look. Then he placed his hand in his friend's hand and allowed himself to be pulled to his feet. "I suppose you think you're pretty funny."

"In point of fact," the blue-furred X-Man replied, "I do find myself rather amusing. Now, let's go. We mustn't keep the professor waiting."

Bobby felt like unleashing a snowball at his friend. However, Hank was right. Xavier had said he wanted to see them pronto.

"Just you wait," he told his fellow mutant as they continued in the direction of their mentor's study. "I haven't even begun to fight."

Hank didn't say anything. He just went on grinning.

Bobby hoped that saving the world wouldn't take too long this time. After all, he had to plot revenge on his big blue pal.

The ionic construct posing as Professor Charles Xavier sat patiently in his study and waited for his X-Men to join him.

When the two of them arrived, they looked flushed with some recent exertion. However, the energy duplicate didn't inquire about it. He had a more important agenda.

"What's going on, sir?" Bobby asked, plunking himself down in one of the posh leather chairs arranged on the opposite side of Xavier's desk.

Hank didn't sit down alongside his friend. With his brawny, strangely-proportioned body, he wasn't comfortable in people-sized furniture. "By all means," he added, "fill us in."

The doppelganger leaned forward, effecting the grimmest demeanor he could manage. "Obviously," he began in a somber voice, "you remember our encounters with the alien called Lucifer."

Bobby grunted. "How could we forget?"

"Indeed," said the construct. "And you no doubt also remember his agenda—to set the stage for his people's invasion of Earth."

"An agenda we thwarted," Hank noted with obvious satisfaction, "which is how he wound up being exiled to another dimension."

"Precisely," the duplicate confirmed.

"Don't tell me Lucifer's gotten loose?" said Bobby.

The construct wanted to steer the pair away from that kind of thinking. "I have no information to that effect. However, I do have some evidence of Quistalian activity on Earth."

Hanks' eyes narrowed beneath his shaggy blue brows. "Has someone set off the alarm in Lucifer's old base?"

"Not exactly," the doppelganger replied. "The base itself has remained untouched. However, its communications equipment has become active. And since no one has invaded the premises to activate it . . ." He allowed his voice to trail off meaningfully.

"It's receiving calls from the outside," Bobby said, attaching a conclusion to the uncompleted thought.

"So it would seem," the energy construct told him. "I am currently in the process of gathering telemetry on these communications. What I believe I will find when I am done is a number of as-yet-undiscovered and previously dormant Quistalian facilities, recently brought to life."

"Sounds like something's about to happen," Bobby observed.

"An invasion?" Hank suggested.

"That is my fear," the doppelganger said.

Bobby frowned. "We've got to figure out where these Quistalian bunkers are and launch a preemptive strike . . . X-Men style."

The energy duplicate held up his hand in a call for patience. "You're as eager as ever to meet trouble head on, Bobby. However, I don't believe an all-out offensive is the best way to approach this problem."

The mutants seemed to accept his assessment at face value. But then, why should they do otherwise? As far as they knew, they were listening to the man who had founded the X-Men and given meaning to their lives.

"The Quistalians may be watching us," he pointed out. "If that's so, we don't dare deploy all our forces at once—or we run the risk of their moving up their timetable."

"So what do we do?" Bobby asked.

"Good question," Hank told him.

The imposter answered it. "We defuse the Quistalians' facilities as soon as possible. However, we do it in a more subtle way—that is, with a small, easily assembled squad."

"Including us, I hope," said Bobby.

"What I had in mind," the energy duplicate told him, "is a quintet—my five original X-Men." He ticked off his reasons for the decision on his fingers. "First, none of you is very far from Salem Center at the moment. Second, only the five of you have had experience with Quistalian technology—which makes you the resident experts on the subject."

Hank nodded. "So it does."

"Third," the doppelganger continued, "you have been working together as a team longer than any of my other students. As a result, you're the best suited for a series of small, surgical strikes."

"Have you summoned the others yet?" asked Hank.

Had the Xavier doppelganger any emotions of his own, he would have been immensely satisfied at how well his deception was being received. "I am doing so even as we speak," he said.

It wasn't true. The imposter didn't have the professor's ability to carry out two tasks at once. However, it was the answer Xavier's mutants would have expected from him.

Hank stroked his furry chin and looked pensive. "Hmm," he said slowly, almost to himself. "I wonder . . ."

"You have a question, Hank?" the doppelganger asked.

The X-Man shrugged his powerful blue shoulders. "I was just speculating, sir . . . could this development be related in some way to yesterday's attack on you and Bobby?"

The imposter took a breath and let it out, pretending to consider the possibility. "I suppose there could be a connection," he conceded. "We will doubtless become better informed as we proceed."

Hank grunted. "I certainly hope so."

"Same here," said Bobby. "I'd like nothing better than to get my hands on the bozos behind that attack."

Hank glanced at him. "As I recall, you said you wanted nothing more to do with them."

"I changed my mind," Bobby retorted.

"I should receive the telemetry results momentarily," the energy duplicate informed them. "In the meantime, the two of you would do well to put on your working clothes."

Bobby looked eager as he got to his feet. "As the saying goes . . . let's get ready to rumble!"

Indeed, thought the doppelganger, *rumble all you want. In the end, Lucifer will emerge triumphant.*

The first thing of which Jean Grey was aware was the roll of gentle waves under her boat. The second thing of which she was aware was the nearness of her handsome, young husband.

Then she became aware of a third thing and she sat up, squinting in the thin dawn light.

Scott stirred and looked up at her. "What is it?" he asked, propping himself up on one elbow and readjusting the goggles he had to wear even in bed. His brow was creased, his voice taut with apprehension.

"Listen," Jean told him, then amplified the transmission and relayed it to him in a way he could understand.

Come home, said the voice. *I need you.*

Scott frowned. "It's the professor."

His wife nodded. *We're at least four hours from the dock,* she replied. *Can you wait that long?*

I can wait, Xavier assured her, though his tone told her he wasn't ecstatic about it.

Jean glanced at Scott. "We've got to go."

Without complaint, the X-Man with the codename Cyclops got out of their v-shaped bed and reached for a pair of khakis in a nearby locker. "I'll start the engine," he said.

"Don't bother," Jean told him, picturing the key and turning it with her telekinetic power. A moment later, she could hear the hum of their inboard as it turned over.

Scott smiled as he pulled on his trousers. "All right. In that case, I'll weigh anchor."

"I'm on it," his wife and fellow X-Man assured him.

Kicking the motor into drive, she slid their boat forward little by little. At the same time, she pulled up their anchor line until the pronged aluminum weight emerged from the water. Then she stowed it in its dedicated compartment near the bow.

Scott chuckled softly as he heard the clatter of heavy chain joining the anchor. "How about if I hoist the sails?" he asked. "Or would you prefer to do that too?"

Jean melted back into her covers with a mischievous grin. "Hoist away, Ahab. Just be careful not to drop your goggles again. We don't need any more perforated mainsails."

Her husband rolled his eyes as he reached for a sweater capable of staving off the morning chill. "Battle one deadly threat after another," he said, "and no one mentions a thing. But drop your glasses just once and they never let you forget it."

"That's what I'm here for, Mr. Summers," Jean informed him coyly. "To keep you honest."

"And you're doing a heck of a job," he responded.

Donning the sweater, Scott slipped his feet into a pair of topsiders at the foot of their bed. Then he made his way through the cabin and up the ladder to the deck.

The mutant known as Phoenix watched him go. After all, watching her husband was one of her favorite pastimes. Then she drew in a pensive breath and let it out again.

Professor X knew how much she and Scott prized their time together. He wouldn't have interrupted their little cruise unless something really urgent had reared its head.

As the sails above her caught the wind and the boat picked up speed, Jean wondered soberly what that something might be.

Warren Worthington III, chairman and principal stockholder of eminently successful Worthington Industries, sat at the oversized mahogany desk in his well-appointed Manhattan penthouse and pored over yet another in a series of daily financial reports.

Up there in his personal eyrie, with the blinds drawn tight against the pale rays of dawn, Wall Street's darling could make himself comfortable. He could sit in his white silk pajama bottoms, bare chested, his great white wings proud and unfurled.

Warren's pinions had first begun to sprout during his early adolescence. Ever since that time, he had been forced to hide his wings from prying eyes, strapping them so tightly to his back that he felt like he was walking around in a straitjacket.

As if that weren't bad enough, his skin had turned blue in the course of an encounter with a powerful adversary. As a result, he had to use an image inducer to cover up his appearance when he went out in public . . . or be identified as an X-Man.

Sometimes, he wondered what was next in store for him. Big red lobster claws? Foot-long antennae with eightballs on the end of them? A neon rash on his forehead flashing KICK ME, I'M A MUTANT?

At the moment, however, Warren Worthington III wasn't thinking about the drawbacks of being born with an unusual set of genes. And contrary to the hopes of his board of directors, he wasn't contemplating the financial reports in front of him either.

He was thinking about the love of his life, who happened to be a mutant as well. He was dreaming about the beautiful, exotic and incidentally telepathic Betsy Braddock, whose *nom de guerre* was Psylocke.

Unfortunately, Betsy was visiting family in England and therefore wasn't around to alleviate his loneliness. He had been tempted to go overseas with her but . . . well, there had been an unfriendly acquisition to fend off and a couple of new product lines to launch and a luncheon full of institutional investors to court.

The mutant bowed his head, sighed and ran his fingers through his thick, yellow hair. He missed Betsy. He missed her gentle presence. And what he wouldn't have given for a decent distraction to take his mind off her.

Be careful what you wish for, a voice told him.

Warren raised his head and tried to be as receptive as possible. *Professor Xavier?* he asked.

Yes, Warren, came the reply. *Something has come up. I need you here in Salem Center as soon as possible.*

Your wish is my command, the winged man assured his mentor.

His best time from his penthouse to Xavier's school was eighteen minutes. He would see if he could come up with a new record.

Crossing the room, Warren opened a secret closet that contained a few of his blue and white uniforms. He removed one and slipped it on, then opened the only set of doors in the room that led to the outside.

Immediately, the wind swept over him. It teased him, inviting him into its embrace like a lover.

Closing the doors behind him, he paused for just a moment to close his eyes and savor the delight ahead of him. Then, before he ran the risk of someone spotting a bird-man standing outside Warren Worthington's penthouse, he opened his eyes, flapped his wings and ascended into the air.

Faster than a human eye could easily follow, the mutant banked and soared over the gargantuan concrete-and-metal spires of Manhattan Island. Up ahead, to the northeast, he could see where the buildings became more modest in size and the land opened up. Somewhere beyond that, along the blue expanse of the Long Island Sound, lay Salem Center.

I'm coming, he told Xavier, though he didn't know if the professor was still listening to his mind. Beating his wings even harder, he thought it again: *I'm coming.*

As Xavier replayed the words in his mind, they were like fingernails drawn mercilessly across a blackboard.

"Have you summoned the others yet?"

"I am doing so even as we speak."

Professor X wasn't certain that his energy duplicate was capable of summoning Scott, Jean and Warren while he was still conversing with Hank and Bobby. However, the thought of the imposter contacting the trio at all was terribly unnerving.

After all, Xavier's X-Men trusted their mentor without

reservation. They would charge innocently into any trap Lucifer and the doppelganger cared to set for them.

And Professor X was still restrained by Lucifer's ionic bonds in the Nameless Dimension, still cut off from everything familiar to him. True, he had mentally penetrated the barrier between dimensions ... but where had it gotten him? He had failed to make any kind of productive contact with Hank.

Then an alternative occurred to him. *Perhaps there is a way out of this predicament yet,* he told himself. To be sure, it was far from a sure thing, but he wasn't going to dismiss the possibility without even trying.

The option he had in mind was Jean Grey, who in some ways was closer to Xavier than any of his other X-Men. To an extent, that was because he had known her since she was a young girl. But it was also because, like him, Jean's powers were psionic in nature.

Without question, she would make the best receiver for the professor's thoughts. If he could contact anyone across the span of the dimensions, it would be her.

However, there was a problem. Hank and Bobby were in Salem Center, a place Xavier knew as well as any on Earth—a place he had been able to locate without difficulty.

Jean was a different story. She wasn't in Salem Center. She and Scott were somewhere else entirely.

Under normal circumstances, Xavier would simply have cast his thoughts like a net and found Jean, wherever she was. However, with the dimensional barrier to hinder him, he would be like a blind man trying to find a penny in a shopping mall-sized parking lot.

On the other hand, what choice did he have? Could he simply accept his fate and let the Quistalian have his way ...

not only with the mutants who made up the X-Men, but with the entire world?

Taking a deep breath, Xavier composed and focused his thoughts. Then he poked a psionic tendril through the dimensional barrier, as he had when he attempted to contact Hank. It came through in the vicinity of Salem Center, exactly as he had intended.

But where to send it next? That was the question.

Fortunately, the professor possessed a few facts that might help him in his task. He knew, for instance, that Jean and Scott had set out on a sailing trip the day of Jeremiah Saunders' funeral.

"Nothing very ambitious," Jean had told him, aware of how quickly a nor'easter could come up this time of year. "Just over to Long Island for a couple of nights."

But Long Island was a hundred miles long. And though Jean's boat wasn't fast enough to take her all the way out to Montauk in that time, it could easily make twenty five miles a day.

Think, Xavier exhorted himself. *Narrow it down.*

It occurred to him that Jean and Scott wouldn't have headed west, in the direction of New York City—not if they wanted to be alone with each other on the water, which was the point of going on the cruise in the first place. And in the other direction, the Long Island side of the Sound didn't have any viable anchorages for quite a stretch east of Mount Sinai.

If they kept to their plan, the professor told himself, they would likely have considered only three locations: West Harbor, a big, secluded basin near the town of Oyster Bay; Lloyd Harbor, a picturesque adjunct to the much larger expanse of Huntington Bay; and Mount Misery Cove, a sand dune-surrounded offshoot of elongated Port Jefferson Harbor.

While Xavier had never actually gone sailing with Jean and Scott, he had heard them mention these anchorages often enough as their favorites. Tempted by the descriptions his X-Men often tendered, he had visited the places in his astral form and found them pleasant . . . even serene.

But this time, he wasn't on a sightseeing expedition. Now, his ability to scour these locales with his mind was all that stood between Earth and Quistalian domination.

Think, the professor told himself again.

Scott and Jean had planned a three-day trip. Most likely, they would either have spent their first night in West Harbor and their second in Mount Misery Cove . . . or they would have reversed the direction. They probably wouldn't have bothered with Lloyd Harbor, since it was situated between the other two sites and less than a day's journey from either.

All right, Xavier thought. *That leaves you with only two locations. Which of them should you seek out first? In which are you more likely to discover Scott and Jean?*

He thought about the long-range weather forecast—something he memorized daily along with a host of other seemingly mundane details—but gleaned nothing from it. No one had predicted the advent of any serious storm systems in the region. And besides, both Mount Misery Cove and West Harbor were protected from wind and waves on all four sides.

The professor scowled. *Keep going,* he told himself.

It wasn't just important that he come to an accurate conclusion—it was critical. Unaccustomed as he was to penetrating the interdimensional barrier, uncertain of how long he could hope to avoid Lucifer's scrutiny, he didn't know how much time he would have to carry out his search. Clearly, he had to make every second count.

Xavier heaved a sigh in his ionic energy confinement. *Which anchorage?* he asked himself. *Which?*

And then it came to him.

Scott had once told him that he liked the first leg of a cruise to be the longest. Then, if there was a problem, he and Jean could always drop their anchor sooner than planned. On the other hand, if the last leg of a cruise was the longest and something went wrong, it could mean a protracted and tiresome trip home—a day that could stretch well into night.

If the professor had divined his X-Men's itinerary accurately, the longest leg of their journey would be between Mount Misery Cove and Salem Center. And since this was to be the day they returned to the mansion, and it was still early in the morning, he would likely find them anchored among Mount Misery's sand dunes.

There was no guarantee, of course. However, it was the best guess Xavier could make.

Reaching deeper into the world of his origin, the mutant sent his tendril of thought flying in a southeasterly direction over the Long Island Sound. The sky above was pale and overcast, the crenelated water beneath it a dark blue embellished with wind-driven flecks of white.

It took some time—how much, Xavier couldn't be sure—but he gradually left the hilly terrain of Westchester behind and began coming up fast on the opposite shore. Long Island looked to him like an immense sleeping dragon, the green of her well-kept lawns and stately conifers the beast's coat of scales and her sandy cliffs its vulnerable underbelly.

He recognized the immense, miles-wide mouth of Hempstead Harbor on his right as he aimed for the shallow beach situated between Oak Neck Point and Rocky Point.

Restricted to their sailboat, Scott and Jean would have had to circumnavigate the peninsula of Centre Island to get into the harbor. However, the professor was laboring under no such limitation. All he had to do was extend his tendril past the beach and the uplands behind it, and the shortcut would deposit him at his intended destination.

Finally, he reached the harbor. But in the same instant, his hopes fell. The boat Scott and Jean had rehabiliated so painstakingly wasn't anchored anywhere in sight. For that matter, neither was any other boat. The place was completely and utterly empty.

Xavier had to face the possibility that he had guessed wrong about the couple's whereabouts. However, his instincts told him not to give up yet. Maybe they had simply gotten underway already, spurred by the doppelganger's urgent summons.

Yes, he thought. *That's it.*

Embracing that possibility, the professor followed the course Scott and Jean would have been compelled to follow—south around Brickyard Point, east in the direction of Cove Neck, and then north toward Plum Point. After that, they would have had to work their way east into Oyster Bay, a route which would have given them access to the Sound.

As Xavier came around Brickyard Point he started to ascend. After all, it was no more difficult for him to go up than to go forward. The professor's hope was that he would be able to spot their ship's sails if he reached a high enough altitude.

This time, he wasn't disappointed. As Xavier approached the dense, overhanging clouds, he caught sight of a white speck on the moody expanse of Oyster Bay. Swooping like a hawk hungry for prey, his thought-tendril reached out for it.

Homing in on the speck, the professor was gradually able to make out the bellied shape of the boat's sails, the dark blue of her hull . . . and eventually, two people standing at her wheel.

One was a dark-haired man wearing a heavy brown sweater and khaki trousers, his eyes concealed behind what looked like a pair of red-tinted sunglasses. The other was an attractive woman in a green windbreaker, her long, red hair streaming behind her in the wind.

Scott and Jean—both of them members of his original team, his original class of teenaged mutants, and therefore imperiled by Lucifer's machinations. Feeling a pang of frustration, Xavier moved his thought-tendril even closer. As he had earlier looked for purchase in Hank McCoy's brain, he now sought it in Jean Grey's.

Again, he felt himself make a light, superficial connection. Again, he tried to dig deeper, to gain entry to an X-Man's consciousness.

And again, he failed.

No, the professor told himself. *I cannot tolerate failure. Not here. Not now. Somehow, I will make Jean aware of me.*

With all his concentration, all his resolve and his mastery of psionics, he pounded on the woman's consciousness. He bludgeoned it with blow after blow, hoping to get her attention even for a moment.

But he couldn't.

Jean continued to gaze north toward the mouth of the bay, the glorious orange banner of her hair rippling on a gust of air. She seemed unperturbed, unsuspecting. If she had even an inkling that someone was trying to contact her, she didn't show it.

Scott slipped an arm around her and she laid her head on his shoulder for a moment. Her only thoughts then were clearly of her husband, not a helpless prisoner of a dimension she had hardly even heard of.

Exhausted, his strength at an end, Xavier slumped in his tight-fitting ionic bonds—and saw his thought-contact with

Earth's dimension severed. For the moment, at least, he had no choice but to admit defeat.

It didn't matter that Jean was a telepath, he realized. Like Hank, she was too complex, too full of distractions to hear him calling her. Her mind was closed to him just like all the others'.

After all it had taken to track down Scott and Jean, his effort had come to nothing. It was hardly the conclusion for which he had hoped. But that didn't mean he was ready to throw in the towel. There had to be a way to beat Lucifer, he assured himself.

All he had to do was find it.

Scott Summers didn't like loose ends. He never had, even as a child. He liked finality, completeness, things he could depend on.

Like his bride. Like the loyalty and affection of his friends. Like the old, stone mansion in which he and his teammates stood, listening to Professor X brief them on his disturbing findings.

"The Andes?" Scott repeated, adjusting the yellow shoulder strap on his mostly dark blue uniform.

"That's correct," said Professor X, who was sitting behind his desk. "Also, Central Africa and Antarctica."

Warren grunted thoughtfully. "Then each of these places is the site of a Quistalian facility?"

"Correct again," said Xavier.

"And you figured this out by tracking the Quistalians' communications activity?" asked Jean, who had taken the time to change into her "working clothes" as well.

The professor nodded. "I checked and rechecked the results. Rest assured they are reliable."

"Of course," said Jean. "I didn't mean to suggest otherwise."

"What do you want us to do?" Scott asked, getting to the point.

After all, he was the field leader of this cadre of X-Men. In fact, he had been their field leader right from the beginning, the day they experienced their gut-wrenching baptism of fire against the powerful mutant marauder known as Magneto.

Xavier was the intelligence behind this operation and always would be. But Scott was the efficient one, the one who never got rattled, the rock his teammates clung to in the confusion of a battle.

"When you arrive at your first destination," the professor told them, "you'll identify and gain entry to the Quistalians' facility. Then you'll remove a critical component of their security system—one you may recognize from our earlier encounters with the aliens—and replace it with a device of my own invention."

"Replace it?" Bobby echoed.

"Yes," said Xavier. "My device is designed to broadcast a 'status quo' signal to the other Quistalian facilities. It should keep the aliens from suspecting our theft."

Hank grinned, exposing his oversized lower canines. "Brilliant, Professor. Simply brilliant."

Their mentor acknowledged the compliment with a subtle inclination of his head. "Finally, you're to bring the component back here."

"So you can study it?" Warren asked, his graceful white wings folding and unfolding reflexively.

"And a good deal more," Xavier replied. "You see, I've designed a machine that will protect Earth from Quistalian invasion permanently. To build it, however, I'll require the security components from all three of the locations I have mentioned."

"Permanently?" Jean repeated, a little surprised. "I've seldom heard you bristle with so much confidence, sir."

"I have seldom *been* so confident," the professor told her. "However, we must move quickly. Now that we have uncovered the Quistalians' offensive, it would be a tragedy if we acted too late to prevent it."

"Time and tide wait for no man," Hank noted cheerfully.

"Indeed," said Xavier. He looked around the room, studying Scott's expression and then those of each of his teammates. "As always, you will find your destination programmed into the Blackbird's onboard computer. Good luck, all of you."

"Thanks," said Bobby, already headed for the door.

The others followed him out of the room, but Scott couldn't help hesitating for a moment. Standing there in front of the professor, he found himself searching the man's face.

"Is there something else?" he asked Xavier. "Something you haven't shared with us, sir?"

The professor's brow furrowed and he shook his head. "No, Scott, there isn't. Why do you ask?"

The X-Man shrugged. "You just seem . . . I don't know. Distracted, I guess. But then, now that I think about it, I guess you've never really looked forward to dealing with the Quistalians."

His mentor frowned slightly. "Again, Scott . . . good luck."

It occurred to the younger man that he might have touched a nerve in Xavier—and in doing so, exceeded the bounds of their relationship. He nodded briskly. "Thank you, sir."

Then he left the professor's office to join his teammates.

*   *   *

The energy duplicate watched the last of the five X-Men depart. Then, reaching out telekinetically, he swung the door to his office closed and allowed himself a smile.

For a moment, it seemed the one called Scott had noticed something was wrong. In the end, however, whatever questions he might have had were laid to rest. And thanks to the imposter's shallow psi screen, which was more than strong enough to thwart a surface scan, Scott's wife Jean didn't suspect anything either.

Soon, if all went well, the X-Men would succeed in their mission. They would bring him the Quistalian components he had asked for.

But he wouldn't incorporate them into a device that would protect the Earth, as he had claimed. Instead, the doppelganger would use the components to engineer Lucifer's escape from the Nameless Dimension.

Clearly, the mutants wouldn't be happy when they realized they had been duped into freeing one of the most powerful adversaries they had ever faced. No doubt, they would be rather cross.

Fortunately for them, the duplicate reflected, they wouldn't have to live long with their regrets.

CHAPTER SIX

Warren Worthington III would have greatly preferred the cloud swept blue freedom of the heavens to the efficient but utilitarian interior of Professor X's private jet.

But then, he was called Archangel for a reason. With his majestic 16-foot wingspan, he could soar to almost 30,000 feet of altitude, achieve horizontal speeds of 150 miles an hour and fly under his own power from the break of dawn until after dusk.

Of course, even as powerful a flyer as Warren couldn't have outraced the professor's specially outfitted jet, especially on an hours-long trip like this one. However, he thought as he peered out a double-thick security window, that didn't keep him from yearning for the wide open spaces, and there was nothing wider or more open than the sky at 20,000 feet.

"Thinking about ditching us?" Jean asked him.

Warren turned to her, saw the smile on her face and smiled back. "These other jokers, sure," he said, jerking a thumb in the direction of Hank, Bobby and Scott. "But you? Never."

"Careful," said Scott from his forward position in the

pilot's seat, his voice flat and distracted and thinned by the hum of the engines. "You'll make me jealous."

"Uh oh," Warren gibed at him. "A sign of emotion. Next thing you know, you'll crack a smile and your face will fall apart."

Scott's seriousness and intensity had long been sources of good-natured amusement to his teammates. That didn't mean they didn't love and respect him and value his services as their leader. If anything, their taunts were confirmations of how they felt about him.

In this original group of X-Men, Warren reflected, you knew everything was all right when your teammates made fun of you. It was when they stopped that it was time to worry.

"Another twenty-two minutes and we'll be in Columbian airspace," Hank announced, hovering over Scott's shoulder to scrutinize the instrument panel. He turned and grinned at the others, exposing the long, sharp teeth protruding from his lower jaw. "Of course, that's just a loose estimate."

"Yeah, right," Bobby chuckled, rolling his eyes. "And Einstein was just a math teacher."

They all laughed at that. Then, for a little while at least, silence reigned in the close quarters of the aircraft. But that wasn't an uncommon state of affairs by any means.

Each X-Man was using that silence to gather himself, to prepare for the perils that might lie ahead. After all, their destination was a facility built by beings from another world.

Though they had encountered Lucifer and his people's technology before, they couldn't say for sure what they would be up against. Even the professor couldn't tell them that.

"You know," said Bobby as he leaned back in his seat, "even now, the thought of Lucifer gives me the creeps. I mean, he was the guy who crippled Professor Xavier."

"I know what you mean," Jean chimed in. "I remember

thinking if he could do that to the professor, he could do it to *anyone.*"

Hank nodded. "I must admit, I was a wee bit intimidated myself in those days." He looked around the cabin at his teammates. "But then, I imagine we all were."

"A lot's happened to us since then," Warren pointed out. "Both as individuals and as X-Men."

"We'll be fine as long as we don't get cocky," Scott rejoined.

"No need to worry about that," Warren assured him.

After all, a member of their extended team—a guy whose codename was Thunderbird—had died on a mission no more dangerous than this one a few years earlier. When it began, he probably hadn't contemplated the possibility that he wouldn't be coming back.

Warren, on the other hand, was eminently aware of that possibility. And though he couldn't read his friends' minds, he was sure that Scott, Jean, Hank and Bobby were, too. They had been playing this game too long for them not to understand how mortal they were . . . powers or no powers.

"Think we'll actually find some Quistalians in this place?" Bobby asked, breaking the silence.

Hank shrugged. "According to Professor X, there wasn't any evidence of voice communications. But one never knows."

"*This* one knows," Warren reminded them, indicating Jean with a tilt of his head. "Or she will, once we get close enough."

Jean nodded. "I won't necessarily be able to tell what they're thinking, but I'll certainly know if there's someone there."

"Hey," said Bobby, "remember the first time we ran into Lucifer? That bash up in the Balkans?"

Hank smiled a toothy smile. "How can I forget? The Avengers must have thought we had lost our minds."

Warren remembered it only too well. Having detected the Quistalians' activities in Europe, Professor X had gone ahead of the team to try to gather information on his own.

What he found was an immense thermal bomb aimed at the North Pole—and attuned to Lucifer's heartbeat. If anything happened to the alien, the bomb would head for the Arctic and trigger an ecological disaster that would bury Earth's coastlines under a series of devastating tidal waves.

As it turned out, the Avengers had realized something was awry in the Balkans as well—and arrived there at about the same time as the X-Men. Naturally, they wanted to find Lucifer and stop him.

But Xavier, who knew they had to keep the alien safe at any cost, ordered his fledgling team to stand in the Avengers' way. It wasn't easy going up against Thor, Captain America, Ironman, Giant-Man and the Wasp, arguably the most powerful assemblage of heroes on Earth. But the mutants kept their older, more experienced adversaries off-balance until the professor could subdue Lucifer safely.

"I'll never forget the look on Thor's face when he heard Professor Xavier in his head," Jean said.

Hank nodded. "Priceless. I thought his noble brow was going to explode."

After Xavier had tendered the Thunder God an explanation, the Avengers had left the X-Men to their own devices, confident that they could handle the problem. Then, following their mentor's directions, the mutants had entered a cleft in a hillside and and descended into a subterranean chasm via some kind of super-advanced elevator.

All except Warren, that is. As usual, he had preferred to spread his wings and fly down.

"And that bomb in Lucifer's underground cavern," said Bobby. "I've seen football stadiums that paled by comparison."

"It was the super economy-size, all right," Warren agreed. He glanced at Scott, whose entire attention seemed focused on flying the plane. "But as I recall, we were more than a match for it."

Actually, Scott and Professor X were the only ones who had been able to do anything about the bomb. Warren remembered circling the thing helplessly as he watched Xavier and his teammate spread themselves flat on the bomb's grey surface and press their faces against it.

Anyway, that was how it looked. In reality, Xavier was mentally probing the device, seeking out its fuse even as it began to hum and throb to life. When the professor found what he was looking for, he told Scott exactly where to focus his optical beam—a narrow seam in the bomb's surface.

A moment later, exhibiting the nerves of a safecracker, the X-Man called Cyclops found the fuse and sliced through it.

"Lucier wasn't too pleased with us after that," Bobby noted.

"You can say that again," Jean responded. "He was like a pit bull on a bad hair day."

"Nor was his pique difficult to understand," Hank put in. "Based on what Lucifer spat at us before he slunk off, it seemed he had been planning Earth's downfall for years ... and we had managed to ruin his scheme in a few scant minutes."

Bobby frowned thoughtfully. "I still don't understand why the professor let him escape that way—without a fight, I mean. It was pretty clear we hadn't seen the last of him."

"Because it didn't matter," Scott remarked, rejoining the conversation at last. "Lucifer was just an advance scout for the Quistalians. If we kept him from leaving, some other scout would've taken his place ... someone we might not have matched up with so well."

"The devil you know?" Warren suggested.

"That's what I'm thinking," said Scott.

"But knowing Lucifer didn't make our second encounter any easier," Hank observed dryly. "In fact, familiarity worked more in our adversary's favor than in our own."

Bobby nodded. "He was ready for us, all right."

"You're referring," said Jean, "to the transparent cage in which Lucifer imprisoned us?"

Warren grunted. "Considering how well he knew us, he wasn't able to keep us there very long."

Hank winked at Jean. "That's because our resident teleki-netic was able to flip a lever without anyone realizing it."

Jean rolled her eyes. "Your resident telekinetic wishes she had thought of that lever on her own. But if memory serves, it took a certain Beast to make the suggestion."

"And to identify the right lever," Warren added.

"It's a gift," Hank told the others, batting his long, blue eyelashes with false modesty.

"Of course," Bobby noted, "we weren't out of the woods yet. We still had all those big green robots to take on."

"Yes," said Jean. She glanced at Warren, her brow creasing over the bridge of her delicate nose. "And a little confusion to overcome."

"Confusion?" Bobby asked.

Warren knew exactly what Jean was talking about. "Over whether to try to knock out Dominus," he elaborated.

Bobby's eyes narrowed with obvious discomfort as it came back to him. "Oh yeah," he said. "That."

Warren hadn't forgotten a single detail. As he and his teammates made their way through endless corridors of sin-ister-looking alien machinery, they finally came across Lucifer's main chamber—a space defined and surrounded by a single, sprawling Quistalian machine.

Suddenly, they heard Xavier's voice in their heads, warning them not to damage the machine—which he called Dominus. However, Warren wasn't so sure it was the professor who had sent the message. After all, Lucifer had demonstrated telepathic abilities as well. What if the Quistalian had impersonated Xavier to deceive them and save Dominus?

With that in mind, Warren had gone after the machine. But before he could do any damage, he felt something slam him in the back with stunning force. It had taken him a moment to shake off the effects—and to realize that Scott had walloped him with an optical beam.

He still remembered how it felt—the psychological pain as well as the physical. It seemed to Warren that he had been betrayed. Stabbed in the back, if only with an energy blast.

By that time, Bobby was making an attempt to destroy Dominus with a well-placed projectile made out of ice. However, Jean stopped it in mid-air with her power of telekinesis.

It was the first time one member of the team had found himself pitted against another—not just in one of the professor's danger room sequences, but for real, in the outside world.

Then they saw why Xavier might tell them not to attack Dominus. One of Lucifer's robots, trying to tear into a bouncing Hank, shot past him and struck Lucifer's machine instead. Instantly, the robot was torn apart—though Dominus remained unscathed.

Had it been Warren who plowed into the machine, there would have been nothing left of him but gristle and gore. Clearly, Scott had done him a favor by pounding him with his optical beam.

Still, it had taken Warren some time to forgive his teammate—to get past the bitter feeling of being double-crossed by someone who was supposed to be his friend.

"Fortunately," said Jean, "Warren's gotten over that shot he took from Scott." She eyed him. "Hasn't he?"

Warren wasn't sure if she had been inside his head the whole time, following his thoughts, or had just arrived at the same endpoint. "Yes," he assured her. "I have."

Jean looked satisfied. "That's what I thought."

Warren sighed. If he was going to hold something against Scott, it wouldn't have been that optical blast. It would have been the fact that his teammate stole the heart of the first woman Warren had ever loved.

The woman he was looking at right now.

"Of course," Warren went on, glancing at Scott and smiling a conspiratorial smile, "that doesn't mean I don't get the urge every now and then to give him a shot in return."

Jean grinned. "Who doesn't?"

"Thanks a lot," said Scott.

And again, they all laughed.

It had been a long time since the being called Lucifer had something to laugh about.

But as he floated in the Nameless Dimension and listened to the X-Men gloating over past victories, he couldn't help delighting in the irony. Time and again, the mutants had neutralized and defused his Quistalian initiatives. Time and again, they had stood in his way as he attempted to lay claim to their world.

But this time would be different. This time, Lucifer wasn't counting on his people's advanced technology to help him obtain his objective. This time, he was relying on the talents of the X-Men themselves.

Every moment they unknowingly did his bidding appealed to his bottomless hunger for retribution. Every second they inadvertently served his cause was a source of deep, heartfelt satisfaction.

On Quistalium, the dark, regimented world-complex of his birth, there was a name for such an exalted feeling. It was called "the secret victory"—and it was prized above all other kinds.

Why? Because other kinds of victory didn't require the same sort of subtlety on the part of the victor. They didn't demand the same level of complexity and imagination. And as a rule, they were a good deal easier to secure.

It was the kind of thinking that prevailed among Lucifer's people, a dour, relentlessly aggressive race dubbed the Arcane by one of the first sentient species to feel the Quistalians' boots on their necks. It was an example of the philosophy that had made them conquerors.

For an agent of the Arcane, victory might arrive in a heartbeat or it might take a century of planning. But in the end, it always came.

Lucifer himself had overseen many a successful campaign. He had identified dozens of unsuspecting species and methodically plotted their downfalls, pursuing each of his schemes with painstaking care and diligence until the time came when he could activate the machine called Dominus and deaden the wills of the populace.

Back on Quistalium, his efforts brought him glory and prestige. They earned him a large, well-appointed estate by the dazzling Falls of Fire, medals enough to fill a sleeping chamber and long parades before cheering throngs in the immense synthetic canyons of the capital.

They also propelled Lucifer to the top of Quistalium's military hierarchy, garnered him the admiration of lesser agents and gave him access to his government's secret inner councils. They made him a bright, blazing symbol of all that his people aspired to.

It was a far cry from his beginnings in the lowest stratum of Quistalian society, a caste that occupied the several barren asteroids in orbit around the homeworld. Lucifer's parents, whom he hardly remembered, had been part of the faceless multitude that worked the asteroids' radioactive mines, serving their civilization in the most mundane and mechanical way possible.

Lucifer would certainly have shared their fate had his brain enzymes not revealed an enormous potential for strategic intelligence—the kind theretofore undocumented in the spartan domiciles of the asteroid belt. From that point on, he was trained with the sons and daughters of aristocrats . . . whom he outshone on a regular basis.

And every time he did so, he was forced to endure physical punishment at their hands. Clearly, they resented his demonstrations of superiority. But he didn't stop demonstrating it and he didn't balk at the beatings—far from it. To Lucifer, the physical torment was merely another rite of training, an exercise that would make his will stronger with each passing day.

In the end, his approach served him well. His meteoric rise to prominence as an advance agent was proof of that.

But power and renown were never ends in themselves to Lucifer. The mantle of commendation always seemed to sit a bit heavily on his shoulders, as if it were a burden rather than an honor.

In truth, the only reward he ever coveted was conquest itself. His only desires, his only goals, were to serve to the Supreme One and to expand the Quistalian empire.

The images imprinted on his eyes when he slept weren't those of riches or splendor. They were the eyes of his myriad victims—always wide with expanding fear, or fixed listlessly on an eternity of unrelenting oppression.

And well they should have been. Once a species was taken in thrall by the Arcane, there was no possibility of its rescue or redemption. There wasn't even the slightest ray of hope.

Year after year, Lucifer had pursued the same ambitious course, like a comet streaking through the heavens. He had established base after secret base, network after hidden network, yoking world after unsuspecting world to the cause of Quistalian domination. And he had never failed in his mission.

Until he came to Earth.

The alien's teeth ground together as he remembered the first time he had seen the blue-green sphere. It had seemed so innocent, so vulnerable, so eminently available for the taking.

Prior to his departure, he was called to the mighty chamber of the Supreme One and warned that Earth might prove a nettlesome acquisition. After all, its population was large and scattered across its globe, and it seemed to exhibit a high level of intelligence.

Lucifer saw now why he had been granted not one chance to conquer mankind, but three—the first time such a thing had happened since his people took their boundless aggression into space.

But even three opportunities had not been enough. The acquisition turned out to be even more difficult than the Supreme One predicted. Lucifer had failed and failed miserably.

And after he squandered his last chance, he was exiled to the place known as the Nameless Dimension. It was necessary, expected—a grim warning to the Arcane's other advance agents never to underestimate any species they sought to enslave.

At first, it had galled Lucifer to think that someone else might reap the harvest he had sown on Earth, learning from his mistakes and using that knowledge to complete Lucifer's conquest. The very notion had gnawed at him like a worm in his brain.

But to his surprise, the Supreme One hadn't sent a replacement to Earth. He had allowed mankind to remain free and unscathed, despite its having been identified as a prime target population.

Lucifer had puzzled over that decision for a long time, turning it over and over in his mind—and at last come to a startling conclusion. It seemed he wasn't the only one who had miscalculated the difficulty of enslaving Earth. The Supreme One had miscalculated as well.

He had sent an agent of the Arcane on a mission for which he was unprepared. And as a result, he had been forced to sacrifice that agent, costing Quistalium a piece of valuable property in the process.

Did that mean the Supreme One deserved to be punished too?

Lucifer cackled uncontrollably at the thought, his gloved fists pressed hard against his mouth. The all-powerful Supreme One, cast aside as Lucifer had been cast aside, forced to live out his solitary existence in a drab, featureless limbo . . . it was too amusing for words.

He wished he had conjured such an image when he was first dispatched to the Nameless Dimension. He could have used a reason to laugh then. He could have used a great many of them.

The present moment was a different matter entirely. Lucifer didn't need to find reasons to be amused. He had all the entertainment he needed, all the diversion anyone could ever hope for.

Xavier's mutants were seeing to that.

CHAPTER SEVEN

The hot Columbian sun beat down on Scott Summers with oven-like intensity as he manipulated the visor that kept his optical beams in check.

The visor opened only the slightest bit, little more than a hairsbreadth really. However, it was enough to release one of the most potent biologically generated energies known to man.

The thick, exotic foliage in front of him ripped away before his optical onslaught, revealing an eight-foot high slab of dark, oily-looking metal built into the side of the mountain. His job done, Scott closed his visor.

Hank approached the slab and touched it with a blue forefinger as the smell of chlorophyll permeated the air. "Quistalian manufacture if I've ever seen it," he observed.

"Looks like we came to the right place," Jean remarked.

"Any sign of life in there?" Scott asked her.

His wife closed her eyes and concentrated. After a second or two, she shook her head. "Nothing even approaching sentience."

"So we could still find some daytime talk show hosts," Hank quipped, readjusting his bulging yellow backpack.

Scott shot him a disparaging look.

"Sorry," said his furry friend, shrugging his massive blue shoulders. "I couldn't resist."

Warren pointed to a tiny hole in the center of the door. "Looks like this is the lock. Where's that key?"

Scott opened one of the utility pouches on his shoulder strap and removed a device the size of a ballpoint pen. Professor X had given it to him before the team left Salem Center.

Inserting the device into the hole, he pressed a stud on the side of it. There was a green glow from inside the hole. Then the slab began to slide down, barely giving Scott time to remove his key.

The dimly lit corridor that stretched out past the threshold was rife with the somber, oily-looking metals and strangely serpentine circuitry they had seen in other Quistalian bases. Replacing the key in his pouch, Scott turned to the others and beckoned.

"Come on," he said.

"Right behind you," Bobby told him.

Scott entered the tunnel, his eyes adjusting gradually to the lower light levels. Its cool embrace felt refreshing after the moist, steamy heat of the Columbian highlands.

Warren flapped his wings and soared ahead of his teammates in accordance with their plan.

As Bobby followed Scott into the corridor, he transformed into his icy form. "You know what's interesting?" he asked.

"What?" Scott responded, his eyes focused on the stretch of passageway directly ahead of them.

"That the professor was working on all this stuff," said Bobby, "and he never told anyone."

Scott spared him a glance. "By stuff, you mean *this* thing?" he asked, patting the pouch that held the Quistalian key.

"That's part of it," Bobby replied. "There's also the machine Hank's lugging around that's going to broadcast the status quo signal to the other bases . . . and whatever it is the professor's going to cobble together once we bring him his components."

Scott pondered his teammate's comment as he led the way deeper into the tunnel. "What are you saying? That Professor Xavier has gotten a bit more mysterious lately?"

"When it comes to the Quistalians," said Bobby, "yes."

Scott frowned as he saw where his friend's remarks were going.

"It must have been pretty traumatic," he said, "when Lucifer dropped a slab of stone on the professor's legs. I can see why he'd devote some extra effort to defending Earth against that kind of power."

Of course, he hated the idea that Xavier was as vulnerable as the rest of them were. But there was no avoiding it. The professor wasn't a god, after all. He was just a man.

They continued to make their way along the corridor, following its twists and turns. Scott and Bobby remained in the lead, poised for trouble. Trailing them, Jean "listened" for any as-yet undetected signs of life. And Hank brought up the rear, carrying the professor's counterfeit broadcast component in his backpack.

Then Scott heard something that sounded like the beating of wings. He exchanged glances with his wife, an unspoken question on his lips.

She answered it just as silently. *It's Warren, all right. And he doesn't seem to be in any danger.*

A moment later, their fellow X-Man was on top of them, his wings spread from one wall to the other in a braking action. "I found the part we're looking for," he said.

Scott nodded. "Good. How far?"

"Another hundred meters," the winged man estimated. "This passage snakes so much, it's hard to tell."

"I can live with a hundred meters," said Bobby.

"Same here," Scott told him. "But let's pick up the pace a little. The sooner we're out of this place, the better I'll like it."

Again, Warren went on ahead. But this time he stayed in sight, hovering at each bend in the corridor until the rest of the team caught up.

Finally, they reached their destination—the entrance to an immense, cylindrical chamber, the upper reaches of which were lost in darkness. The lower portions of its towering walls were lit by long, opalescent strips, revealing serpentine circuitry that was even thicker and more twisted than what they had already seen.

The place brought back memories of the Quistalian facilities Scott had explored early in his career as an X-Man. None of those memories were especially pleasant ones.

At the opposite side of the chamber, a series of smaller cylinders comprised what the professor had described as the base's communications system. The majority of the cylinders were solid gray in color. Only one was a dusky gold with a series of scarlet striations running through it. Scott recognized it as the component they had come for.

Bobby regarded the device, his eyes glinting in the opalescent light. "Well," he said softly, "here we are."

Despite his attempt to keep his voice down, it echoed

ominously. Eventually, it was lost in the vastness of the enclosure.

"Still no sign of anyone," Jean reported, adding to the echoes.

Hank cocked a pointed blue ear. "I don't hear any gears moving," he remarked. "Always a good sign."

Scott eyed the place. It looked safe enough, but he knew from experience that appearances could be deceiving.

"Hank," he said thoughtfully, "wait a couple of seconds before you make the swap. Jean, Bobby and I will take up positions at intervals, just in case we've missed a security feature. Warren, you go aloft for a bird's-eye perspective on the chamber."

His teammates followed his orders without comment. At the same time, Scott himself moved toward the curved wall on his left. He could hear the soft shoosh of Warren's wings, the sound of his own breathing, the scrape of his boots on the smooth, seamless floor.

"All right," he told Hank.

The mutant known to the world as Beast moved forward, the slap of his bare feet on the alien surface echoing hollowly. When he reached the communications cylinders, he zipped open his backpack and took out the professor's fake component. Then he laid it gently on the floor.

Next, he lifted the gold cylinder from its resting place and looked around. There was no alarm. The place was silent except for the whisper-like beating of Warren's wings.

Obviously relieved, Hank placed the component in his yellow backpack and slung it over his shoulder. Finally, he retrieved the substitute cylinder from the floor and snugged it into place.

Taking a deep breath, the furry blue X-Man turned to

Scott. "Mission accomplished," he announced with a measure of satisfaction.

"Well done," said Scott. "Now let's get the—"

Before he could finish his imperative, he heard Warren cry out and looked up to see what was the matter. Suddenly, the winged mutant came swooping down from the heights of the chamber, followed by a dense, dark swarm of twitching, chittering spider-things.

They were even oilier and blacker than the labyrinthine circuitry on the walls, each of them boasting eight legs and two bright green, faceted eyes. As they got closer, Scott could see that the smallest of them was the size of a compact car.

The mutant didn't waste time trying to figure out what the things were or where they had come from. He just went into action as Professor X had trained him to do.

Opening his visor, he shot a ruby-red optical beam at the nearest of the spider-things. The shaft of destructive force hit it squarely and sent it pinwheeling wildly across the chamber. Taking aim at a second monster and then a third, he sent them spinning backwards as well.

But there were far too many of the things for Scott to knock them all out. Before he knew it, twenty-five or thirty of them had landed on the smooth, dark floor. As they hit the ground, deadly black claws emerged from the ends of their forelegs.

They skittered toward him with insect-like speed and determination, their eyes blinking an eerie green. Fortunately, the X-Man called Cyclops wasn't on his own.

As he hammered away at one spider-thing after another, his teammates did their part too. Warren wove in and out of the swarm, keeping the eight-legged monsters occupied as

Bobby encased them in heavy blocks of ice and Jean telekinetically sent them smashing into each other.

Hank was the only one doing his best to avoid the things altogether. But then, he was the one who held the backpack with the Quistalian device in it. It was his job to get out of there and make sure the component got back to Salem Center.

Scott, Jean called to him, her thoughts flooding his brain. *These things aren't alive. They're robots.*

That explained her inability to detect their brain functions when the team was approaching the chamber. It also gave Scott a better idea of what he and the others were up against. Sensors instead of eyes and olfactory systems. Programs instead of instincts. Bodies a good deal more durable than the flesh and blood variety.

It was the first time the mutant had been forced to fight machines shaped like Terran arachnids. However, it was far from his first taste of Quistalian battle technology.

In fact, Scott had squared off against the aliens' robots on several different occasions—and he had taken away from these encounters one very valuable piece of intelligence. Like biological organisms, the Quistalians' creations had a single, central power generator. Once that generator was shut down, they would stop functioning.

As he responded to his wife's insight, he had that information very firmly in mind. *Jean,* he thought back at her, *find their power conduits and start ripping them out.*

Done, she assured him, then broke the link.

Next, Scott closed his visor and turned to Bobby, who was piling ice on top of another spider-thing. "We need a barrier across the midpoint of the chamber," he bellowed, his voice rebounding off the walls.

"Gotcha," his crystalline teammate called back. At the same time, he began building a wall of ice at the appointed spot.

By then, Hank had leaped and vaulted his way to the vicinity of the chamber's exit. But the other X-Men were still in the thick of the fight, not far from where Bobby was piling up his barrier.

"Fall back, Jean," Scott told his wife. "We're going to seal up half of them behind an ice wall."

Good idea, she responded telepathically.

Next, Scott waved to get Warren's attention. As quickly as the winged X-Man was moving, it wasn't easy. Finally, as Warren emerged from a cluster of attacking spider-things, he noticed Scott's gesture.

"Talk to me," he yelled as he shot across the chamber, his voice echoing back on itself.

"Lure as many as you can to the far side of the room," Scott shouted. Then he pointed to Bobby.

Studying their Iceman for a moment, Warren seemed to understand what Scott had in mind. Once more he wove his way in among the spider-things, daring them to snatch him out of the air—but when he eluded them this time, he drew them further away from the exit.

Satisfied that everyone was doing his or her part, Scott turned his attention to Hank again—and saw that his friend needed some help. Despite Hank's remarkable speed and agility, his path to the exit had been blocked by a knot of chittering robots.

Opening his visor again, Scott drove his optical beam into the midst of the spider-things, sending one and then another skidding across the floor of the chamber. A couple of them forgot about Hank and came after him instead, and he punished them as well.

But try as he might, he couldn't clear an adequate path for his teammate. Hank looked frustrated as he bounded from one spot to the other, seeking something resembling an opening.

Obviously, the furry X-Man didn't like the idea of falling back—not when he had come so close to getting away with his stolen component. But in the end, he had to clutch his yellow backpack to his chest and retreat from the monsters' grasping claws.

Fortunately, Scott wasn't the only one who had been hard at work. As he closed his visor to scan the chamber, he saw Bobby complete a glistening, fifteen-foot-high ice wall. A moment later, Warren came surging over the top of it, wings spread imposingly, leaving almost half the enemy's forces trapped behind him.

Jean had done her share as well. Four of the Quistalian spider-things lay crumpled around her on the chamber floor, their internal workings hopelessly mangled and disrupted.

Another four were still trying to crack the ice blocks with which Bobby had burdened them. That left fewer than a dozen of the robots still functioning, most of them clustered near the exit. Scott had to admit he liked those odds a good deal better.

Still, they had to capitalize on the situation quickly. Bobby's frozen barrier wouldn't remain intact forever.

"Clear them out!" Scott roared to his teammates, pointing to the spider-things blocking their exit. Then he opened his visor again and leveled a crimson blast at one of them, sending it tumbling end over end.

Bobby encased two more in a block of ice. Jean took the fight out of a third one. And on it went, victory by hard-fought victory until—at least for a moment—the way out was unobstructed.

"Let's go!" Scott bellowed, his voice joined by an army of echoes.

"Onward and outward!" Hank replied, launching himself out of the chamber and into the passageway beyond.

Warren was right behind him, cradling Jean in his arms as he flew. Then came Bobby, laying down a savage barrage of ice pellets as he backpedaled. Scott placed a few last shots among the robots who came pouring after them like a black tide, then took off down the corridor as well.

As soon as he was clear of the chamber, Bobby clogged up the opening with as much ice as he could muster. But he had already taxed his powers to their limits. He was fatigued and it showed.

"That's enough!" Scott told him as the spider-things began breaking through the ice. "We're out of here!"

Closing his visor and grabbing his friend's arm, he pulled Bobby down the corridor. They ran as quickly as they could, following the dark, serpentine curve of the passage as their pursuers punched through the obstacle Bobby had left behind.

But Scott could tell they weren't moving fast enough. The clacking of the robots began to grow louder in their ears, telling him the things were narrowing the gap between them.

One of the mutants would have to stay behind and cover their escape. Scott already knew who it would be.

"Keep going!" he told Bobby as they negotiated a bend in the corridor—and thrust him in the direction of freedom.

The other X-Man whirled. "No way!" he shot back.

"That's an order!" Scott told him.

Bobby hesitated, pain and anger etched into his icy features.

"Go!" Scott insisted.

With obvious reluctance, Bobby turned away from him. Then he pelted down the hallway as quickly as he could, leaving the team's leader to confront the horde by himself.

Bracing himself, Scott faced his adversaries. Then he opened his visor and unleashed his optical beam, pounding the first eight-legged thing that came around the bend. As it caromed off the wall in back of it, another filled the breach. It received the same rough treatment.

But pretty soon, the pace picked up. The monsters began coming at him in pairs, then crowding the corridor three at a time. It got harder and harder to figure out which one was closest to nailing him, more and more difficult to keep the robots at bay.

Still, Scott didn't panic. Even when his head started to swim with the intensity of his effort, he stood his ground and kept at it—and not because he was thrilled about dying there like some mutant Horatio.

There was another reason he was able to maintain his position. As the robots got closer to him, close enough almost to reach out and slice him with their claws, he heard the approach of that reason.

At first, it sounded like a gentle surf, hissing softly over the sand. Then it became louder, like a bellows. And louder still, like the beat of a strong, insistent pulse in his ears.

Just as Scott was about to go down under the press of the robot spiders, he felt himself grabbed under the armpits and swung away.

Closing his visor, he looked up—and saw Warren's blue-skinned face above him. It showed the sweat and strain of carrying a hundred and eighty-pound burden through the narrow, snaking corridor.

"Cut it a little close, did we?" Scott asked evenly.

Warren looked down at him, the slightest gleam of amusement in his eyes. "Sorry. I had to tie my shoelaces."

"You don't have any shoelaces," Scott pointed out.

Warren feigned exasperation. "Now you tell me."

In a matter of seconds, they reached the opening and emerged into the heat of the outside world. With a flourish of his wings, Warren slowed their progress and descended to the plateau below them.

Professor X's sleek, black jet awaited them there, its idling engines already warmed up. Scott could see Hank sitting in the pilot's seat with Bobby beside him. But Jean was standing outside the plane, clearly refusing to get in until she was certain her husband was safe.

Had their positions been reversed, Scott would have done the same thing. He couldn't imagine a time, place or circumstance when he would even contemplate leaving Jean behind.

Warren let Scott down beside her. Relieved, Jean brushed Scott's face with her fingertips. Then she got into the jet and he followed her. Folding his wings, Warren came last and pulled the door closed behind him.

Then, with Hank at the controls, they took off.

"Not too bad," the furry X-Man said, patting the new bulge in his yellow backpack. "That is, for an assemblage of diverse talents that hasn't worked together in a while."

Bobby, who was in the process of de-icing, turned to his friend. "Of course, there was one weak link. I'm not mentioning any names, mind you ... but his initials are Hank McCoy."

Hank cast a sidelong look at him. "Droll, Robert. Very droll."

"Hey," said Bobby, grinning at him, "it's nothing a couple hundred hours in the professor's Danger Room won't cure."

Jean leaned back in her seat and closed her eyes. "We did pretty well at that," she remarked, "didn't we?"

Scott slipped his fingers into hers and squeezed. "No complaints here," he assured her.

He couldn't help but take pride in the way the five of them had meshed their efforts. They had certainly come a long way since their struggle against Magneto all those years ago. Now there wasn't a collection of costumed heroes alive—mutants or otherwise—who could put them to shame.

"One Quistalian base down and two to go," Warren announced.

Hank cast a glance over his muscular shoulder. "Your grasp of mathematics is impeccable, Mr. Worthington."

Warren couldn't help chuckling a little at the comment. "Just shut up and fly the plane, okay?"

"Your wish," said Hank, "is my command."

As they climbed into a cloudless sky, he set the controls for their next destination.

CHAPTER EIGHT

More than anything else on Earth or in the heavens, Charles Xavier hated feeling helpless.

When Lucifer stole his ability to walk in a Tibetan cavern many years earlier, he had made it his business to be as self-sufficient as anyone with two good legs. In addition, despite his physical handicap, he had launched a one-man offensive against hatred and oppression. He had mobilized a squad of young mutants and showed them how to take care of themselves in any situation.

But even Professor Xavier could make mistakes, it seemed. Even he could allow his vigilance to lapse. After all, he had left himself open to an attack by one of his oldest adversaries . . . and now he found himself paying the awful price.

Still, Xavier hadn't given up. It wasn't his nature to do so—especially when the lives of those he loved hung in the balance. All along, as he floated in the awful silence of the Nameless Dimension, he had been working on a plan to turn the tables on his captor and free himself.

And now, at long last, he believed he had come up with something.

True, the professor hadn't had a great deal of success trying to communicate with Hank or Jean. But then, as he had learned to his chagrin, their minds were too complicated, too full of competing thoughts for him to make his presence known.

But there were simpler minds on Earth's side of the dimensional barrier. Considerably simpler. And of all of them, there was one with which Xavier had established a rapport not so long ago—a consciousness that happened to reside in a remarkably capable and dexterous body, making it even more useful for the professor's purposes.

What's more, Xavier knew where this body would be. All he had to do was push his tendril of thought through the dimensional barrier and send it to Westminster House.

That was where Jeffrey Saunders lived.

As Professor X willed his thought-tendril over the wooded autumn hill country that stretched northwest of Salem Center, the early morning sun casting long shadows on the land, he hoped fervently that his plan would work this time. If it didn't—if his friend Jeremiah's grandson proved as unreceptive to his psychic overtures as Hank and Jean had been—he didn't know what he would do.

But he wasn't going to focus on failure. He was simply going to find Jeffrey and hope for the best.

Fortunately, the professor had visited Westminster House once before, in the days when it was the estate of a wealthy philanthropist. It was only in the last several years that the place had been converted into an institution for the mentally challenged.

Before too long, he caught sight of Westminster's main

edifice, a stately red brick structure with green shutters and a great deal of ivy covering its southern exposure. He extended his tendril toward the manicured grounds behind the building, where several of the home's residents were sitting or strolling with the help of escorts.

Jeffrey didn't appear to be among them.

Where is he? Xavier asked himself. Then he heard the tinny sound of a ball bouncing and he was able to fashion a guess. Making his way around the red brick building, he found an asphalt basketball court with a single figure moving across it.

It was Jeffrey, of course. He was dribbling in remarkably precise circles, first clockwise and then counterclockwise, with his right hand and then with his left.

Unfortunately, he looked as if he was having some trouble. After a moment or two, the professor realized what the problem was. The basketball, a bright orange specimen with a colorful team logo emblazoned on it, didn't look as if it had been completely inflated.

Jeffrey's brow was creased. Clearly, he knew there was something wrong. He just didn't know what to do about it.

Professor X carefully extended his thought tendril into Jeffrey's mind, seeking the kind of purchase there that he had been denied on earlier occasions.

Immediately, the professor knew that this time would be different. He found no formidable distractions in the retarded man's consciousness, no serious competition for his attention. If anything, the fellow's mind was even more open than Xavier remembered.

Jeffrey? he thought. *It's Professor Xavier—your grandfather's friend. I need your help.*

The young man stopped dribbling his basketball and listened to the voice in his head. There wasn't any fear or distress in him—no negative emotion at all, in fact.

I'm sorry to bother you, the mutant thought. *I know you're just getting used to your new home. However, this is a most urgent matter.*

Jeffrey didn't move. He just listened.

You must make a long trip for me, Xavier told him. *A trip that will take a great deal of courage and effort on your part. Unfortunately, there's no one else to whom I can turn. You may be my last hope.*

The retarded man seemed to understand how badly Xavier needed his help, if not the magnitude of the sacrifice that was being asked of him. What's more, he recognized the professor's presence and trusted it as he would have trusted his grandfather's.

After a moment, Jeffrey nodded. He seemed willing to do whatever his friend deemed necessary.

Thank you, Xavier told him.

But even as he projected the thought, he experienced a twinge of guilt. He was, after all, asking Jeffrey to take on a challenge he couldn't possibly grasp in its entirety. If the situation had been any less dire, the professor wouldn't even have considered the fellow an option.

But the situation was as desperate as they came. Lucifer wouldn't hesitate to use every weapon available to him—and Xavier couldn't afford to be any less hardnosed than his enemy.

If we are to do this, he told Jeffrey, *I need to assume control of your mind. I hope this isn't too uncomfortable for you.*

The retarded man didn't know what the professor was talking about, of course, so he couldn't exactly give his permission. Still, Xavier had felt compelled to announce what was coming.

After all, Jeffrey wasn't a mindless pawn in this game. He wasn't one of the unwitting dupes Lucifer had used in the past. He was a human being . . . and the professor was determined to treat him that way.

Scanning the Nameless Dimension to make sure the Quistalian was nowhere in sight, Xavier tightened his grip on Jeffrey's consciousness. He proceeded quickly, firmly.

Of course, he could have pursued the process slowly, allowing the younger man to gradually gain some understanding of what he was getting himself into. But like a parent faced with the removal of his child's adhesive bandage, the professor didn't want to give Jeffrey time to become frightened.

As it happened, the retarded man became frightened anyway. His mind reeling like a wild, unbroken horse trying to throw its rider, he struggled against the psychic link— struggled so mightily, in fact, that Xavier almost lost contact with him.

But in the end, the mutant hung on. Despite the tumultuous power of Jeffrey's panic, despite the burden imposed on the professor by the dimensional barrier, he maintained control. Then, little by little, Xavier calmed the retarded man down. He showed Jeffrey that playing host to a telepath wasn't all that difficult once one got used to the idea.

Xavier had the youth take a breath and let it out. *Easy,* he thought. *There's nothing to be frightened of, nothing for you to worry about. Just allow me to guide you.*

And guide him the professor did.

In accordance with Xavier's directions, Jeffrey took a look around to see if anyone was watching him. At the moment, every attendant in sight seemed to be taking care of one of the other residents. None of them was looking directly at Jeffrey.

The professor knew he might never get a better opportunity. Without hesitation, he had Jeffrey fling his ball at the thick line of fir trees that bordered Westminister House to the south. Then, making certain that the throw hadn't roused anyone's suspicions, Xavier sent his host loping innocently after it.

When Jeffrey caught up with the ball, he glanced around again. Still, no one had moved to stop him or even wonder what he was up to. And by then, he was only about ten yards from the trees.

Going for broke, Xavier had him dash the rest of the way to the tree line and take shelter behind one of the thickest trunks he could find. After a moment, he had Jeffrey look back. No one was coming after him, it seemed. So far so good, the professor thought.

Then he turned the retarded man around and had him make his way through the untended woods. The ground was uneven and rife with exposed roots and rocks, but it barely slowed Jeffrey down.

After a mile or so, the professor and his host came to a four-lane macadam highway. As before, Xavier had Jeffrey look around to make sure no one was coming after him. Then he stuck his thumb out and waited for a vehicle to come rolling by.

The professor knew the retarded man was in exemplary physical condition. However, it was almost twenty-five miles from Westminster to Xavier's mansion. A lift from a passing motorist, especially at this early juncture, would go a long way toward ensuring the completion of Jeffrey's journey.

On the other hand, Xavier couldn't linger too long at the side of the road. Once the people at Westminster realized their charge was gone, they would call the police—and it would only be a matter of time before the area was thick with patrol cars.

The first two vehicles that passed him were family vans in bright metallic colors. Neither driver even glanced at him. The next vehicle was an expensive black sports car that slowed down but didn't stop.

The professor had Jeffrey glance over his shoulder. No sign of a police car, he noted—at least not yet.

He resumed his attempts to thumb a ride. Two more cars went by, a white station wagon and a small blue sedan. Then came a couple of motorcyclists, and a pizza delivery vehicle in what appeared to be a great hurry.

Finally, an eighteen-wheeler with a red cab surmounted the rise in the highway. It slowed down as it got closer to Jeffrey. Then its driver pulled it off the road and onto the shoulder.

Xavier had his host approach the driver's side of the cab. The trucker rolled down the window and stuck his head out. He was a burly black man with a salt-and-pepper beard and a beige and black baseball cap.

He seemed to size up the hitchhiker at a glance. "I'm headed for the Taconic," said the trucker. "How about you?"

The professor had Jeffrey assume a hopeful expression. Then he had him gesture down the road.

The man's brow creased. "Can't you talk?"

Xavier shook his host's head from side to side.

"Really?" the trucker asked.

The professor had Jeffrey nod.

Frowning, the man appeared to weigh the information for a moment. Then he reached way over to the passenger's side of his cab and swung his big, red door open.

Xavier had his host walk up to the vehicle, climb in and

pull the door closed after him. When he offered his hand to the trucker, the man shook it with a good strong grip.

"My wife has a cousin who can't talk," the trucker explained. "His name's Reggie. Heck of a poker player."

The professor nodded Jeffrey's head, doing his best to make his host look interested in the trucker's comments.

"If Reggie was havin' trouble," the man said, "I'd want someone to pick him up. Know what I mean?"

Xavier made Jeffrey's head go up and down.

"Tell you what," the trucker told him, putting his vehicle into gear and snaking back onto the road, "you see a sign for the place you want to go, you point to it."

The professor was grateful for the suggestion. He made an "okay" sign with his thumb and forefinger.

Then he and his benefactor went barreling down the road, leaving Westminster House behind.

CHAPTER NINE

The Atlas Mountains loomed above Jean Grey, looking like giant camel gods resting after a journey across the sands of the Sahara. They were proud, angular, devoid of color and life except for the few tenacious scrub plants hardy enough to survive on their flanks.

"And I thought Columbia was hot," Bobby remarked, half his words stolen by the wind.

Hank, who was lugging another bogus component in his backpack, combed some sand out of his fur with his fingers. "Professor X sends us to only the nicest places," he said.

Jean heard the remark, but she didn't laugh. She didn't make any comments of her own, either. She was concentrating too hard on finding the Quistalian base buried in these sand-swept foothills.

Scott stood beside her, watching her silently. Though he was the team's field leader, he was also her husband. He knew better than to say anything until he saw an expression of triumph on her face.

They had followed the professor's directions to the letter,

landing the Blackbird on a conveniently exposed table of rock almost a quarter mile away. But with the wind hooting at Jean and stinging her face with sand, it was harder to find the base than she had imagined.

Come on, she told herself. *Reach deeper.*

Warren circled overhead like a white-winged vulture. But he was only exploring, having never visited a place like this before.

Deeper, Jean urged herself.

And suddenly there it was, something hard and unyielding, something vertical and perfectly flat. She felt along its smooth, unpitted surface and made certain of her discovery. Only then did she turn to Scott.

"I've got it," she said.

But he was smiling already. "I know," he told her.

Hank gestured to Warren. "Paydirt!" he bellowed.

Of course, Jean's job wasn't over yet. Locating the base was one thing. Exposing its entrance was another.

Again, she applied her telekinetic abilities—but this time, she didn't focus any deeper than a foot or two. *Dig,* she thought. Suddenly, the sand in front of her began to fly away in frantic haste. It looked as if some desert genie were blowing on the spot with all his strength.

Bobby chuckled. "You go, girl!"

Jean kept blasting away, digging deeper and deeper, driving the sand out of the hole she was making faster than the desert could pour it back in. Her progress was slow but steady.

Three feet. Four. Five . . .

And then she saw it—a dark, oily-looking metal surface. The same kind of door they had found in South America, except this one was below the level of the ground. *Of course,* Jean reflected, *the sands probably shifted all the time here, so the entrance might have been above ground when the Quistalians first built it.*

She continued to dig, exposing more and more of the alien metal, until she could begin to make out the door's outlines. But at the same time, it got harder and harder for her to keep the sand back.

"Bobby," said Scott, "we need some ice walls."

"Coming right up," said his teammate. "But don't expect them to last too long in *this* place."

A moment later, he was driving icy wedges into the hole Jean had created, securing the product of her labors. The last wedge, which faced the aliens' door, had chiseled-looking steps so the X-Men could descend into the hole without any trouble.

Scott was the first one down. Opening his pouch, he took out the Quistalian key he had used to gain entry to the Columbian base. Then he located the tiny hole in the center of the door.

Inserting the tool the professor had given him, he pressed the stud on its side. Jean saw a green glow emerge from the aperture. Almost instantly, the slab of alien metal slid down out of sight.

Bobby chuckled. "Gotta love that thing."

Scott beckoned. "Let's go."

As before, Warren darted inside to reconnoiter. Then the others followed him, glad to be out of the arid wind.

As Scott put away his "key," Jean probed the corridor for signs of life. She only needed a moment to satisfy herself that there weren't any—and to inform her husband of the fact.

"I don't hear anything either," Hank reported enthusiastically. "But as we've learned the hard way, that doesn't rule out intruder-killing spider-robots."

"True," said Scott. "And if one base had them, there's a

good chance the others will too. So we'll have to be on our guard."

"No problem," Bobby told him with forced cheer. "Being on guard is one of my specialties."

Again, Scott led the team inside. Jean trailed in his wake through bend after bend, scouring the alien venue for living antagonists she might somehow have missed.

She found that the experience wasn't any less ominous for her having been in a similar facility so recently. The narrow, echoing passageway and its dark, serpentine bundles of circuitry still sent chills up and down her spine.

Then, all at once, the telepath realized that Warren was on his way back, his reconnaissance of the place complete. She inspected his mind for signs of anxiety, but she couldn't find anything specific—just a general undercurrent of wariness.

Hank cocked an ear. "Here comes Warren," he announced.

A moment later, Jean heard it too—the soft, slightly sibilant sound that their teammate made when he flapped his majestic white wings. Before she knew it, Warren swooped around a bend in the corridor and alighted on the floor in front of them.

"Any surprises?" asked Scott.

"None that I can see," Warren told him. "I checked the ceiling and there wasn't any sign we'll be attacked from above."

Jean read his mind. "But you're still not confident about our entering the chamber," she said.

Warren looked at her. "That's right."

Scott frowned. "It's not as if we've got a choice."

One of the things Jean loved about the X-Men's field leader was his ability to cut through doubt and uncertainty, reducing a situation to its most basic premise. Another was his understated courage.

"Let's continue," Scott told them.

The team moved through the corridor without incident and arrived at the Quistalians' chamber. It was just like the other one—immense and cylindrical in shape, illuminated by long iridescent strips, its dark walls crowded with twisted circuitry.

Jean looked across the chamber and saw the collection of smaller cylinders that made up the base's communications system. One of the cylinders was a muted gold with veins of scarlet running through it.

"There it is," Scott said, his voice echoing wildly.

"Right where it's supposed to be," Bobby added.

Again, Jean cast about for sentient life. As far as she could tell, they were still alone.

Scott didn't like the silence any more than the rest of them. His wife could tell. "Same positions as last time," he said.

Warren went aloft as the others spaced themselves around the chamber. Jean positioned herself along the right-hand wall, just beyond Bobby. Then Hank looked to Scott and got a nod.

"Here goes nothing," said the furry X-Man.

He crossed the chamber more cautiously than the last time, his blue hide gleaming sleekly in the alien light. On reaching the communications cylinders, he removed the professor's substitute component from his backpack and placed it on the floor.

You're okay so far, Jean assured him telepathically.

So far, Hank echoed fatalistically.

Wresting the gold cylinder from the system's embrace, he tucked it into his backpack and tossed the pack over his powerful shoulder. Then, every muscle in his amazing body alert, he picked up the bogus cylinder and placed it in the empty slot.

This time, Jean noticed, Hank didn't pause to report his success. He just took off for the exit, moving briskly on palms and feet.

But before he had advanced halfway to his goal, a series of pits opened in the floor—and a fleet of small, dark figures floated up from them. *Machines again,* Jean determined instantly. Each of them featured a glowing yellow orb, the purpose of which wasn't immediately clear to her.

She sampled Hank's thoughts and found her teammate was actually relieved. To this point, he hadn't known what kind of defense the chamber would spring on then. Now he knew—and to Hank's mind, at least, the hovering machines didn't look all that formidable.

Then, as if in response to the mutant's thought, their yellow eyes pulsed with power and unleashed a barrage of sizzling, white energy beams. Just in time, Jean threw herself to the hard, smooth floor—and saw a beam wallop the wall behind her.

It didn't do any damage to the dark bundles of circuitry there—possibly because they generated some kind of protective force field. But if it had hit a flesh and blood target....

Jean didn't want to contemplate the possibilities. Instead, she went into action—not with her body, but with the power of her mind. Taking hold of one of the assault machines telekinetically, she sent it slamming into the nearest of its fellow defenders.

The impact ruined both machines' aim. However, they didn't have enough mass to do any damage to each other, so the maneuver didn't really accomplish anything. Jean had to find another way to put a dent in them.

It occurred to her that she could tamper with their insides, as she had done to the spider-robots in Columbia. But as she looked around, she saw that her teammates were in bad straits, the Quistalians' energy beams keeping them on the run.

Bobby, for instance, was too busy erecting ice shields to go on the offensive. Hank was leaping and tumbling at a frantic pace, pushed to the limits of his considerable agility, and Warren was slicing through the air so fast he was just a blur.

None of them could keep it up for long. If Jean was going to make a difference in this battle, she would have to do it quickly.

Then she caught sight of Scott. Of all her teammates, he was the only one holding his ground, using the bludgeoning power of his optical beams to go after one attack machine after the other.

And to Jean's surprise, he was making some progress. Whenever her husband hammered one of the chamber's defenders, the thing sparked and fizzled and fell to the floor, inert. *If only the rest of us had Scott's kind of power,* she told herself.

Then it came to her. They *did* have that kind of power. All they had to do was apply it.

Concentrating her telekinesis on the nearest flying machine, Jean used her mental powers to swing it around— and aim it at one of its comrades. At the last moment, it occurred to her that the devices might have a failsafe proto- col to keep them from firing at each other. If so, her scheme was doomed to fail.

But it *didn't* fail. In fact, it worked beautifully. The machine's energy beam lanced out and battered its fellow defender, sending it to its "death" in an eruption of sparks.

Flushed with success, Jean tried it again. And again, her beam smashed one of the flying machines, sending it plum- meting to the floor.

Warren, she called out with her mind. *See if you can grab one and turn it on the others. That's what I'm doing.*

The telepath couldn't linger to hear her friend's response. But as she took aim at a third victim, she saw him snatch one of the assault machines and swing it about in mid-air.

Before she knew it, the tide of battle had begun to turn. While Jean, Scott and Warren thinned the ranks of their adversaries, Bobby was able to make easier targets out of others by weighing them down with ice.

It was a good thing, too. Hank was wearing down from all his gyrations, finding it harder and harder to elude the machines' beams. When he finally saw the opening he needed, he didn't hesitate to make a break for it.

Three of the flying defenders went after him. Jean used her machine to take one of them out, then another. But she didn't think she could get to the third one in time.

Fortunately, she didn't have to. Scott blew it out of the air with a seething red beam of his own—giving Hank a chance to spring and somersault his way to freedom.

"Fall back," Scott cried out, his voice folding back on itself in waves. "I mean now!"

Continuing to use her captive machine as a weapon, Jean backpedaled in the direction of the corridor. Scott, Bobby and Warren retreated as well. After a moment or two, they converged on the exit.

With all their targets clustered in one place, the machines concentrated their firepower there. But the X-Men's efforts had taken their toll. If there had been thirty of the defenders at the outset, there were only a dozen left of them—and two were in the X-Men's possession.

"Icewall!" Scott barked, ducking an energy beam and returning fire.

But Bobby was way ahead of him. He built a frosty barrier

from the ground up while his teammates kept the machines at bay. In a matter of seconds, the ice shelter grew tall enough and sturdy enough to limit the defenders' angles of attack.

That gave the mutants the advantage. They put it to good use, picking off their adversaries one by one, while Bobby's barrier kept them from harm. Only Warren declined the protection of his teammate's creation, preferring to rely on his remarkable speed and maneuverability.

Jean did the most damage of all since her machine could move without exposing itself to risk. She focused hard on taking out as many defenders as she could—so hard, in fact, that she was surprised to find a lack of targets after a while.

Only two of the machines were still discharging energy beams. One was in Warren's possession. The other was Jean's.

As the echoes in the chamber died, she turned to Scott. *That's it?* she asked telepathically.

He poked his head out past the right-hand edge of their ice barrier. *Seems like it,* he replied after a moment. *Except, of course, for the ones you and Warren enlisted.*

"Go ahead," she told Scott.

Without hesitation, he turned his beam on the machine and blasted it out of the air. It was a hunk of sputtering junk by the time it hit the floor. Then Scott signaled for Warren to release the device he had been holding and instantly gave it the same treatment.

Warren's protector crashed to the ground and lay still. Only then did Bobby come out from behind the barrier.

"We get to leave now?" he asked.

Scott closed his visor and nodded. "Before this place throws something else at us."

As the team made its way back through the corridor, Jean felt a surge of satisfaction. After all, they had come two-thirds of the way toward getting Professor X the parts he needed.

After a quick stop at home to refuel, they would strike out on the last leg of their mission. But as well as the first two legs had gone, Jean didn't foresee any real problems.

It seemed the third component was as good as theirs.

Maryellen Stoyanovich stood by the sunlit stand of conifers at the edge of Westminster House's property, her heart pounding, and considered the basketball in her hands.

"It wasn't my fault," insisted Mohammed, the gangly attendant who had noticed that Jeffrey Saunders was missing. "I just looked over at the court and the boy was gone."

Stoyanovich felt numb. In all her years at Westminster House, she had never lost a client. Not once.

"You hear what I'm saying?" asked Mohammed, his voice rising an octave. "It wasn't my fault."

"I believe you," she said.

After all, Jeffrey was a good deal more athletic than any of their other clients. He presented a special problem in that respect—a problem Stoyanovich had apparently underestimated.

"If it's anyone's fault," she added, "it's mine."

Jeffrey had seemed so cooperative to her. So tranquil. So stable. Stoyanovich would never have guessed he would try to run away the first chance he got.

But she *should* have guessed. She had been at this job long enough to know that anyone under her care could run away.

"I have to call the police," she said.

If poor Jeffrey got hurt, she would never forgive herself.

CHAPTER TEN

Xavier had approached the gates to his private academy thousands of times. However, he had never done it in the body of another person.

From the dark, wrought-iron gates to the long asphalt drive to the dignified, red brick exterior of the mansion; the estate looked alien . . . unfamiliar—or so it seemed, as the professor considered it through the eyes of a tired Jeffrey Saunders, who had been asked to jog the last six miles of his journey here.

But one aspect of the place felt exactly right to Xavier— and that was the presence of his X-Men. At the moment, there were five of them inside the mansion, the five who had comprised the professor's first fledgling team: Scott, Jean, Hank, Warren and Bobby.

It was they who had defeated Lucifer not once, but twice. And it was on them the Quistalian aimed to avenge himself.

Stop, Xavier told his host. *We must consider our next move.*

After all, his mansion was guarded by a number of

advanced security systems. With his intimate knowledge of them, he reflected, he might be able to avoid detection.

However, he decided not to try. If he did, his energy duplicate might discover his arrival anyway and destroy Jeffrey out of hand. By the time the professor's X-Men got wind of the intruder, he would be dead and unable to help them.

It would be better, Xavier decided, if he let himself be detected right from the start. Then everyone in the mansion would become aware of his presence . . . and the imposter's hands would be tied.

Yes, Xavier thought. *That's the best course open to us.*

He was about to move Jeffrey forward when he felt a pang of fear—an emotion he had long ago trained himself to transcend. It surprised him . . . until he realized that it had come from the mind of his host.

But how could Jeffrey know what they were about to face in Xavier's Institute for Higher Learning? Had some of his thoughts about Lucifer managed to seep into Jeffrey's mind?

Xavier didn't know for certain. After all, he had never shared anyone's consciousness for such a prolonged length of time. But one thing was crystal clear to him: if he allowed Jeffrey's trepidation to increase, his link with the youth would be compromised.

And the professor couldn't afford that. Not when this might be the only chance he got to drive a stake into Lucifer's plans.

Jeffrey stared at the mansion as if it were a death's head. Adrenalin pumped through his system. His heartbeat increased and his breathing came noticeably faster.

No, Xavier told him. *You need not be afraid, Jeffrey. Whatever we face, we face together.*

Jeffrey wavered, still caught in the arctic, stomach-clenching grip of fear despite the mutant's attempts to calm him. He swallowed back a spurt of panic.

Come, Xavier thought soothingly. *Put one foot in front of the other, Jeffrey. I will do the rest.*

The youth trusted him. The professor had no doubt of that. The only question was whether Jeffrey would find the courage to overcome his dread.

For a moment, Xavier wasn't sure which way his host's inner struggle would go. Then Jeffrey took a deep breath and started walking again. Before long, he had passed through the gates of the professor's estate and was well on his way to the mansion's front door.

Now, thought Xavier, *comes the hard part.*

Professor X's doppelganger, comfortably ensconced in the sleek, golden anti-gravity chair that Xavier used in the privacy of his mansion, pointed to a couple of compartments in the elaborately honeycombed wall of his underground storage room.

"You may deposit them there," he said.

"As you wish, sir," said Hank McCoy.

He crossed the floor with his strange, bowlegged strides, a cylindrical Quistalian component tucked under each powerful, furry arm. When he reached the far wall, he placed his burdens in the compartments the imposter had indicated—in the midst of hundreds of other high-tech parts that Xavier employed on a regular basis.

"Thank you," said the energy duplicate.

"No trouble at all," Hank assured him.

"So when are we going to see this machine of yours?" Bobby asked—innocently, no doubt. He tilted his head in the direction of Xavier's lab, which occupied the next room.

Lucifer's simulacrum favored him with a sympathetic

look. "In good time," he replied. "I have yet to perfect its security shields and I would not want to unnecessarily endanger any of you."

It was the sort of answer Professor X had given his X-Men on other occasions, so it seemed safe to give it to them on this one. The truth, of course, was that the energy duplicate didn't want any of them inspecting the device too closely.

If they did, they might realize that it wasn't powerful enough to protect the Earth from an invasion. They might guess that it was intended for a different purpose entirely.

"When I am finished," the imposter promised them, "you five will be the first to inspect my—"

Before he could finish describing his intention, a whooping sound filled the room. The energy duplicate recognized it as the mansion's security alarm. Apparently, someone or something had tripped one of the real Xavier's exterior detection systems.

"Anyone expecting a visitor?" Warren asked, exchanging sober looks with his fellow X-Men.

At the same time, Hank loped over to a computer station in the corner of the room. "Looks like a single intruder," he said, glancing at the data as he stopped the whooping. "I'll call up a visual."

The doppelganger pressed a couple of studs on the armrest of his anti-grav unit and maneuvered his way to the computer station as well. Peering over Hank's massive, furred shoulder at the monitor, he saw an image of the interloper in question.

The imposter wouldn't have been shocked if one of the mutants' many enemies had made an attempt to invade their stronghold. After all, there was ample precedent for that sort of thing. But as it turned out, it wasn't one of the team's enemies after all.

It was a tall, handsome young man in a navy blue warm-up suit and white basketball sneakers. What's more, with all Xavier's memories at his disposal, the doppelganger recognized the fellow.

"Jeffrey?" said Bobby, who had crossed the room to join Hank and the doppelganger at the monitor. "What's he doing here?"

"Who's Jeffrey?" asked Scott.

"His grandfather was Jeremiah Saunders," the energy duplicate was compelled to explain.

"Saunders was the professor's friend," Bobby noted for the benefit of Scott, Jean and Warren. "We went to his funeral the other day."

"And didn't quite make it back in one piece," said Hank. His furry, blue brow scrunched up in confusion. "But didn't you report that Saunders' grandson was mentally handicapped?"

Bobby nodded. "He is."

"Then how did he get here?" asked Jean.

"Good question," said Bobby. "I mean, the institution where he's staying must be twenty-five miles from here."

"He looks flushed, sweaty . . ." Scott observed. "As if he made it to Salem Center on foot."

"All that way?" asked Hank, sounding skeptical.

"And how could he have known where to find us?" Jean added.

"Come on," said Warren. "Somebody must have driven him over. Is there a car somewhere on the grounds?"

Hank switched the image on the monitor to a view of the drive that led up to the mansion. Then he returned to the picture of Jeffrey. "None that I can see," he replied thoughtfully.

"A mystery," Scott announced. But the mutant didn't say it as if he really meant it.

"It's easy enough to clear up," Warren said. "All we have to do is answer the door."

The energy duplicate stared at the monitor. Something was amiss, he told himself. It hardly seemed likely that Jeffrey would show up on Xavier's doorstep when he didn't even know what a street address was.

He was inclined to deal forcefully with anything that might derail his master's plan. That was his nature. It was the modus operandi with which Lucifer had endowed him.

However, the presence of Professor X's mutants constrained him from doing as he wished. After all, the real Xavier would have treated Jeffrey kindly, with great concern for his welfare—even if he had no idea how Jeffrey had gotten there.

"Yes," he said, responding to Warren's suggestion. "By all means, let's answer the door."

And with that, he sent his anti-grav unit sailing in the direction of the exit, trusting Xavier's team to follow in his wake.

CHAPTER ELEVEN

Floating in the slow, monotonous tides of the Nameless Dimension, his mind acutely receptive to events on Earth, the being called Lucifer cursed vividly beneath his breath.

Despite Jeffrey Saunders' complete and utter lack of a reason to visit Salem Center, despite his severe mental limitations, he had made his way to the mutants' doorstep. The more the Quistalian thought about it, the more certain he was that the boy's appearance wasn't just a coincidence.

Somehow, he reflected, Charles Xavier had had a hand in this development. Though the mutant had arrived in the Nameless Dimension less than a day ago, he appeared to have already discovered a way to carry on communications with the outside world.

But why he had chosen a retarded man to be his agent? Lucifer hadn't finished posing the question before the answer occurred to him. Jeffrey Saunders' mind was simpler and therefore more open than that of a normal human being. He was the perfect vessel for an intruder like Xavier.

And why was he at the mansion? Why had he gone to

the trouble of making such an arduous journey? There could be only one reason—to expose the doppelganger as a fraud.

Lucifer scowled. His enemy had come a long way, but he would get no farther. Gathering up some of the ionic energy with which he had become so murderously skillful, the Quistalian propelled himself through the viscous liquid of the Nameless Dimension.

I am coming, Xavier, he called out telepathically. *And it won't take me long to reach you. We'll see how deftly you can manipulate your proxy when you've got more a immediate concern on your mind.*

Survival, for instance.

Professor X heard his enemy's telepathic threat. As a result, he knew that Lucifer was coming for him long before he saw the murky speck of crimson in the distance.

The alien was standing upright as he advanced, his cape billowing behind him, the same expression of hatred and anger twisting his bearded face. No doubt, he intended to give the mutant the kind of beating he had given him before—perhaps even worse, considering what Xavier was trying to accomplish back on Earth.

Still bound in the chains of ionic energy that had been imposed on him, the professor frowned. He wanted desperately to guide Jeffrey Saunders into the presence of his X-Men, where he would at least have a chance to expose Lucifer's scheme. But to do that, he would have to defeat the Quistalian here in the Nameless Dimension as well.

Fortunately, Xavier had done more in the time allotted to him than send Jeffrey dashing through Westchester County. He had acclimated himself to his surroundings. He had made adjustments.

But would they be enough against someone as powerful

as Lucifer? He eyed the rapidly growing figure in crimson and purple. Apparently, he wouldn't have to wait long to find out.

Suddenly, a thought branded the professor's mind like a white-hot poker: *How dare you!*

In the same instant, the Quistalian unleashed a barrage of ionic fury. But unlike the last time, his attack never reached his adversary—because Xavier threw up a psionic shield against it.

It wasn't the best defense the mutant had ever erected, nor did he think he could be quite so effective with it a second time. But then, he had no intention of using it a second time.

Lucifer's features twisted with anger. Reaching back, he hurled another fiery energy wave at Xavier.

This time, however, the professor didn't attempt to ward it off. Instead, he reshaped it, refocused it, turned it into a pencil-thin stream—and used it to shatter the ionic shackles that bound him!

Before the Quistalian had any idea what Xavier was up to, the mutant was free. What's more, he was able to return Lucifer's fire with a volley of powerful mental bolts. They slammed into the alien one after the other—driving him back, staggering him . . .

And finally causing him to lose consciousness.

But Xavier could only do so much at one time—especially in such a strange and troublesome environment. As he dealt Lucifer that final, stunning blow, he felt himself lose contact with his agent on Earth.

Jeffrey . . . he thought as he felt their telepathic link slip away—and at a most critical juncture.

The mutant tried desperately to restore it, to find the man's mind again and extend his consciousness into it. But there wasn't enough time. The Quistalian's eyes were already beginning to flutter open.

Clenching his jaw, Xavier swam away from Lucifer with all the speed of which his crippled body was capable. If he could put enough distance between himself and his tormentor, he might be able to establish his psychic link with Jeffrey again . . .

Before something awful happened.

The false Charles Xavier was in the dark, elegant foyer of his red brick mansion, settling into his wheelchair with the help of Jean Grey's telekinetic abilities, when he lost contact with his other-dimensional master.

Lucifer? he called out with the power of his mind, attempting to fill the vacuum the Quistalian's absence had created.

But there was no answer. Not even a faint one. Something had happened to Lucifer, the energy duplicate realized. Something had separated them, if only for the moment.

Fortunately, he had been given an unconditional agenda to follow—and follow it he would.

"Is everything all right, sir?" Jean asked him.

The imposter turned to her as if he were genuinely surprised. "Everything is fine, Jean. Why do you ask?"

She frowned ever so slightly. "I caught a stray thought . . . or at least, I thought I did. It seemed you were looking for someone."

He dismissed the notion with an economical wave of his hand. "I was reaching out to Jeffrey," he lied. "That's all."

Jean's expression lightened. "Of course. I should have known."

"After all," the doppelganger went on, wheeling himself

toward the heavy wooden front doors in advance of the mutants, "the young man is in a strange place. He cannot help being frightened, no matter the circumstances under which he arrived."

"No doubt," Hank agreed, making his way around the wheelchair to open one of the doors for his mentor.

Outside, the heavens were a bright blue. The estate's sprawling front lawn was host to a scattering of crimson and golden-brown leaves. And Jeffrey Saunders was standing stock still in the middle of them, his expression one of disorientation.

As the energy duplicate wheeled himself down the concrete ramp next to the mansion's front steps, he regarded Jeffrey—and vice versa. Jeffrey brightened a little when he recognized what he believed was his grandfather's friend— but only for a moment. Then he seemed to close down again, lost on a sea of confusion.

If the youth had ever been in contact with Xavier, their link seemed to have vanished already—just as the imposter's link with his creator had vanished. It occurred to the false Professor X that there was a connection between the two events, though he couldn't be certain of it.

The doppelganger was accompanied by Scott, Jean and Bobby as he made his way across the lawn toward Jeffrey. Hank and Warren stayed behind in the house, however. After all, the former was undisguised and the latter hadn't hidden his wings—and they all believed there was enough mutant hysteria in the world without taking a chance on inciting more.

Stupid genetic accidents, the imposter thought. *Pitiful twists of nature. They cower from mere human beings, who can't hope to match their power, while a much greater threat insinuates itself among them.*

In the end, he mused, all Earthmen would fall to his Quistalian master. The X-Men would be the first, to be sure, but no one on the planet would escape Lucifer's domination—especially helpless, handicapped individuals like young Jeffrey Saunders.

He stopped his wheelchair in front of Jeffrey and looked up at him. "Jeffrey," he said in the most sympathetic voice he could muster, "what an unexpected surprise."

The youth didn't respond. Clearly, he wasn't equipped to understand what was being asked of him.

Bobby put a hand on Jeffrey's shoulder and smiled at him. "Hey, pal. Remember me? From the funeral?"

Again, Jeffrey was silent.

"He's scared," Jean observed, no doubt taking the opportunity to plumb Jeffrey's mind. She turned to the energy duplicate. "Just as you said he would be, professor."

The imposter nodded. "Jeffrey is like a child, I'm afraid. I don't suppose your examination of his thoughts has turned up anything useful?"

Jean shook her head. "Not a thing."

Good, thought Lucifer's pawn.

Outwardly, however, he frowned. "For the time being," he announced sagely, "Jeffrey's appearance here may have to remain unexplained. It is more important that we see him returned safely to Westminster House than that we satisfy our curiosity."

"Agreed," said Scott.

"Me too," Bobby added.

"Do me a favor," the doppelganger told Jean. "Call the police and tell them we have a visitor who needs a ride home."

"Of course," Jean responded.

As she retreated into the mansion, the false Xavier considered Jeffrey Saunders. *You'll be home soon enough,* he thought privately. *For all the good it will do you.*

For just a moment, the youth almost looked as if he knew what the imposter was talking about. Then the moment passed and he seemed as lost and innocent as ever.

By the time Lucifer regained consciousness in the thick, foggy waters of the Nameless Dimension, Charles Xavier was gone.

Cursing to himself, the Quistalian clenched his gloved fingers into fists. He had believed the mutant to be helpless, at his mercy. And yet, it was Xavier who had gotten the upper hand.

But my enemy hasn't won anything, Lucifer consoled himself. *Not really. And I haven't lost anything. Xavier is still trapped with me in this hideous place. He is still my prisoner.*

The Quistalian's only concern was Jeffrey Saunders— whose assistance the mutant had enlisted, if Lucifer's suspicions were at all correct. He didn't imagine a retarded man could do any significant damage to his plans, but he vowed to stop the fellow nonetheless.

His first step, of course, was to reestablish his link with his ionic energy construct. That way, he could find out how far the situation at the mansion had progressed.

It wasn't all that difficult for the alien to extend his consciousness through the dimensional barrier and find the one he sought. After all, he had had years to perfect the skill, and the doppelganger had received explicit instructions to remain in Salem Center.

Sure enough, Lucifer found him on the lawn of Xavier's mansion, along with three of the professor's X-Men and a couple of uniformed state police officers. Jeffrey, the Quistalian noticed, was already sitting in the officers' vehicle with a concerned look on his face.

". . . darnedest thing," one of the officers was saying, a bemused expression on his face. "The missing person report says this Westminster place is almost twenty-five miles from here."

"Yes," said the energy duplicate. "We are aware of that."

"And you say you haven't got a clue as to how our friend got here?" the other policeman asked.

"Not a clue," the imposter assured him. "Though, as you can imagine, I wish it were otherwise."

The first officer grunted. "That makes two of us. Like I say, it's the darnedest thing. Well, thanks for the call, sir. We'll see to it he gets back where he belongs."

"I trust you will," said the doppelganger.

As the policemen made their way to their car, Lucifer reached out to his puppet and restored their connection. Immediately, he felt the renewed flow of information and knew what had transpired.

You did well, he told his construct.

I live to serve you, the imposter replied.

It was nothing more than the truth, of course. Still, the duplicate's acknowledgement of it gave the Quistalian a measure of satisfaction—as did the knowledge that Xavier had lost his best chance to interfere with his enemy's plans. With Jeffrey Saunders out of the way, the mutant no longer had the tool he needed to derail Lucifer's efforts.

"You know," said Bobby Drake, "I'm still dumbfounded."

The doppelganger looked at him. "By the fact that Jeffrey made the trip from Westminister House?"

Bobby nodded. "It's just crazy."

Jean chuckled softly at the remark. "And that's from a guy who makes icicles in August."

Bobby looked sheepish. "When you put it that way . . ."

He seems suspicious, Lucifer told his pawn.

Indeed, the energy duplicate agreed. *But not so much so that he suspects your involvement.*

The Quistalian mulled over his puppet's conclusion. *I suppose not,* he decided. *However, if that changes . . .*

I will eliminate him, the imposter replied crisply. *Without so much as a second thought.*

Lucifer was pleased with his construct. It was precisely the answer he had been looking for.

"Come," the energy duplicate told the three X-Men who had accompanied him out to the lawn. "Our labors are not yet complete. We still lack one of the Quistalians' components."

"It's as good as done," Scott Summers promised him.

That, too, was the answer Lucifer had been looking for.

CHAPTER TWELVE

As soon as Xavier believed he was beyond the range of Lucifer's power, he attempted to pierce the dimensional barrier and make contact with Jeffrey again. But Jeffrey wasn't on the leaf-covered front lawn of the professor's mansion anymore.

He was gone—and Xavier didn't know where.

All kinds of possibilities came to mind. First, the professor imagined that the imposter had confronted Jeffrey alone . . . and destroyed him with a series of mental bolts, then concealed his body in the bushes.

No, Xavier told himself. Jeffrey's presence on the lawn had to have tripped alarms all over the mansion. The X-Men couldn't have helped knowing about it.

And if Xavier's mutant protégés had been alerted to Jeffrey's presence, Jeffrey would have been safe from the imposter's worst intentions. More than likely, he had simply been comforted and sent back to his room at Westminster House.

But by whom? Along what route? And in what sort of

conveyance? Xavier had to know these things if he was to intervene.

If he had been back on Earth, he could have done without such information. He could have scanned the area for Jeffrey's unique mental signature and located him in a matter of moments.

But with the dimensional barrier standing between the professor and the object of his search, it became a more difficult and painstaking enterprise indeed. He would have to comb every automobile in town if he was to find Jeffrey—and even then, he had no guarantees.

What's more, it was critical that he locate Jeffrey quickly. Once the youth reached the high-speed Cross Westchester Parkway and headed west, Xavier's problem would become a good deal more complicated—because even if he managed to free Jeffrey at that point, it would take a long time to get him back to Salem Center.

Lucifer would be using that time to move his nefarious plan forward. He would be taking advantage of every minute, every fraction of a second, to steer Xavier's original team of mutants in the direction of humiliation, defeat and death.

So it was with a finely honed sense of urgency that the professor propelled his thought tendril in the most promising direction he could find—that of his office at the mansion, where he sensed the presence of the energy duplicate and his five unsuspecting X-Men.

Xavier saw Scott, Jean, Hank, Warren and Bobby standing in the large, well-appointed room. They were wearing their uniforms, ready for action. Bobby was covered with slick, faceted ice and Warren's wings were flexing. The imposter looked thoughtful as he sat in his anti-gravity chair by the window, giving them last-minute instructions.

"I need not tell you how important this mission is," he

said evenly. "Or how much more difficult it will be if the Quistalians have discovered our efforts despite our best precautions."

"In other words," Scott responded, "if your status-quo projectors haven't done the trick."

"But we always knew that was a possibility," Jean noted. "No machine is foolproof—even yours, sir."

"Indeed," the energy duplicate acknowledged. "All I ask is that you tread cautiously. I trust that you will come home safely, as always. But above all, bring me that third component."

Hank nodded. "Will do, professor."

Xavier wanted to cry out. He wanted to block the doorway with his body. But he was still a prisoner of another dimension, so he couldn't do either of those things. All he could do was wait patiently and hope someone gave him the clue he needed.

"Good luck," said the ersatz Professor X.

"Thank you, sir," Warren replied, speaking for all of them. Then, folding his magnificent white wings, he exited the room.

Jean left next. Then Hank and Scott followed her out. It appeared to Xavier that Bobby would do the same . . . until he paused at the threshold, obviously bothered by something.

The doppelganger regarded him. "Something on your mind, Bobby?"

The youngest of the original X-Men returned his scrutiny. "Sir, when we found Jeffrey . . ."

"Yes?" the duplicate prompted.

Bobby frowned. Then he dismissed the balance of his question with a wave of his hand. "Nothing, professor." And he swung around the doorpost to catch up with his teammates.

Xavier's heart sunk. When he heard Bobby mention Jeffrey, it seemed to him he might obtain the information he so desperately needed. Now he had to follow his X-Men to their plane and continue to hope that they might drop a hint.

And all the while, Jeffrey was getting farther and farther away. The professor imagined Jeffrey diminishing with distance on a long, multi-lane ribbon of black asphalt—and with him, Xavier's faintest hopes of stopping Lucifer.

Unaware that he was being watched, the imposter smiled to himself. Then he made a pyramid of his hands and gazed out the window.

Suddenly, Bobby reappeared in the professor's doorway. "Do me a favor, sir?" he asked the doppelganger.

The counterfeit Xavier turned to him in his antigrav unit. "Of course," he replied benevolently.

"Call Westminster House," Bobby requested, "and make sure Jeffrey got home all right?"

"I had every intention of calling," the duplicate assured him. "However, I'm certain Jeffrey will arrive safely. The police don't often lose a missing person once they've found him."

The police! the professor exclaimed inwardly.

Faster than a hawk stooping to take a field mouse, he withdrew his thought tendril from his mansion and sent it flying across Salem Center. Now he knew what he had to find—a police car. And it had to be a state police car, since local officers seldom traveled beyond town limits.

Xavier just hoped he wasn't too late.

As Lucifer monitored his enemy's X-Men from the depths of the Nameless Dimension, he could come to only one conclusion—that everything was moving forward again as he had planned.

Xavier's mutants had already exited the underground rail

vehicle that connected their mansion with a subterranean aircraft hangar. Now they were refueling their sleek, black jet in preparation for an assault on the last of their Quistalian objectives.

And in the process, coming that much closer to their doom.

"I wonder what they're wearing these days in Antarctica," said Beast. He was hanging upside down, applying oil to one of the plane's landing flaps.

"Blue fur, I think," replied the mutant called Archangel, who was sitting on his haunches below the jet's wing. "So a guy like you should be right at the height of fashion."

"Me?" Hank rejoined. "I was thinking more along the lines of Bobby. After all, what could be more more haute couture in the Antarctic than nice, cold ice?"

"Yeah," said Bobby, who was leaning against the plane's fuselage. "For once, I'm dressed for the occasion."

How blithely they wasted time and energy, thought Lucifer. How easily they allowed themselves to be distracted. A team of Quistalians would never have acted so inefficiently.

They would have done what was absolutely necessary and been on their way as quickly as possible. Any conversation would have been curt, economical, and directly related to their objective.

Of course, the mutants and their banter would soon be forgotten, ground beneath the star-spanning machinery of the Arcane. And on that swiftly approaching day, Lucifer's travails would all be rewarded, his struggles brought to a final, satisfying conclusion.

The Quistalian smiled to himself. The crafty Xavier had come within a hair of outmaneuvering him again, hadn't he? But this time, the mutant had fallen short of his goal.

Forced to defend himself against Lucifer, he had relinquished control of his pitifully limited pawn—and thereby forfeited any possibility of stopping his enemy's energy duplicate. Soon, despite all Xavier's labors, Lucifer would be liberated from his dimensional prison.

I have the upper hand again, the Quistalian reflected, his mouth twisting beneath the edge of his helmet in a cruel parody of a grin. *And unlike Xavier, I won't hesitate to use it.*

Professor X scoured the hamlet of Salem Center with his thought tendril, following one twisting, tree-lined road after another in the hope of spotting the police car with Jeffrey Saunders in it.

Bustling Main Street boasted a steady stream of afternoon traffic, but not a single police car. Elegant Highland Avenue displayed a couple of patrol vehicles, but neither of them had state markings.

Undaunted, Xavier sent his thought tendril soaring over Chappaqua Road, the third and last of the village's thoroughfares that fed into the Cross Westchester Parkway. He scanned its two-lane span from end to end. And this time, he found what he was looking for.

It was a black and white car with the words "state police" painted in bold black letters on its side. Swooping almost to ground level to peer into a rear window, the professor's psionic projection detected a single passenger in the vehicle's backseat.

It was Jeffrey. And from all appearances, he had emerged from his confrontation with the doppelganger unharmed.

Relieved, Xavier penetrated the window and made contact with Jeffrey again. All was well, he assured himself. He had discovered Jeffrey in time to retrieve him and reenter the fray.

As it turned out, his celebration was premature.

For when the professor tried to take the reins of the young man's mind as he had before, he found that Jeffrey's mental state had changed. Fear and mistrust assailed Xavier, cloying about him like a cold, foul-smelling mist, chilling him to the depths of his soul.

The mutant believed he knew the reason. Having been daunted once, his host was no doubt reluctant to confront Lucifer's doppelganger a second time. But as he plumbed deeper, he found to his surprise that it wasn't Lucifer's doppelganger whom Jeffrey feared.

It was Xavier himself.

The professor recoiled from the realization. *Me?* he asked himself numbly. The boy fears *me?*

But the more he mulled it over, the more he understood Jeffrey's reaction. After all, Xavier was the one who had invaded his mind, asking him to do things he had never done before . . . asking him to leave the safety of the familiar and venture into the dark, dangerous unknown.

As the professor considered this, Jeffrey's mind seemed to sense his presence . . . and like an eye with a painful irritant in it, it squeezed itself shut. Suddenly, Xavier was forced back to the outskirts of the young man's consciousness, a murky place from which he could observe Jeffrey's thoughts but was unable to direct them.

The mutant wasn't pleased with this turn of events. He would have to do something drastic to win back Jeffrey's cooperation. What's more, as much as the prospect chilled him, Xavier knew what that something would have to be.

He would have to make plain to Jeffrey how alike they

were, despite appearances to the contrary. The professor would have to show the younger man the constant price he was forced to pay to maintain his facade of calm and self-assurance.

In short, he would have to bare the raw interior of his soul—the intense suffering, anger and regret he had kept bottled inside ever since Lucifer deprived him of the use of his legs, the dark corners of himself of which even his X-Men were unaware.

He detested the idea of exposing his weaknesses, of inviting pity. But he would do it anyway, he resolved—because the alternative was to watch Lucifer destroy his X-Men step by step, and the professor couldn't live with so hideous a conclusion.

Gritting his teeth, he projected an image into Jeffrey's mind—an image of his innermost fears and insecurities, his most private stock of resentments and frustrations. And yes, an image of the hatred that raged in his heart from moment to moment.

Hatred for those who saw how he held himself apart and felt sorry for him. Hatred for those who looked at his mangled legs and dismissed him as a cripple. But most of all, hatred for himself, because Xavier wished desperately to be above such base emotions.

Here I am, he thought. *This is my essence. In the end, I am like you—incomplete, afraid, terribly and unutterably alone.*

You feel pain, Jeffrey's mind observed on a plane that transcended any spoken language.

Yes, he admitted. *I feel pain such as you have never known.*

You made me feel pain, Jeffrey remembered.

I couldn't help it, the professor said. *I needed your help. I still need your help.*

You will make me hurt again? came the response.

There will be pain, yes, Xavier responded. *Perhaps more than before. But if you don't help me, the world will feel even greater pain.*

The whole world . . . ? Jeffrey wondered.

That's right, the professor told him. *You, me, Mrs. Stoyanovich . . . everyone. But you and I, together, can prevent that.*

Jeffrey shook his head. *But the pain . . .*

For what seemed like a long time, Xavier forced his spirit to remain naked and vulnerable, enduring the childlike scrutiny of Jeffrey's mind. He allowed Jeffrey to see him for what he was, not how he wished others to think of him.

But the professor received nothing in return—which made him more and more concerned that he was going to fail in his effort. Despite all he had put into it, despite the awful indignities he had permitted himself to suffer, he began to despair.

Then, as if the young man's psyche sensed his heartsickness, it started to unclench. Not a great deal, but enough to give Xavier hope. Then it unclenched a bit more, and a bit more than that. And as the mutant looked on in that strange, dim world of the mind, Jeffrey's consciousness opened up to him like an exotic flower.

But it didn't just give him access again. It gave him a lot more.

To Xavier's surprise, Jeffrey did exactly what the professor had done. He bared the raw, red recesses of his soul, showing Xavier all the pain and terror and frustration he had endured in his life.

Jeffrey painted a picture of a loving home, a place where both his parents were alive and doting on him. A place with a basketball backboard nailed to a closet door and a little ball that fit in the basket, and a joyful clatter of applause every time he put the ball in the hoop.

It was a scene of warmth, of contentment. A scene that promised to go on forever.

Then the young man showed the professor a different picture. He showed Xavier how it felt when he realized he would never see his parents again.

The blackness. The emptiness. The awful, unexpected weight of loneliness.

The boy had tried to understand what happened to his mother and father. He had tried to figure out if he had perhaps done something to make them go away. But there hadn't been any answers to his questions—just a hole in his life where his parents had been, a hole that nothing could seem to fill.

Fortunately, his grandfather had been there to help him through the bad time. He had cared for Jeffrey, provided him with a home and an adult-sized, outdoor basketball court, given him as much love as an old man could give. It wasn't like a mother's love or a father's love, but it was love nonetheless, and it was all that the boy had.

In time, Jeffrey had allowed himself to trust in his grandfather's permanence. Maybe his parents had gone away, for some reason he still couldn't understand. But his grandfather wouldn't do that to him. He would stay and love him always.

And then, to the young man's utter confusion and dread, his grandfather had left him too. He had left without saying goodbye, without giving Jeffrey any reason for his departure.

The boy was older than the last time. He was able to cope with the pain of loss a little better. But he was alone again, as alone as a person could be, and he had to wonder . . . who would love him now? Who in the world was left?

The professor felt Jeffrey's sorrow and fear as if they were his own. He felt the way the world had been ripped apart for the young man, not once but twice, leaving him wary and distrustful.

And more than ever, Xavier had to question whether he was doing the right thing. He wondered if he had the right to ask someone like Jeffrey Saunders to help him.

To trust him.

Are you sure you want to go through with this? he asked Jeffrey. *Are you willing to pay what might become a terrible price?*

If you can do it, the younger man's mind replied, *I can do it too.*

Outside, in the material world, the police car conveying Jeffrey came to a stop. In control of his host again, Xavier looked out the window and saw the reason. There was a red light up ahead—the last one they would encounter before they reached the ramp to the highway.

There was no time to waste, the professor reflected. After all, he couldn't ask Jeffrey to fling himself from a car going fifty miles an hour. If Xavier was going to make his move, he would have to do it now.

First, he directed Jeffrey to close his eyes and groan as loudly as he could. Then he had the youth clutch at his stomach and double over, as if he were in pain.

There were two police officers in the front seat. The one on the driver's side was tall and rawboned, with a spray of freckles and thick red hair. His partner was a much bulkier man with a neatly trimmed moustache and dark hair graying at the temples.

At the sound of Jeffrey's discomfort, the dark-haired police officer turned around, his forehead creased with concern. "What's going on?" he asked Jeffrey.

Xavier had Jeffrey groan again, even more loudly than the first time.

"Is he all right?" the redheaded officer asked.

"I dunno," said the dark-haired one. He turned in his seat and put his hand on Jeffrey's shoulder. "Hey buddy, you all right?"

The youth couldn't answer, of course. But the professor had him place his hand over his mouth.

The officer with the freckles glanced at Xavier's host in his rear view mirror. "Looks like he's about to get carsick or something. I'm pulling over before he spews on the seat."

"Good idea," his partner told him.

A moment later, the professor could feel the police car swerve to Jeffrey's right. Then, with a squeal of tires and a jerk, it came to a stop on the road's asphalt shoulder. Both officers got out and came around to open the door for Jeffrey.

As he felt the cool air on Jeffrey's skin, Xavier had his host groan a third time.

"Aw, jeez, let's get him outta there," said the officer with the freckles. "He's gonna toss his cookies for sure."

"I hear ya," his partner responded. He reached in, grabbed Jeffrey's arm and tried to pull the young man out.

The professor didn't ask Jeffrey to resist. In fact, he had him lean in the officer's direction to make the fellow's job that much easier. Seconds later, Jeffrey was standing outside the police car in the thin autumn sunshine, an arm around him for support.

"Easy," the dark-haired policeman told him. "Take a deep breath, son. Maybe it'll help."

"You think he understands you?" asked his freckled partner, clearly skeptical of the possibility as he leaned back against his patrol car. "The kid's not all there, remember?"

"I dunno what he understands," the dark-haired one said.

"But I gotta do something, right? I can't just stand here and—"

Xavier chose that moment to make Jeffrey bolt. The young man's body moved so quickly, so unexpectedly and with such power, he was fifty feet up the road before the officers had any idea what was happening.

The policemen cursed volubly and shouted for him to stop, but the professor didn't have any intention of complying with their wishes. Instead, he kept Jeffrey running as fast as he could, knowing that the officers couldn't catch up with the youth on foot and would need several seconds before they could get in their car and turn it around.

Several undeveloped acres of dense woodland opened immediately to Jeffrey's right. Propelling his host into the thick of it, Xavier increased the odds of their eluding the police officers.

Fortunately, the professor knew intimately the ins and outs of Salem Center. He was confident that that familiarity, coupled with Jeffrey's considerable speed and endurance, would get them back to the grounds of his academy unmolested.

Then Xavier and his host would see if they could improve on the results of their last visit.

CHAPTER THIRTEEN

A half-mile short of Xavier's estate, Jeffrey stopped. He was flushed and wet with perspiration, his blue warmup suit soaked through at his armpits and in the middle of his back.

But then, he had already dashed four miles across one stretch of private property after another, constantly on the lookout for indications of police pursuit. Even someone in the best of shape couldn't have accomplished that without showing a few signs of fatigue.

Suddenly, a sound drew the professor's attention—a loud sound, reverberating in the nearly cloudless autumn sky.

It was a small black plane knifing through the air—and not just any plane, Xavier realized. He recognized it as the Blackbird, his X-Men's preferred means of long distance travel.

The professor's heart sank. *I'm too late,* he thought.

If the Blackbird had left its carefully concealed underground hangar, Scott and the others were no longer at the mansion. They were on their way to the Quistalians' base of operations in the Antarctic, unwittingly serving the doppel-ganger's nefarious purpose.

Then Xavier realized he had a chance to stop Lucifer after all. If he could remove the energy duplicate from the equa-tion, he could bring the Quistalian's scheme grinding to a halt.

It would not be an easy thing to accomplish. The imposter enjoyed all or most of the professor's psionic abili-ties, not to mention all the surveillance technology Xavier had installed at his estate over the years. Lucifer's pawn would be a formidable adversary indeed.

But the professor had defeated more than his share of formidable adversaries. He wouldn't shy away from this one, no matter how badly the odds were stacked against him.

With that thought in mind, he had Jeffrey run the last half-mile separating him from Xavier's school. In a matter of minutes, the professor again found himself at the gates to his estate, looking through Jeffrey's eyes at his red brick mansion.

But it wasn't his mansion any longer, he reminded him-self. It was the doppelganger's fortress. He would have to think of it that way if he was going to have a chance at dis-abling his enemy.

In the privacy of Jeffrey's mind, Xavier ticked off the estate's defenses one by one. First and foremost, there was Cerebro, the mutant-detection device he had developed years ago. But he didn't have to worry about Cerebro for the time being, since Jeffrey wasn't a mutant and the professor himself was still imprisoned in the Nameless Dimension.

Then there were the concealed electric eye beams set up at intervals around the grounds. The first ring of beams, positioned in the woods some sixty-five yards from the man-sion, was set at a height of three feet. The next ring, hidden among some bushes at a distance of twenty-five yards, was set at a height of two feet.

A bit closer to the house, an intruder would have to get past a checkerboard of pressure-sensitive pads lying a couple of inches below ground, as well as two dozen tiny surveillance cameras covering almost every angle of entry. And to detect swiftly approaching airborne visitors, there were four separate radar dishes concealed on the roof.

All in all, it was a rather thorough array of security systems. Until this moment, it had always worked to Xavier's advantage. Now, for the first time, he had to look at it as his enemies looked at it.

As an obstacle.

Before he could attack it, however, he had to visualize the few small blind spots behind the mansion that the video surveillance cameras didn't cover. By making his way from one of those areas to another, he could minimize the odds of his being spotted by the doppelganger.

Unfortunately, the professor didn't have a lot of time with which to work. The police might call the energy duplicate at any moment and alert him to Jeffrey's flight. In fact, they might have called already.

The professor was glad there was no one around to see Jeffrey as he crawled across a patch of grass, or as he made a sharp left turn to take advantage of a camera-blind section of the lawn. He was glad there was no one to question his behavior as he rose, sprinted forward, then dove for the ground again and wriggled forward on his belly.

To Jeffrey's left, the breeze pulled dead leaves from the highest branches of the trees and sent them fluttering earthward. They would soon fall across the same laser beams the professor was diligently trying to avoid. But they wouldn't trip any alarms; the mansion's security systems were programmed to respond to much larger bodies.

Once past the inner electric eye perimeter, Xavier had Jeffrey scramble to his feet again. Then he had him spring for the back door with all the speed at his disposal.

If it was unlocked—and there was no way for the professor to know that in advance—it would provide Jeffrey with an entrance into the house. But even if the doppelganger had seen fit to bolt the door, Jeffrey could still clamber up a copper drainpipe alongside it and slip in through a second story window.

Either way, it seemed the professor had made it through his estate's security gauntlet—and inched that much closer to his enemy.

The Xavier doppelganger had barely finished monitoring the X-Men's departure in their Blackbird when something in the top drawer of his desk began to produce a soft beeping sound.

Opening the drawer, the energy duplicate pulled out a dark metal cylinder about the length and thickness of his thumb. It was the control device for the Quistalian surveillance system he had secretly installed when the X-Men were away in South America. A small amber screen in the cylinder confirmed the reason for the alarm.

There was an intruder on the grounds.

Pressing a button on the arm of his anti-gravity unit, the doppelganger swiveled around to face his desktop computer. Then he tapped out a command, activating a link that would slave the device to his Quistalian sensor network. Instantly, a red and black graphic appeared, showing him the location of the interloper along with some vital statistics.

Armed with that information, he was able to access the

appropriate video camera in Xavier's security configuration. What he saw was instructive, to say the least.

Jeffrey was back, it seemed. And judging by the ease with which he was circumventing Xavier's security measures, the professor's mind was in control of him again.

The energy duplicate scowled as he followed the intruder's progress. He knew that Lucifer would not be happy with this turn of events. He had believed himself rid of Jeffrey forever.

Fortunately, the doppelganger had been warned of the danger in time. As a result, the unsuspecting Xavier would fail as he had failed before. But this time, the imposter vowed, the Terran would fail in a significantly more violent fashion.

Xavier was less than two strides from his mansion's back door when he saw it fly open in his face.

Before the professor could sort out what was happening, his doppelganger came hurtling out of the house in its borrowed antigrav chair. Its hauntingly human-looking mouth was set with determination, its blue eyes narrowed to a deadly intensity beneath its upswept brows.

Instantly, Xavier realized he must have tripped an alarm after all—either through his own miscalculation or because the duplicate had installed a system the professor knew nothing about. He also realized that he and Jeffrey were in a great deal of trouble.

After all, Lucifer's minion enjoyed a wide array of powers, including almost all of Xavier's psionic abilities . . . and had none of the professor's scruples about using them.

Had Xavier been at the helm of some other body, his options would have been pitifully limited at that moment. However, as Jeffrey Saunders had demonstrated, he was in excellent physical condition. If life had been kinder and he had become a professional athlete, his reflexes might have been the envy of his teammates.

So when the professor urged him to dive to his left, he did so with remarkable quickness and agility—and narrowly avoided the bolt of ionic energy hurled at him by the doppelganger. But even then, Xavier and his host were far from safe.

The energy duplicate loosed a second bolt on the heels of the first. This time, the professor had Jeffrey dive to the right—and again, they managed to escape the imposter's assault.

Rolling to his feet, Jeffrey eyed the doppelganger and awaited additional instructions. Xavier scanned Lucifer's puppet from his position in the Nameless Dimension, poised to send Jeffrey tumbling again at the first hint of another bolt.

But the imposter was laying back. Apparently he was dissatisfied with the results of his strategy.

Changing tacks, he gazed at the ground in front of Jeffrey's feet. Abruptly, it began to shudder and groan. Then, with a deafening, leviathan roar of protest, the leaf-strewn earth cracked wide open.

Jeffrey gaped at the yawning, black chasm before him and staggered backward, charged with an almost irresistible desire to run. But the professor anchored him, steadied him— and chased what had to be a mere illusion from the young man's mind.

Look, he told Jeffrey with all the force of his conviction. *Look hard. There is no chasm here. There never was.*

Jeffrey stared at the crack in the earth . . . and struggled with Xavier's contention that it didn't exist. How could it not? After all, Jeffrey could see it. He could smell the earthworm odor of decay coming out of it.

And if he came too close, wouldn't he plummet to its unseen bottom and break his bones?

No, the professor assured him. *It is not real, Jeffrey. And it if it is not real, it cannot hurt you.*

The youth knew that Xavier wouldn't mislead him. Depending on the mutant's ironclad certainty, he held his breath and took a step forward. Then he knelt and extended his hand toward the chasm . . .

And felt hard, solid ground instead of empty air.

You see? said Xavier. *There is no crack. It was only an illusion created by our enemy.*

Jeffrey looked up at the energy duplicate, whose features had twisted into a distinctly unXavierlike mask of anger and frustration. Balling his fingers into fists and raising them in front of him, the imposter launched another barrage of ionic bolts.

The professor was ready for them. After all, it was precisely the tactic he himself would have chosen. He sent Jeffrey tumbling this way and that, eluding one blast after the other.

But this time, Xavier didn't merely keep Jeffrey out of harm's way. With each maneuver, each narrow escape, he moved his host a step or two closer to his tormentor.

Suddenly, the sky began to gather into something dark and fearsome, something that roiled like molten rock . . . and from the midst of it came a seething, unnatural rain of fire. Jeffrey became frantic as hissing balls of flame fell around him, searing the ground wherever they landed.

Stay where you are, Xavier insisted. *There's no darkness in the sky, Jeffrey, just as there was no chasm a moment ago. The balls of fire cannot hurt you. It's all just another illusion.*

But it was a better illusion, a more dramatic and compelling one. And it had the professor's host cringing, his hands raised against the horror, his mind a red flood of panic.

Look up, Xavier told him. *Look at the sky. It's blue, Jeffrey. It's the most pleasant day of the entire year.*

Jeffrey couldn't look. He wanted to believe the professor, but the pit in the sky and the fireballs were too real.

Listen to me, Xavier said, seeing that the situation was rapidly deteriorating. If it went on that way much longer, it might become imposible to salvage it. *There isn't any rain of fire. I'll show you.*

And with all the force of will he could muster, he compelled Jeffrey to stomp on one of the fallen fireballs. His host cried out as his foot came in contact with the thing, convinced that it would be consumed in agonizing flames.

Then Jeffrey saw that his foot wasn't harmed at all. And once he came to that realization, the illusion was no longer quite so terrifying. It no longer held any power over him.

No doubt, that was why the energy duplicate dropped it. To Jeffrey's relief, the rain of fire vanished as suddenly as it had appeared, and the sky brightened again. But that didn't mean the professor and his charge were out of danger.

Thwarted at every turn, the imposter resorted to barrages of ionic bolts again, hurling them at Jeffrey with redoubled fury. As before, Xavier helped his host dodge the duplicate's attacks, moving him closer to his adversary each and every time.

Unfortunately, Jeffrey was only made of flesh and blood. His journey from Westminster House had taken a lot out of him, and fighting for his life was taking even more.

As a result, each ionic blast was coming closer than the

one before it. If the professor was going to take the battle to the doppelganger, he was going to have to do it quickly. That much was clear to him.

Then, with heartbreaking suddenness, Xavier's opportunity was lost. In trying to dive to his right, Jeffrey slipped and took an ionic bolt dead on. It made his bones shudder and shocked his nervous system, blackness eating hungrily at the edges of his vision.

But it was the second bolt that knocked him flat on his back, his head aching as badly as if it had been smashed with an aluminum baseball bat. The pain was so bad it was an effort for the professor just to open the young man's eyes.

And when he did, he was sorry—because all he could see was the doppelganger hovering over him in his anti-gravity chair, a smug smile on his all-too-familiar face.

Get up, Xavier urged his host. *We cannot let him beat us.*

Jeffrey clenched his jaw and did his utmost to comply. Muscles quivering, perspiration streaming down the side of his face, he managed to prop himself up on an elbow.

However, he had absorbed too much punishment at the hands of the professor's duplicate to support himself for long. After a moment, he slumped to the ground again, weak and helpless.

In the Nameless Dimension, Xavier felt a lump in his throat. After all, it wasn't Jeffrey who had failed him—it was he who had failed Jeffrey. And now, unless the professor could think of a way out, Jeffrey was going to pay the penalty for his failure.

"Is this the best you could do?" the imposter asked scornfully. "In all this overgrown, overpopulated world of yours, was this the best ally you could possibly find?"

Xavier had no answer for him. And even if he did, his host didn't have the ability to deliver it.

"Pitiful," said Lucifer's puppet, smiling wickedly.

And to the professor's horror, the doppelganger began gathering his ionic energies for a death blow.

CHAPTER FOURTEEN

Lucifer's energy duplicate had been correct. When the Quistalian saw Jeffrey approaching Xavier's mansion from his vantage point in the Nameless Dimension, he wasn't happy.

Not at all.

Fortunately, his servant had managed to neutralize the threat the mutant posed to them. And in a matter of seconds, as soon as the doppelganger built up sufficient power for a lethal blast, he would make sure that threat never reared its head again.

Do it! Lucifer cheered inwardly, unable to wait another second. *Pound the wretch to paste!*

Suddenly, something caught Lucifer's attention—something he could see only out of the corner of his energy pawn's eyes. A flutter of blinding white feathers. A flash of blue and white . . .

"*No!*" the Quistalian screamed miserably in the murky confines of the Nameless Dimension—and turned with the imposter to see the mutant called Archangel alighting gracefully on the grass.

The X-Man's expression was one of surprise and concern as he took in the sight of Jeffrey. "Hey," he exclaimed, "that's Jeffrey!"

"It is indeed," Lucifer responded through the mouth of his doppelganger, doing his utmost to contain his anger and frustration.

The Quistalian's mind raced as he struggled to absorb this new development. Clearly, he had been too busy dealing with Xavier's puppet to take note of the winged man's approach.

But why, had Warren Worthington decided to return to Professor X's estate? And had he done so on his own, or were his mutant teammates on their way to join him?

Abruptly, at least one of his questions was answered, as Hank McCoy came bounding out of the mansion on knuckles and feet. His furry brow was knotted with apprehension.

"Is he all right?" Hank asked.

Through his doppelganger's eyes, Lucifer watched Scott, Jean and Bobby catch up with their teammates. Their reaction was much the same as that of Warren and Hank.

Obviously, they were worried about Jeffrey. But then, they would have been worried about anyone who was stretched out on the ground a few yards from the professor's mansion.

Jean knelt at Jeffrey's side. "He's hurt," she observed.

Lucifer took a closer look at Jeffrey and noticed the bruises on his face—a result of his battle with the doppelganger. He didn't have a good explanation for them, so he simply feigned ignorance.

"So it would seem," the energy duplicate remarked, agreeing with Jean. "However, I don't know how it happened."

"How did he get back here?" Bobby asked.

"I'm afraid I don't know that either," the fake Professor X lied. "Clearly, he escaped the police somehow. I wouldn't be surprised if they were on their way to retrieve him."

"Me either," Scott muttered, his face obscured by his mask but his tone full of sympathy for Jeffrey.

Lucifer decided that it would be a good time to change the subject. Besides, there was something he very much wanted to know. "What made you all return?" he asked through the doppelganger.

"Engine trouble," Hank responded absently. "But nothing horrendous." Like Jean, he knelt alongside Jeffrey. "We can effect repairs," he said, "then start out again."

"I wish he could speak to us," said Scott.

"Same here," Bobby added. "I mean, who knows? He might be hurt even worse than we think."

As far as Lucifer was concerned, the mutants were paying entirely too much attention to Jeffrey's injuries. That could lead to trouble, he reflected—the kind he couldn't afford.

"The more I think about it," he said through his energy duplicate, "the more I believe it would be imprudent to wait for the police. We need to get Jeffrey to a medical facility."

"I could fly him there," Warren suggested.

"No," said Lucifer—a bit too quickly, he realized, and cursed himself for it. "As Bobby points out, Jeffrey may have suffered internal injuries. An ambulance would be a preferable form of transportation."

"Wait," said Bobby, dropping down to his haunches. "Jeffrey looks like he's trying to tell us something."

Indeed, Jeffrey was staring up at Jean and moving his mouth. He was having difficulty making any words come out, but Lucifer knew that was merely a temporary setback. Eventually, Xavier would find a way to reveal to his X-Men what had happened to him.

Unless Lucifer's doppelganger did what he was about to do before the team showed up . . . and destroyed Jeffrey with a powerful ionic bolt. That would put an end to Xavier's scheme once and for all.

With the mutants' attention focused squarely on Jeffrey, Lucifer mustered the explosive ionic energies at his disposal. Then he focused them, intending to unleash them in a single devastating blast.

One which no one but Xavier would ever notice.

But before he could finish his task, Jean looked up at him with a wide-eyed expression of alarm on her face. Pointing at the energy duplicate, she cried out, "Bobby was right!"

Seeing that the other X-Men were staring at him, Lucifer had his doppelganger retreat a couple of feet in his anti-grav unit. "Right about what?" he asked innocently.

"About *you*," said Warren.

"About your not being who you appear to be," Scott added.

"Not what I . . . that's insane!" Lucifer stammered through the mouth of his energy puppet.

Then it occurred to him that Professor Xavier would never have sputtered like that. He would have remained calm, even-tempered, even under the most nerve-wracking circumstances.

"What's insane," said Bobby, "is that you were able to get away with it for so long."

"Easy, Bobby," Hank told him. "Don't be so hard on yourself. After all, it was *you* who first became suspicious of this scalawag."

Reining in his turbulent emotions, Lucifer made the doppelganger shake his head from side to side. "You're making a mistake," he told the X-Men solemnly. "A terrible mistake."

"No," Bobby insisted. "It's you who made the mistakes. I suspected something was wrong from the moment I saw Jeffrey show up here, but I didn't know who was responsible for it. Then I saw you call the police to have them take Jeffrey back to his institution."

The mutant frowned, frozen vapor issuing from his mouth. "He was your friend's grandson—a guy you showed a lot of kindness back at your pal's funeral—and yet you didn't offer to take him home yourself. That got me thinking about you. And suddenly, I began to see a motive in the way we were attacked the other day.

"I began to wonder," said Bobby, "what if the professor had actually been kidnapped while I was lying there unconscious? What if he had been replaced with someone else?"

"Someone like *you*," Warren said, finishing his comrade's thought.

"But I didn't tip my hand right away," Bobby continued. "I didn't know what kind of mental surveillance you were capable of, or what kind of listening devices you might have hooked up. So I kept my suspicions to myself until I got a chance to talk to my teammates alone."

Scott jerked a thumb over his right shoulder, indicating the Blackbird's underground hangar. "Right after we took off on another of your missions," he noted bitterly.

"By then," said Bobby, "I knew you couldn't be monitoring us. That's when I told my friends here what I was thinking."

"At which point," Hank remarked, "we decided to turn back and evaluate the evidence firsthand."

"And found you hovering over Jeffrey," Warren said, "looking like a spider picking over his prey."

Lucifer saw there was no use in denying it anymore—no use in pretending the doppelganger was really Xavier. On the other hand, there was still a use for his energy construct.

Using the ionic force the imposter had gathered, he began to direct it at Jeffrey. After all, without Xavier's living link to this world, the X-Men could never learn where the professor was imprisoned or who had abducted him. And if they remained ignorant of such information, Lucifer could still find a way to salvage his scheme.

But before he could reach Jeffrey's mind, something got in the way of his assault. It was another telepathic presence, one that no less powerful than his own.

Perhaps Xavier himself could have penetrated that presence, forced his way through it. However, the doppelganger was not Xavier. At best, he was only a faint copy of the original.

"No!" groaned Jean, her features contorted suddenly with concentration. "No, I won't let you!"

"What's going on, Jean?" Bobby demanded of her, his faceted brow creased with concern.

"Let her be, Bobby!" said Scott. "She's fending off an attack!" He pointed to the doppelganger. "From *him!*"

And with that, he started to open his visor.

Knowing what was going to happen next, Lucifer gave up on Jeffrey for the moment and had the doppelganger stab the controls on his anti-gravity unit. The vehicle lurched sideways—and Scott's ruby-red beam missed its target by inches, carving a furrow into the ground instead.

But before Lucifer could recover, he heard a rush of air and felt something hammer the doppelganger's chin. He sprawled backward out of his anti-grav chair, stunned. And as he lay there on the grass, trying to gather his senses, he felt himself pinned by something hard and extremely cold.

Ice, he thought. *A great mass of it.*

Lucifer was unable to move the doppelganger's head, unable to catch sight of his enemies much less attempt to strike back at them. But a moment later, two of them appeared in front of him anyway.

"That should hold him," said Bobby, expelling a wintry breath from his crystalline countenance as he loomed over the energy duplicate. "At least until we can get a containment cube ready for him."

Hank was standing next to his teammate, examining the doppelganger's icy bonds with a long, blue finger. He looked down at the false Xavier with an almost bestial wariness— one that seemed to be the result of instinct as much as experience.

"So it would appear," the furred mutant agreed.

Hank McCoy watched Scott Summers tap commands into a black computer console in a large, brightly lit chamber.

A titanium cube with a small, reinforced window on each side took up more than half of the enclosure. Located beneath the professor's mansion like so many of the team's other resources, the cube had been designed to restrain hostile mutants.

Of course, even a material as durable as titanium was no match for some of the X-Men's worst enemies. That was why Xavier had further equipped the cube with a complex configuration of wave and particle emitters, each one capable of producing several different forms of energy in an array of tight, intensely focused beams.

As luck would have it, ionic energy was one of those forms.

Lucifer's doppelganger was sitting inside the cube, still restrained by a thick, doughnut-shaped band of blue-white ice. He glared at Jeffrey and at the X-Men, no doubt plotting his revenge on them.

However, Hank reflected, it was unlikely that the duplicate would ever escape to deliver on his plot. He was about to be imprisoned by the very principles that had given him his limited life.

"Clear the area," Scott told the others.

The X-Men stood back from the cell. So did Jeffrey, no doubt at Professor Xavier's instigation.

"Consider it cleared," said Hank.

"Let's light this candle," Bobby added.

A moment later, the air around the cube began to seethe with a network of silver beams. Hank couldn't see the floor below the cell, but he knew that there was an ionic energy grid down there as well. After all, he had helped with its installation.

The doppelganger eyed the beams through the transparent portions of his prison. He didn't seem overjoyed at the sight of them. But then, any contact he made with them would compromise his corporeal integrity, tearing him apart the way a storm wind might tear apart a plume of smoke.

In other words, the furry blue mutant assured himself, *Lucifer's energy duplicate isn't going anywhere.*

Scott got up and turned to his teammates. "That takes care of our first order of business." He glanced at the only person among them that lacked a costume. "Now let's see what Jeffrey can tell us."

Hank was eager to determine that as well.

Sitting Jeffrey down behind the desk in his study, Xavier looked at his X-Men, who were scattered across the room. All five of them were intent on him, willing to learn whatever he could teach them.

He wished he could simply speak to them about Lucifer's plot. However, his host was a mute, unable to effectively utilize his vocal cords, and that was a hurdle the professor couldn't seem to overcome.

Scott turned to Jean. "Ready?" he asked.

Jean nodded. Then she regarded Jeffrey in a way that told Xavier she was trying to plumb the young man's mind.

Unfortunately, the professor couldn't do anything to help her. True, he had managed to gain access to Jeffrey's consciousness—but it didn't allow him to grant access to others.

As an alternative, Xavier could have tried to reach Jean with his own mind. However, he already knew where that would lead. The dimensional barrier would prevent him from carrying on any significant dialogue.

For several seconds, Jean concentrated. Her brow bunched in a small knot of flesh above the bridge of her nose.

"Anything?" Scott asked finally.

Jean sighed heavily and shook her head. "If the professor's in there, I can't find even a hint of him."

"He's *got* to be in there," Bobby insisted. "Jeffrey couldn't have showed up at the mansion on his own."

Xavier wished that Jean had been successful in her efforts to communicate with him. However, they hadn't yet expended all their options. There was at least one more open to them.

He pulled out one of the drawers on the side of his desk and removed a sheet from a sheaf of fine writing paper, which he had gotten as a Christmas gift the year before. Then he reached across the desk for a gold-plated pen that had been part of the same present.

"The professor's going to write something," Scott observed.

"An excellent idea," said Hank. "Perhaps we'll finally get to the bottom of this conundrum."

It was difficult for Xavier to make Jeffrey's fingers wrap themselves around the writing implement. After all, they weren't accustomed to such fine motor activity. However, he hadn't come this far to be stymied by a few inexperienced muscles.

Slowly, laboriously, the professor managed to scratch out a word with the pen in Jeffrey Saunders' hand. Then, just as laboriously, he scrawled another, and a third.

"What does it say?" asked Warren, craning his neck to get a better look at the piece of paper.

"Lucifer . . . kidnapped . . . me," Jean read out loud.

Warren swore beneath his breath. *"Lucifer . . . ?"*

"So that's who's behind this," said Scott.

"I thought Lucifer was dead," Bobby remarked.

"So did I," Warren chipped in.

"Apparently not," Jean replied.

"Hence, the need to obtain Quistalian technology," Hank deduced, his eyes bright with enlightenment. "A need, it seems, that had nothing to do with an impending invasion after all. But what did Lucifer plan to do with the stuff when he got it?"

Xavier looked up at him, wishing he could answer his X-Man's question out loud. But he couldn't, of course, so he compelled Jeffrey to resume his clumsy efforts at writing.

"He . . . wants . . . to . . . *he wants to come back!*" Bobby exclaimed, reading Jeffrey's scrawl. He looked at the others. "Lucifer must still be in the Nameless Dimension—and he's trying to get out again!"

Scott nodded grimly. "That sounds plausible. He's pulled the strings from that place before."

"Then where's the professor?" asked Warren. He looked directly into Jeffrey's eyes. "Where is he holding you, sir?"

Again, Xavier required his host to apply pen to paper. Unfortunately, the process wasn't getting any easier. In fact, Jeffrey's fingers were beginning to cramp.

Bear with me, the professor told him. *Please, just a little longer. Then you can rest all you like.*

He sensed Jeffrey's willingness to help. No, Xavier reflected—it was more than willingness. It was determination.

"I'm . . . there . . . too," Hank announced. He turned to Jeffrey, understanding dawning in his furry, blue face. "My god . . . the professor is in the Nameless Dimension as well."

Silence reigned for a moment as the team absorbed the implications of Hank's statement—none of which were very cheerful. Finally, it was Jean who spoke up.

"How can we get you back?" she asked Jeffrey. Of course, she was really asking the question of Xavier. "What do you want us to do?"

As before, the professor made his host's hand scratch out an answer, and this time it was longer and considerably more painful than before. But in the confines of his mind, Jeffrey didn't complain; understanding how terribly important this was to the man in the wheelchair.

"The . . . third . . . piece," Jean said, interpreting what she saw. "Put . . . with . . . others."

"Of course," said Hank, stroking his chin with powerful, blue fingers. "The professor wants us to obtain the third Quistalian component and configure it with the first two."

"But why?" asked Bobby. "Unless . . ."

Scott tacked an ending on his teammate's thought for him. "Unless it was with the assistance of the resulting machine that Lucifer was hoping to return to Earth."

Warren nodded. "Except we'll be using it for a different purpose—to bring the professor back instead."

Jean looked at Jeffrey. "That's it, isn't it, sir? We need to complete Lucifer's machine in order to bring you back?"

With consummate resolve, Professor Xavier carved out one more word below the others: "Yes."

Scott scanned his teammates' faces. "Then it's settled," he said. "We head for the Antarctic after all."

"What about Jeffrey?" asked Bobby.

Warren frowned. "We can't just leave him here."

"Indeed," Hank agreed. "Especially when Lucifer might have some other tricks up his sleeve."

"But we don't know what we'll find in the Antarctic," Scott pointed out. "Jeffrey might be in more danger if he comes with us."

"There's another consideration," said Hank. "After all, Jeffrey is our only means of access to Professor Xavier. His input may prove invaluable when we reach our destination."

Jean regarded Jeffrey. "We should leave this up to the professor. He'll know what's best for everyone."

Bobby nodded. "Good idea."

Warren eyed Xavier's host. "What should we do, sir? Should we take you and Jeffrey along?"

Jeffrey nodded emphatically. *Yes,* Professor X thought. *By all means, Warren, take us with you.*

Lucifer watched the X-Men from the not-here-and-not-there reality of the Nameless Dimension . . . and nearly choked on his red-hot fury.

His ionic energy duplicate had been exposed as a fraud and incarcerated by those he had duped. The Quistalian's own involvement in the plot had been unceremoniously revealed. And the details of Lucifer's scheme to regain his freedom had been laid bare for all to see.

Under such circumstances, why *wouldn't* he be angry? Why wouldn't his rage be savage and all-consuming, like the heat of a raw young sun?

But even through the haze of his wrath, the Quistalian could see all was far from lost. In dispatching his mutant underlings to Earth's Antarctic region, Xavier had made a critical mistake. He had given his adversary an opportunity to rise from the ground and emerge victorious despite everything that had gone before.

Lucifer hadn't ascended to a high and exalted rank in his people's galaxy-spanning interplanetary hierarchy by ignoring such opportunities. By the Supreme One who had sent him to Earth in the first place, he wasn't going to ignore *this* opportunity either.

CHAPTER FIFTEEN

Fletch Cuppy was a man who was going places.

All his life, he had been certain of that, as certain as the sun coming up in the morning. Even when other people made fun of him for hunting squirrels day-in and day-out, and never bothering to look for a proper job, he held onto the notion that he would do himself proud one day.

It was just a matter of time, Fletch always told himself. He was like a big old mess of dynamite, waiting patiently for the right match to come along and light his fuse.

And now, he believed, it had.

Fascinated, Fletch turned the page of the magazine some trucker had left in Fletch's regular booth at the Interstate 84 All-Night Diner and Gas-Right. He had only come in for a cup of coffee and some chewing gum, like always, but the magazine had been lying there on the pale blue seat as if Providence had set it down especially for Fletch to find.

And so as to leave nothing to chance and the devil, Providence had opened the darn thing to an article about Silicon

Valley. Of course, Fletch had heard people mention the place before, but he hadn't ever been curious enough to learn more about it.

The magazine article said people were getting rich in Silicon Valley, one right after the other. They were starting up companies and getting their faces on television. And as far as Fletch could tell, they weren't any smarter or handsomer or more charming than he was. The only thing they had going for them was they were handy with computers.

If I was handy with computers, Fletch had reckoned, *I could get rich too. I could drive a fancy car and live in a fancy place and get some respect . . . even if I did decide to take off and hunt squirrels for a while.*

Unfortunately, he didn't know a computer from a second-hand waffle iron. That had presented a bit of a problem, at first.

Then Fletch saw the ad on the page opposite part of the article. It told him he could learn about computers in no time. Anybody could. All they had to do was send away for a book and a set of tapes.

It sounded like school learning to Fletch, and he hadn't ever paid much attention to school learning. But the ad made it sound real easy—as if the tapes did all the work, and all someone like Fletch had to do was sit back and let everything sink in.

He believed he could handle that just fine. His only remaining obstacle was paying for the book and the tapes, which came to the modest sum of $59.95 plus postage and handling.

Fletch's mom worked behind the counter in Stemmeyer's Convenience Store in town, which was how Fletch got money for coffee and chewing gum and bullets for his gun. Of course, he hated to ask her for anything special, because she always got so ornery about it and told him he was a good-for-nothing slug like his daddy.

But this time, it was different. Fletch needed that money as he had never needed anything in his entire life. And he was going to get it even if he had to beat his mother worse then he did that other time, when the sheriff had to come and put him away for a day or two.

"More coffee, hon?" asked his mom's friend Inez, coming along to give him a free refill.

Fletch shook his head emphatically from side to side, shaking loose a lock of blond hair. "No, thank you, Inez. I believe I've got me something to do today. I'm a fella who's going places, you know."

The waitress looked at him squinty-eyed, as if she thought he might be joking with her. "You? Going places?"

Fletch felt a spurt of anger. "That's right," he told her, rolling up the magazine and sticking it in the back pocket of his jeans. "You just wait and see if I don't."

Then he slid out of his booth, laid down a dollar for the coffee and the gum, and left his mom's friend standing there with her mouth open. He didn't have time for people who looked at him like that—not anymore, he didn't. He had his eye on the future now.

Fletch's dark brown pickup truck was waiting for him in front of the diner, the autumn sun accenting the spots where its paint had rubbed off. He opened the driver's side door, swung himself in and pulled the door closed behind him. Then he started the engine and pulled out onto the broad asphalt ribbon of Interstate 84.

Off to his right, he could see the highest parts of the Salmon River Mountain chain, a dusky purple blur with a gleaming mantle of white. Funny, he thought. As long as he had lived in this part of the state—all his life, really—he had never had occasion to visit those mountains.

And now, he probably never would. After all, the Salmon River was a long way from Silicon Valley.

Fletch grinned at the thought, immersing himself in the idea of running a big old company with his name on the outside of the building. *And maybe a fountain out in front,* he thought. He had always liked fountains.

Fletch was so intent on his glorious magazine dream, so wrapped up in his prospects for quick success, he almost didn't notice the flash of silver in the cloudless sky—the flash that cut through the roof of his pickup truck like a hunting knife from Heaven and lodged in the soft chewy center of Fletch Cuppy's brain.

For a moment, he thought he had imagined the whole thing. After all, he didn't feel any different. He was still driving as steadily as ever, still making progress down a straight patch of westbound Interstate 84. Then he heard the whispers.

You are mine.

Fletch cast a glance over his shoulder at the truck's empty bed. "Who's talking to me?" he demanded.

You will do as I tell you.

"The heck I will," Fletch blurted, and tried to pull over onto the shoulder of the road.

But he couldn't make his hands turn the steering wheel. It was as if they were no longer part of him, no longer under his control.

You will remain on the road.

Fletch's hands shook with fear. What in blue blazes was happening to him? Was he going insane the way his daddy did, the way his mother always told him he would too?

"Please," he groaned, "I don't deserve this. Whoever you are, you've got to know that."

But the voice didn't show him any mercy. It went on the same as before, hissing like an angry snake inside his brain.

You will help me gather others.

Fletch could feel hot tears rolling down his cheeks. "What do you want from me?" he pleaded.

The voice gave him no answer. It had fallen silent. But he had a feeling it knew what he had done to his mom.

Suddenly, Fletch felt an irresistible pressure on his foot, forcing him to push down harder on his gas pedal. A moment later his old pickup truck shot forward, its chassis vibrating, its engine roaring as it had never roared before.

There was no longer any question about it. Fletch Cuppy was clearly a man who was going places.

Following the instructions Lucifer's doppelganger had laid out for them, Warren and his teammates soared over the immense blue and white ice fields of southern Antarctica.

The terrain below them was blindingly beautiful, a series of sculpted mountain ranges rising precipitously from wide, unbroken plains. There was no other place on Earth that could match it for sheer splendor.

It was here that the Quistalians had established one of their secret bases years earlier.

"If you were an Antarctic crevasse," said Hank, who was sitting in the pilot's seat and deftly guiding the Blackbird, "where would you be?"

"Wait," said Bobby. "I think I see it." And he pointed to a spot ahead and to their right.

Warren followed his teammate's gesture and spotted a bluish line that cut a swathe from one range of ice crags to the next. "I see it too," he announced to the others.

Hank must have caught sight of the crevasse as well,

because he decelerated, banked the Blackbird and headed right for it. "Please stow your trays and bring your seats to an upright position," he quipped. "Remember to take all carry-on luggage with you when you leave the aircraft. And thank you for flying Air McCoy."

They all smiled at their friend's jest—with one notable exception. Jeffrey, who was sitting in the back of the cabin, remained as expressionless as when they left Salem Center. Only his soulful, dark eyes were alive with interest and curiosity.

Warren leaned across the aisle and put his hand on the young man's shoulder. "It won't be long now," he said reassuringly, though he wasn't sure if he was talking to Jeffrey or the professor . . . or both.

"I hope that ice field is as solid as it looks," Hank remarked with mock solemnity, "because it's the closest thing to a landing strip your pilot is likely to find."

"We'll know how solid it is soon enough," Bobby told him.

As it turned out, the ice field was every *bit* as solid as it looked. After descending in a gentle loop, Hank eased the Blackbird into a soft landing and cut the engines not a hundred meters from the crevasse. Then he turned back to his passengers and grinned a toothy grin.

"Bundle up, kids," he advised his teammates. "I'm guessing it's a bit nippy out there."

"A bit," Scott echoed ironically.

Jean glanced at Bobby as she zipped up her thermal jumpsuit. "It's times like these I wish I had a nice coat of ice."

Bobby returned the glance. "Sorry, Jeannie, but there's only room for one ice person in this bunch."

"Believe me," Hank returned with a toothy grin, "one's enough."

As on their other flights, Warren found the banter soothing. But he had to wonder if Jeffrey felt the same way.

Jeffrey looked a little frightened as he gazed out his window at the wintry wastes that surrounded them. No doubt, he would have been overwhelmed completely if not for the professor's influence on him.

"You'll be safe here," Warren told him. "With luck, we'll be back before you know it."

Jeffrey looked up at him and nodded slowly. *Yes,* he seemed to say, *I'll be safe. Do what you have to.*

"Any last-minute instructions?" Warren asked.

Jeffrey's head moved from side to side.

"Then let's go," said Scott.

With that, he swung the door to the plane open, letting in a blast of frigid air that made him wince despite the protection afforded by his jumpsuit. Then he jumped out onto the snowy surface and made a crunching sound as he landed.

Jean came out next, dropping into Scott's waiting arms. She was followed by Hank, who no longer needed his yellow backpack now that the doppelganger's scheme had been exposed, and then by Bobby. Warren brought up the rear, unfurling his wings with such untrammeled eagerness that his feet never touched the ground.

With a powerful thrust of his feathery appendages, he sent himself hurtling upward into a dazzling blue and white sky. Reveling in his freedom, which was that much more satisfying after his confinement in the Blackbird, Warren had to remind himself that he was there for a reason.

Gazing down on his teammates, who seemed tiny as they made their way across the frozen waste, he reflected that only Hank stood out against the ice. But then, blue fur was a lot easier to spot than Bobby's faceted ice-form or the white jumpsuits worn by Scott and Jean.

Like Bobby and Hank, Warren didn't need thermal outerwear. After all, his body was equipped to handle the subzero wind chill factors he often encountered at high altitudes.

Folding his wings close to his body, he allowed himself to plummet earthward. At the last moment, he came out of his dive and glided parallel to the ground until he had caught up with the others.

"Showoff," said Bobby.

Warren smiled. "Eat your heart out."

The closer they got to the crevasse, the more it seemed to open up to them. By the time they reached its brink, they could see how immense it really was—a hundred meters across at the very least.

And deep, Warren thought. Deep enough for its bottom to be lost in a haze of soft blue shadows.

Unfortunately, the Quistalians' facility was at the bottom—or so Lucifer's energy duplicate had told them. If they were going to secure the last component, they were going to have to make the descent.

The last time the X-Men had been forced to negotiate a chasm to reach a Quistalian hideout, the aliens had been considerate enough to supply them with an elevator. This time, there was no sign of such a conveyance. They were completely and utterly on their own.

Too bad, Warren thought. As cold as it was for his teammates, he wished there had been an easy way down.

Scott turned to him, frozen vapors issuing from his mouth. "Warren," he said, "take Jean."

The winged mutant didn't answer. He just scooped Jean up in his arms and hovered over the crack in the ice.

Next, Scott turned to Bobby. "Can you get Hank and me down there safely?" he asked.

The polar light glinted in Bobby's crystalline eyes. "Could Joe DiMaggio play centerfield?"

Scott smiled at the quip—but only a little. He had already assumed his "field leader" frame of mind.

"I'll take that as a yes," he said.

Before he got all the words out, Bobby had begun building something icy at the edge of the crevasse. At first, Warren couldn't tell what it was. But after a few seconds, it became clear to him.

It was a slide—one that wound its way out past the sheer drop of the cliff and back again in a tight spiral, with raised sides and sufficient width for a grown man to negotiate it.

As Warren looked on, Bobby leaped onto the slide and began to surf it as only he could, all the while adding ice onto its lower extremity so it wouldn't end up flinging him into thin air.

Satisfied with Bobby's approach to the problem, Scott clambered on and slid down after his teammate. Hank came last, opting to cling to the lip of the slide with his hands and his dexterous feet instead of playing it safe and staying in the middle.

"Hang on," Warren told his passenger.

"I'm hanging," Jean assured him.

Then he described a spiral of his own, flapping his mighty pinions slowly, almost languidly, as he wafted down into the frigid depths of the crevasse. Little by little, the blue haze yielded to them, giving up more and more of its secrets.

Finally, after what seemed like a long time but couldn't have been more than a minute, they came to the bottom of the icy chasm. As Hank joined Bobby and Scott on a surprisingly level surface, Warren lowered Jean into their midst. Then he landed on the ground beside them, giving his powerful wings a well-deserved rest.

"There's the door," said Bobby.

He pointed to a vertical surface covered with a thick, slick-looking veneer of ice. But it was clear that there was a dark, regular surface beneath it—and that it was about the size of the portals they had opened in Columbia and in the Sahara.

Of course, it would be useless to the X-Men if they couldn't penetrate the ice that covered it. But then, they had Scott with them to take care of things like that.

Opening his visor a bit, he unleashed an optical beam that cracked away the ice in a matter of seconds. Suddenly, the dark, oily-looking slab was eminently accessible to them.

Scott closed his visor, cutting off the ruby-red beam. Then he reached into the pouch on his shoulder strap and produced the alien key the doppelganger had given him. Inserting it into the tiny hole in the door's center, he pressed the stud on the side of the key.

Instantly, Warren saw a familiar emerald glow in the aperture, and Scott took that as his cue to remove the key. For a moment or two, nothing happened, and it occurred to the winged man that the Quistalian metal might have frozen into place.

Then the slab began to slide down into the living ice, revealing the entrance to a narrow, dimly lit corridor. Scott glanced back over his shoulder at his teammates.

"We're in business," he said, his normally resonant voice strangely muted by their surroundings.

"I'll check it out," Warren volunteered, assuming their

strategy would remain the same as in their previous explorations.

Scott nodded. "Be careful."

"Always," said Warren. And with that, he launched himself into the Quistalians' passageway, feeling its serpentine environs envelop him like the arms of an unwelcome lover.

The corridor he traveled was just like all the others—constructed of dark, slick-looking metal and packed with serpentine circuitry. Alert for boobytraps, he penetrated deeper and deeper, flapping his powerful wings in quick, economical bursts . . .

And finally found what he was looking for.

As Warren alighted, he inspected the cylindrical chamber before him. It was every bit as massive, every bit as imposing as the first two he had seen—like a foreboding alien sepulcher full of Quistalian ghosts.

And the usual collection of communication cylinders was sitting across the way, exactly where he had expected to find it. The gold and scarlet specimen stood out invitingly from the rest.

"Eureka," Warren said under his frozen breath. "Flip 'em, trade 'em, collect the whole set."

Spreading his wings again, he flew inside and took a look around. Skirting the walls as closely as he could, he scanned the place bottom to top, alert for the least sign of an intruder response system.

He didn't find a thing. The chamber appeared to be defenseless, ripe for plucking by a blue-furred thief. But then, the other chambers Warren had scouted had looked that way as well, and they had turned out to be chock full of surprises.

What are you hiding? he asked the mammoth facility,

gazing into the shadows at the top of it. *Another plague of spider-robots? Another swarm of flying laser-beam generators? Or some new kind of treat—one you've been saving up for us?*

They wouldn't know for certain until Hank removed the gold and scarlet cylinder from its pedestal. With that in mind, Warren veered in the direction of the corridor.

Then something occurred to him.

To this point, Hank had been the key to their acquisition of the cylinders. With his strength and dexterity, he was the logical choice to lift what they needed and replace it with its status quo-transmitting replica.

But they no longer had to worry about a replacement, since the doppelganger had lied about the need for a status quo broadcast. So why was it necessary to get Hank involved at all?

For that matter, why get *any* of his teammates involved . . . when Warren could snatch the cylinder by himself and be on his way in record time?

He could hear Scott's rebuttal in his head, an echo of previous conversations. *The X-Men work best when they work as a unit.* And in most cases, Warren wouldn't have argued the point.

But in this case, when speed might be all they needed . . .

Making his decision, the winged man came to a hover in front of the gold and scarlet cylinder. Taking a last, quick look around, he made certain that he hadn't tripped any alarms yet.

Then he whisked the component off its dark metal pedestal and took off in the direction of the exit, his great, white pinions beating as hard as they possibly could.

For the space of a heartbeat, Warren wondered if he had lucked out and gotten away scott free. Then he heard a slithering sound behind him and risked a glance over his shoulder.

What loomed behind him wasn't at all pretty.

Hank peered down the alien corridor and found himself frowning. "Warren's been gone a long time," he observed.

"Maybe we ought to go in after him," Jean suggested.

"Just in case," Bobby chimed in.

Scott considered it for a moment, then nodded. "Let's go."

Hank bounded ahead as if he had been shot from a cannon. After all, he was the fastest of them with the exception of Warren. If his winged friend needed help, he was determined to be the first to provide it.

As it happened, he hadn't covered a hundred meters of winding corridor before he saw something up ahead. Unfortunately, even with his superior intellect, he couldn't quite figure out what it was.

Then Hank got closer and gained a deeper appreciation for Quistalian ingenuity. The passageway ahead of him was choked with a battalion of large silver globules, each one as determined and relentless as a white blood cell attacking a raging bacterial infection—and as physically impressive as a well-fed St. Bernard.

And in their midst, imprisoned and all but suffocated by their bulk, was none other than Warren Worthington III.

Hank didn't think he would have much time to act before the globules attacked him as well. So instead of slowing down, he did his utmost to accelerate—and hit the mess of silvery globes with all the force his mutant body could muster.

His strategy turned out to be the right one. Jarred by the impact, the globules released Warren—and something else along with him. Hank's eyes widened as he realized what it was.

The third component.

Warren lay sprawled on the smooth, dark floor beside it, dazed and battered, drawing breath in huge, wracking draughts. Clearly, his body was trying to compensate for his near-smothering—which meant the mutant was in no condition to use his wings.

Before the globules could surround them again, Hank grabbed both his friend and the Quistalian device and leapfrogged back down the corridor for all he was worth.

Bobby, who was riding a crest of ice not far behind him, looked confused for a second as he saw what was headed his way. Then his training took over and he sent a volley of ice darts whizzing over Hank's shoulder.

Jumping aboard the frozen path that Bobby had left in his wake, the most agile of the X-Men allowed his momentum to carry him and his burdens along. Darting a glance behind him, he saw that his frigid teammate was fleeing the globules as well.

Bobby cupped his hands to his mouth and bellowed, "What are they?" His voice echoed savagely in the narrow corridor.

"I wish I could tell you," Hank growled back at him. "My advice is to reach the exit before we concern ourselves with such analyses."

He looked forward again to see where he was going—and his eyes were seared by a flash of seething, red light. *Scott,* he thought, blinking away after-images. Sure enough, he caught sight of the team leader and his mate pelting down the corridor to join him.

"Retreat!" Hank cried out as he went whooshing past on Bobby's slide. "I've got the component!"

But retreat wasn't Scott's strong suit. Instead, he adjusted his visor again and blasted the pursuing globules.

Jean stood her ground as well, using her telekinetic abilities to slow the alien entities by sending them smashing into each other like pinballs.

Hank sighed. He would have liked to stay and join in the mayhem. But with Warren and the component in his arms, he had to remain more escape-minded. So he continued to glide along Bobby's ice trail, glimpsing the battle at an ever-increasing distance.

Finally, he reached his destination—the exit from the installation. As the ribbon of ice neared its end, Hank bounded off and leapt through the open doorway. The brilliance of the Antarctic landscape made his eyes hurt, but not so badly that it slowed him down.

The huge, roller coaster style ice slide that had gotten the team down the crevasse looked even more impressive as Hank gazed up at it. Unfortunately, without gravity on his side, going up wouldn't be nearly as effortless a proposition as coming down.

What's more, his arms would be full, since Warren wasn't yet strong enough to fly. But almost since he was born, Hank's feet had been more powerful and more dexterous than other people's hands. With luck, they would be equal to the task ahead of them.

Making sure he had a good grip on both Warren and the cylinder, the X-Man took a running leap at the ice slide. As he sailed over it, he hooked it with his right foot. Then he executed a loop-de-loop around it and used centrifugal force to propel himself to the next level.

Again and again, he repeated the maneuver, swinging ever closer to the dazzling upper reaches of the ice structure. He twisted deftly, even gracefully, exercising a muscle control and a sense of balance to which other humans could only aspire.

However, even Hank's amazing body had its limits. Little by little, the rigorous nature of his gymnastics took their toll on him. With each swing, each circus turn, his breathing came that much harder, and his muscles grew heavier with fatigue. Sweat dampened his face and his fur and almost instantly stiffened with cold.

But still, Hank went on, flipping dizzily from one level to the next, putting his pain and his weariness out of his mind lest he miss a toehold and plummet back down. And eventually, by refusing to even consider the possibility of defeat, he reached the top.

From there, it was simplicity itself to lope across the frozen terrain and return to the plane. Flipping the cylinder high into the air, he swung the door open and placed Warren inside. Then he caught the device before it could hit the ground and stowed that away as well.

Jeffrey had obediently remained behind in the Blackbird. He sat there in the back of the cabin as silent as ever, darting glances at Hank and the exhausted, still-gasping Warren. But there was no mistaking the deep, questioning concern on his face.

"It's all right," Hank assured him. "Warren will be fine. And I'll be back with the others before you know it."

Jeffrey seemed to take a moment to absorb the information. Then he nodded his head up and down, indicating that the professor inside him understood what he had heard and accepted it.

As Hank scampered back across the icy landscape to lend his teammates a hand, he still believed what he had told Jeffrey—that he and the rest of the X-Men would return to the plane in no time. But when he reached the beginning of Bobby's ice slide and started his descent, he saw that his teammates were in more trouble than he had thought.

Some of the silver globules were escaping from the entrance to the Quistalian facility, squeezing their way out into the open. Certainly, that was bad enough. But to add to Hank's chagrin, he could find no sign of Bobby, Scott or Jean.

With his teammates' lives in danger, he had no time to spare. Clenching his jaw, the furry mutant launched himself out over the space described by the icy spiral and plummeted like the proverbial stone.

At the last possible moment, Hank latched onto the lip of the slide with powerful blue fingers and swung around it, expending the kinetic energy of his drop. Then, his fingers still hooked around the ice, he slid the rest of the way down.

By the time he reached the entranceway, even more of the globules had squeezed themselves out. Leaping without hesitation into their midst, he wedged himself between two of them and pushed as hard as his muscles allowed. As the silver spheres parted, he lowered his shoulder and tried to insert himself between a couple more up ahead of him.

It didn't work. As soon as Hank let up on the pressure between the first two globules, they snapped back together. The effect was to squirt him back to square one.

Worse, there were additional globules pouring out of the entrance every second, placing the entrance further and further out of reach. They looked like silvery detergent bubbles from the world's biggest and most overloaded washing machine.

Had Hank been a character in an old black-and-white situation comedy, he might have sighed at his misfortune while the rising tide of bubbles took over his kitchen. How-

ever, this was anything but a sitcom. His friends' very survival was at stake.

With that in mind, he threw himself at the globules with
redoubled resolve. He wedged himself between a first pair
and, with great effort and concentration, made it between a
second. But it wasn't until he inserted himself between a
third pair that he began to feel encouraged.

Hank's progress was slow, painstaking, laborious—but it
was progress all the same. Eventually, he told himself, he
would wrestle his way back inside the corridor.

However, would he get there in time to help his teammates? That was the *real* question.

Just then, Hank felt a significantly greater pressure
behind the globules. Unable to resist it, he felt himself moving backward, starting to lose the ground he had fought so
hard to gain.

He pushed against the pressure for all he was worth. But
it was no use. He wasn't strong enough to oppose it.

Then he saw a crimson glow beyond the silver spheres,
and it took the edge off his disappointment. *It's Scott,* he
told himself. His friend was still fighting, still struggling to
escape.

A moment later, Hank saw a buildup of ice between some
of the globules, and he realized that Scott wasn't the only
one still on his feet. Bobby was still battling too. And if Scott
and Bobby were doing their best to get out of the corridor,
Jean must have been with them, because neither of them
would ever have contemplated leaving her behind.

"This calls for a change of tactics," he decided, his breath
streaming from his mouth in steamy white vapors.

Backing off a good thirty meters, Hank got a running
start, lowered his shoulder and hit one of the spheres with
all his might. The thing shot backward with the impact, then

slowly changed direction and bounced forward again to rejoin the heap. But in the meantime, a wedge of ice had insinuated itself in the globule's place.

A second time, Hank retreated and came hurtling at the pile-up like a furry, blue cue ball. And a second time, he managed to dislodge one of the spheres, giving his team-mates a chance to make more headway.

He took three more shots at the cluster of silver globules, each assault harder than the last. Then his efforts were rewarded . . . as his friends' escape process began to acceler-ate before his eyes.

Scott's potent optical beams provided the first indication of it. They cast a gaudy crimson brilliance over the scene as they thrust away one stubborn sphere after the other.

Then some of the other globules began to move apart, driven by an invisible force that could only have been Jean's telekinesis. And still others became bogged down with thick coatings of ice, compliments of Bobby Drake's remarkable freezing powers.

Jean was the first one to squeeze past the cluster of Quistalian spheres. Then came Scott, and Bobby last of all.

But their struggle wasn't over. Far from it, Hank observed with trepidation. The globules were piling out after the X-Men in a frantic rush to reclaim their prey.

"Ice wall!" Scott bellowed.

But Bobby had anticipated his comrade's words. He was already translating them into action. As Scott, Jean and Hank held the globules at bay, each employing his or her special mutant abilities, Bobby painstakingly heaped the ice higher and wider.

One by one, the spheres were immobilized. Bit by bit, their curved silver surfaces disappeared under a frosty veneer.

Before long, Bobby had encased the spheres completely. But to make sure they didn't break out again, he took some time to reinforce the barrier, doubling and even tripling its thickness.

Finally, he took a step back and surveyed his work. There was a distinct expression of pride on his faceted face. But then, Bobby Drake was nothing if not a craftsman.

"Not bad," Jean quipped. "And in this part of town, I don't think it'll be melting anytime soon."

"There's a lot to be said for permanence," Hank remarked in turn. "But just in case those globules are stronger than we think . . ."

"We ought to haul our rear ends out of here," Scott said, picking up on his friend's thought.

"I hear you," Bobby told them. "Next stop, the penthouse."

If he was fatigued from all he had done, he gave no outward indication of it. Directing a flow of ice at the ground, he created an icy platform beneath their feet. Then he built up more and more ice beneath it, gradually raising them off the ground.

In a minute or less, Bobby had elevated them out of the crevasse and enabled them to look out over the frozen landscape. The slender dark shape of the Blackbird was easily visible in the distance.

Warren was just emerging from the plane. *A good sign,* thought Hank, when it came to his friend's well-being. But as it happened, the winged man's services were no longer needed.

Hank gestured for Warren to stay where he was. Then he bounded eagerly across the icy waste.

After all, he mused, the sooner he got into the pilot's seat, the sooner they could get home with their third cylinder.

* * *

Billy Ray Meekin was a prisoner.

That was the truth he was forced to admit as he tried to coax another dollop of soft chocolate ice cream out of the big tin dispenser with the red and white Dairy Dip logo on the front of it.

He pumped the machine's plastic-handled lever a dozen times, opening and closing the ice cream aperture, but it was no use. The darn thing had gotten gummed up, and the back-up dispenser was on the blink.

That meant Billy Ray would have to take the cover off the machine, stick his hand into the ice cream tank and try to dig out whatever was clogging up the works. And there was nothing he hated as much as the cold, goopy feel of that ice cream.

"That cone almost ready?" asked the guy who had ordered it, a fat, balding fella with a fat, whiny kid.

"No, sir," said Billy Ray, "it ain't almost ready. I'm afraid there's something wrong with the machine, sir."

"Well, hurry up and fix it," said the fat man, slapping the counter with his fat hand as if he owned the place. "My boy here's been asking for a chocolate ice cream cone all day."

"Has it gotta be chocolate, sir?" asked Billy Ray. "Because we got a vanilla ice cream machine, and I believe that's working just fine."

The guy shook his head. "It's got to be a chocolate cone. My boy don't like vanilla." He glanced at his son. "Isn't that right?"

"That's right," the kid whined.

Billy Ray wanted to tell the guy where he could stick his chocolate ice cream cone. He had no use for fat, whiny kids. In fact, he had no use for kids at all.

Unfortunately, he was on parole from the state penitentiary for holding up McGunnigle's Drug Store back in Horse

241

Shoe Bend, and his parole officer wouldn't tale kindly to his upping and leaving the only paying job he had been able to find.

So even though Billy Ray wasn't living in a prison anymore, he was still a prisoner. The only difference was there were no gummed-up ice cream dispensers in the state penitentiary.

"Hey," said the fat fella, "you gonnna fix that machine or not?"

Billy Ray looked at the guy and realized that he'd been stewing instead of getting a move on. "I fully intend to fix her," he said. "I just gotta get the stepladder so I can reach on in and unclog the opening."

The fat guy's fat kid made a face. "Is he gonna stick his hand in the ice cream?" he asked his father.

"I don't know," the guy said. Then he turned to Billy Ray. "You gonna stick your hand in the ice cream?"

"Well, yessir," said Billy Ray. "As far as I know, that's the only way to get the stuff moving again, sir."

The fat kid shook his head from side to side. "I don't want no ice cream somebody stuck his hand in."

His father frowned—and Billy Ray knew why. The guy had already promised the little monster an ice cream cone, and if he didn't get it at Driscoll's Dairy Dip, he would have to find it someplace else.

Not that it made the least bit of difference to Billy Ray. Either way, he was going to have to reach down into that cold, chocolate slop and get the stuff flowing again.

"I believe I'm going to have to cancel that order," said the fat fella. "You know another place around here that sells ice cream?"

"No, I don't, sir," Billy Ray answered politely.

Of course, he knew half a dozen places. He just wasn't

inclined to be helpful to people who talked to him like he was dirt.

Swearing beneath his breath, the fat guy took his kid and exited the Dairy Dip. As the glass door closed behind them, Billy Ray cackled. He loved knowing that other people were having trouble. It made his own misery a little easier to tolerate.

But his amusement was short-lived. After all, it was a warm day for autumn. Somebody else was bound to come in and ask for ice cream. With a sigh, Billy Ray fetched the stepladder from the supply closet in the back and unfolded it next to the stuck-up dispenser.

Mounting the stepladder, he took the top off the machine and slid it aside so he could reach in. Then he scowled and submerged his hand in chocolate glop up past his wrist.

That was when Billy Ray heard the sound of a motor running too loud and saw a brown pickup swing into his parking lot. *That's just great,* he thought. *Someone else can stand here jabberin' at me while I'm tryin' to get this blasted dispenser unclogged.*

Then he saw that it was worse than he had thought. As the pickup turned its dented flank to Billy Ray, he noticed that there were six or seven people sitting in its bed—maybe ten people in all, including the driver and the person next to him.

That was a lot of ice cream cones—and a lot of complaining when his customers didn't get what they wanted. Billy Ray bit his lip and concentrated on squishing his fingers around the opening, trying to find whatever was clogging the thing up.

Finally, he felt something with his fingertips—a big, honking piece of ice, it seemed to him. Working it out of the aperture, he extracted it from the glop and held it up where he could see it.

It was ice, all right. Just like the last time.

And he had found it just in time. After all, at least some of those people in the pickup weren't going to like vanilla ice cream any more than the fat fella and his whiny kid.

Having one impatient so-and-so at the counter was bad enough, Billy Ray told himself. Having eight or nine was downright nerve wracking.

But as he replaced the top of the ice cream machine and got down from the stepladder, he saw that the people in the pickup hadn't gotten out of their truck yet. They were just sitting there, looking like they were waiting for something to happen.

Well, thought Billy Ray, *they'll just have to go on waiting. We don't provide no parking lot service. They want ice cream, they're gonna have to come in like anybody else.*

Then it occurred to him that the men in the truck might have been there for more than just ice cream. They might have been after what was in the Dairy Dip's shiny new cash register—which was considerably more than usual for this time of year.

The more Billy Ray thought about it, the more the fellas in the pickup reminded him of guys he had met in the state penitentiary—hardcore types without much to lose, which was why they would cut your throat as soon as look at you.

Parole or no parole, he wasn't going to fight anybody like that. Not when it was eight or nine against one. Billy Ray wanted to stay on the outside plenty, but not if it cost him his life.

"Go ahead," he would tell them, "here's the flippin' cash register, all opened up for ya. Knock your socks off."

Funny, Billy Ray thought, *It was a holdup that got me*

thrown behind bars back in Horse Shoe Bend, and it was going to be a holdup that gets me in trouble a second time. Except this time, I'm going to be looking down the wrong end of the gun barrel.

But if that was what the people in the pickup had in mind, they were sure taking their time about it. They had hardly moved since they got there. They were just sitting, cooling their heels.

It made Billy Ray nervous—even more nervous than if they had just come in and asked for the day's receipts. He felt like walking out to the parking lot and asking them to get it over with already.

When he held up that drug store, he hadn't kept anybody waiting. He'd been considerate enough to get in and get out. He wondered if that store manager he pistol-whipped had appreciated all the time Billy Ray had saved him.

Maybe not, he thought, remembering the thud of the gun against the guy's head. But then, there was no pleasing some people.

Billy Ray snuck another look at the pickup truck. Still nothing—but that didn't mean anything. Maybe they were waiting for a customer to come in, so they could rob him too.

Well, he told himself, *maybe I'll put in a little call to the police. They can't fire you for being careful, can they?*

Billy Ray was just about to go for the pay phone when he saw a flash of something silver in the sky.

Before he could punch a single number into the phone, before he could even blink, the flash seemed to reach down and pierce the roof of the Dairy Dip. And it didn't stop there, either. It stabbed down right into his brain, like a silver bolt of lightning.

At least, that was how it seemed to Billy Ray.

He felt the top of his head with his fingertips, expecting

to find some blood there. But there wasn't any—not even a little bit. And yet, he was almost sure something had happened up there.

Darndest thing, Billy Ray thought.

Then he caught sight of something out of the corner of his eye. The people in the back of the brown pickup had gotten up and were shuffling all around, looking like they were trying to make room for someone or something else in the truck bed.

While they were doing it, they were staring at Billy Ray. The pair on the front seat was staring at him too. And for the first time, Billy Ray realized there was something funny about their eyes.

They were silver, like the flash in the sky.

Before he could figure out how anyone's eyes could be that color, he heard a soft, insistent whisper in his head. *You are mine,* it told him. *You will do as I say.*

Suddenly, Billy Ray Meekin knew something with heart-stopping certainty: if he wasn't a prisoner before he saw the flash of light, he was most definitely one now.

CHAPTER SIXTEEN

Professor Xavier lifted Jeffrey Saunders' hand with what had become practiced ease, extended a forefinger and pointed to a location more than halfway up the timber-covered mountainside.

"There?" asked Jean.

Xavier nodded Jeffrey's head. *Yes,* he answered silently, *there.* Then he had Jeffrey turn his head so he could watch Warren ascend into the heavens again.

The winged X-Man had already deposited Jeffrey, Jean, Bobby and Scott on the slope, which was at least five miles from the plateau where they had been forced to set down the Blackbird. He had also carried over the three Quistalian components they had secured, each one hidden in a bright yellow backpack. Now, as his flying figure diminished rapidly with distance, he was on his way back to get Hank.

"The professor says the transport chamber is just up there," Jean told her teammates. She pointed to the spot Jeffrey indicated.

"Then this shouldn't take long," Scott observed.

Bobby looked around at the dark, dramatic sweeps of pine forest that surrounded them. "Sure," he agreed with a hint of irony in his voice, "what could possibly go wrong?"

"Hey," said Jean, "it can't be any more dangerous than the last few places on our itinerary."

"Can't it?" asked Bobby. "If the professor's right about this facility, Lucifer's used it to open a hole between realities. I don't know about you, but that gives me the creeps."

Xavier shared the sentiment, though he might not have chosen the same words to express it. Interdimensional transport required a precise exchange of energies. Even a small miscalculation might cause significant damage to both the Nameless Dimension and this one.

Which was why the professor had made certain that Hank would be the one to retrofit the transdimensional transport device. If anyone was likely to be precise, it was Henry McCoy.

Xavier's host was excited to be here, but also a little afraid. After all, having lived his entire life in the more civilized parts of Westchester County, he had never been on such a long, steep incline.

Be patient just a little longer, the mutant told Jeffrey. *Soon you'll be rid of me.*

But to his surprise, Xavier didn't sense any eagerness on the young man's part to be free of him. Apparently, Jeffrey had grown accustomed to the professor's influence.

Then he probed a little deeper, and he realized that his host had become *more* than accustomed to the association. Indeed, he had begun to find comfort in it, as he had in his relationships with his parents and his grandfather.

The discovery pleased Xavier to a depth he hadn't anticipated. *I will miss you too,* he thought, confident that no one but Jeffrey would ever know what he had said.

"Here he comes," Scott announced.

Xavier roused himself from his internal dialogue and scanned the skies above the Salmon River Mountains. Shading his eyes from the sun, he spotted something dark and vaguely v-shaped in the distance.

The casual observer might have speculated that it was some large variety of mountain hawk carrying its most recently acquired prey. However, as the figure got closer, it became apparent that it was a man with wings carrying a furred and much bulkier companion.

In other words, Warren and Hank.

"Our pal's really motoring," Bobby observed, his ice-blue eyes narrowed against the bright sunlight.

"You'd motor too," said Jean, "if you were carrying someone the size of Hank. Warren's wings may be superhuman, but a heavy Beast can't be easy on the arms."

Before long, Warren loomed over them, blocking the sun with his beating pinions. Then he dropped his teammate in the X-Men's midst and alighted on the slope beside them.

"Sorry it took so long," the winged mutant told them, kneading the understandably cramped muscles in his forearms. "I had to give a couple of hikers a wide berth."

"Or else scare them half to death," Hank added.

Warren beat his wings once, as if flexing those muscles too. "Let's face it, gang—it's not every day you see a big blue Sasquatch crossing the sky at a thousand feet."

Hank showed his oversized teeth in an appreciative grin. "Not every day, indeed."

"We can worry about hikers later," said Scott. "Right now, we've got an alien cubbyhole to explore."

For emphasis, he reached down and lifted one of the yellow backpacks, then swung it over his shoulder. Hank, easily the strongest of them, took charge of the second.

Reluctant to let his X-Men do all the work, the professor was about to have Jeffrey pick up the third pack, however, the young man beat him to it. For the first time, it seemed, Jeffrey had taken an initiative.

It took them a while to reach their destination—perhaps as much as twenty minutes, Xavier estimated. He couldn't be precise since Jeffrey wasn't in the habit of wearing a watch.

But he didn't need any mechanical devices to recognize the entrance to the Quistalians' facility. All the professor had to do was recall how the place looked to his astral projection . . . while his true self was lying on a slab in the presence of Lucifer's hologram.

Xavier saw it with Jeffrey's eyes exactly as he had seen it with his astral vision. Each detail came alive for him, separately and in tandem . . .

A pair of tall pine trees with an unusually wide space between them. An oddly shaped boulder protruding from the slope above. A smaller and flatter boulder below. A thick carpet of pine needles, the thickest of any spot on the entire slope.

The professor had Jeffrey lay his heavy backpack down and brush away some of the pine needles. Underneath, there was only dirt . . . but it was freshly turned dirt. And as Xavier probed it with Jeffrey's fingertips, he felt something hard and flat below it.

Looking back over his host's shoulder at his X-Men, he used Jeffrey's knuckles to rap on the metallic surface. It made a dull sound, but it got his point across.

"Bingo," said Bobby.

"In a matter of speaking," Hank added.

Jean knelt beside Jeffrey and helped him clear some of

the dirt away. Her efforts exposed the same kind of dark, oily-looking metal that they had encountered before.

Except there was no keyhole in it.

"How do we get in?" Bobby asked.

Xavier didn't know. He had been unconscious when Lucifer's drones brought him into the facility. However, it couldn't have been very difficult if a pair of ionic energy puppets had accomplished it.

With his X-Men looking on, the professor ran his host's hands over the slab. He examined it that way for a minute or so without any luck. Finally, as he was about to rock back on Jeffrey's heels and try to think of another approach, he felt something . . .

A hole in the metallic surface.

But Jeffrey's eyes told Xavier that it wasn't there. And as he pushed the tip of the young man's index finger into it, confirming its existence beyond any doubt, Jeffrey's finger-tip seemed to vanish into the otherwise solid-looking slab.

A hologram, he concluded.

It was similar to the one Lucifer had made of himself to taunt the professor. However, this one was designed for a different purpose—to disguise the door's keyhole.

"Jeffrey's found an aperture," Jean reported as Xavier withdrew the young man's finger from it. She glanced at Scott. "What do you say we give that key of yours a try?"

Scott opened his pouch and removed the Quistalian device. Then he hunkered down and inserted it into the metallic surface at the point where Jeffrey's finger had disappeared.

The key vanished from sight as well. However, it achieved the desired result. With a low, almost inaudible hum, the slab slid down into the side of the mountain.

Xavier looked beyond it and saw a dark, poorly lit passageway. It expelled a breath of cool, stale air with a metallic tang to it—the same metallic tang he had smelled as Lucifer's prisoner.

Hank nodded approvingly. "Good work, Professor."

Thank you, Xavier thought, hefting his backpack again.

With Scott leading the way, they ventured inside. It took Jeffrey's eyes a while to adjust to the gloom, but after a while he could make out the surfaces of the walls on either side of him.

They were rife with slim, dark conduits arranged in serpentine patterns—a hallmark of Quistalian architecture, it seemed. Clearly, they were on the right track.

The passageway was an unexpectedly straight and short one—no more than forty meters long. At its end, the X-Men found a man-sized, rectangular piece of metal—a door, by all appearances.

However, it didn't require any kind of key. There was a metal pad built into the wall that responded to Scott's touch and slid the door down into a slot in the floor, revealing a large, brightly lit chamber full of dark, angular machines.

The professor had Jeffrey lead the others into the room and look around. He could almost see Lucifer's drones attending him as he lay helpless on a cold metal slab, strangely mechanical in their movements and utterly expressionless. Without question, Xavier told himself, this was the place where he had regained consciousness.

He looked for the semicircular doorway through which he had been carried, and found it at the far end of the room. The enclosure to which it led looked dark and ominous.

"Careful, sir," said Hank, gently taking hold of Jeffrey's arm. "The other facilities we visited possessed rather formidable automatic defense systems. This facility may have one as well."

"Maybe *more* than one," Warren chimed in.

The professor nodded Jeffrey's head to show he understood. He even allowed his X-Men to surround him, offering him protection if a defense system did respond to their presence.

But after a minute had passed, Xavier was reasonably certain they wouldn't have any trouble. Either Lucifer's ionic energy puppets had disabled the facility's defenses when they kidnapped him, or there simply hadn't been any in the first place.

"Looks like we lucked out," Jean observed.

"Looks that way," Scott agreed, though his tone indicated that he would remain cautious despite appearances.

Warren turned to Jeffrey. "Is this where they opened the interdimensional portal, Professor?"

Xavier had his host shake his head from side to side. Then he used Jeffrey's hand to point to the semicircular doorway. *There*, he thought. *That is where they opened the portal.*

Of course, the professor's protégés couldn't hear his thoughts—not when they were all being filtered through Jeffrey's consciousness. But they could follow his gesture.

Scott put the fingertips of his right hand to the switch on his rounded, yellow visor—just in case the team ran into trouble after all. Then he led the way into the enclosure.

Once across the threshold, Xavier's mind was flooded with unpleasant memories all over again. He only glanced at the serpentine tubes and glowing nodes on the walls, and the control panel in the midst of them. But he took his time studying the metal surface to which he had been bound and the lamp-like fixture hovering above it.

In the bizarre reality of the Nameless Dimension, the professor felt a shiver, and thought: *Unpleasant indeed.*

Fortunately, he grasped the basic principles of Quistalian technology—one of the few positive results of his earlier encounters with the aliens. And having seen Lucifer's transdimensional transport in operation, Xavier believed he knew how to use the three cylinders his X-Men had acquired to reverse the imprisonment process.

If he was right, he would soon be restored to his rightful frame of reference. And if not . . .

The professor didn't finish the thought. After all, the alternative was too hideous to contemplate.

Until a few hours earlier, Henry Ballard had been just a normal guy—one who worked as a bookkeeper for the lumber mill during the day and went home to his family at night.

As was his custom, he had stopped to pick up some coffee at the River Rocks Restaurant on his way to work. When he came out of the place, there was an old, brown pickup sitting in the parking lot—a pickup full of people he had never seen before.

And their eyes were flashing silver fire.

Henry had dropped his coffee and tried to run back into the restaurant. But before he could get very far, a sliver of light came out of nowhere and passed through him like a bolt of lightning.

That was when he started hearing the voice. It spoke to him in whispers, telling him that he belonged to the voice's owner, that his life was no longer his own. It told him that he had to pile into the pickup with the others and do his new master's bidding.

But it didn't tell him what his master wanted of him.

Now, Henry and his strange, speechless companions were

speeding up a winding, two-lane asphalt road that took them into the heart of Salmon River Mountain country.

Their truck, which wasn't meant to carry such a load, was rumbling and whining and threatening to drop dead at any moment. In fact, it was a wonder the thing hadn't dropped dead a long time ago.

Henry wished he knew where he was going. He wished he knew what he was going to have to do when he got there. But most of all, he just wanted his nightmare to be over.

Suddenly, the pickup pulled over to the side of the road. Its tires screeched as it came to a stop, jolting everyone in the truck bed. Then the driver's side door opened and a pudgy, baby-faced fellow with greasy blond hair got out.

A moment later, Henry knew he had to leave the truck too. No one told him to—he just knew.

When his feet hit the ground, it occurred to him to try to run away. More than likely, it would be his last chance to do so. But Henry had a bad feeling he wouldn't get very far. And even if he did, it was an awfully long trek back to civilization.

Before the bookkeeper could think anything else, he heard the whispering in his head again. So did everyone else, judging by their expressions.

Listen carefully, the whispers told him. *I know who you are. I know the things you have done in the course of your miserable existences . . . the things of which you are ashamed to speak. . . .*

Inwardly, Henry protested. He hadn't done *anything* he was ashamed of. He was a good employee, a good husband, a good father. He even helped deliver turkeys to poor families on Thanksgiving.

Of course, there were the Friday nights he spent at Emmett Dodge's place, watching his pitbull Sonny tear those other dogs apart. But that was just Henry's way of letting off steam. And besides, fighting was what those animals were meant for.

I know you, the whispers repeated. *And I know you will stop at nothing to survive. That is why I offer you a proposition.*

So there was a way out after all, Henry thought. He listened carefully, not caring what it was he would have to do. If it meant going home again, he would do it.

I have enemies on the mountain. They are powerful, without question—but I have made you even more powerful.

For a moment, Henry didn't know what the whispers were talking about. Then he felt a surge of energy so intense that it threatened to rip him apart. He felt as if he could do anything, move anything . . .

Destroy anything.

You will battle my enemies in my name. If you win, I will let you go free. If you lose. . . . The whispers faded ominously.

Henry followed the fir-covered sweep of the mountain up to its summit. It was a long way up, he thought. A normal guy would never make it without stopping for food, drink and rest.

But Henry Ballard was no longer just a normal guy.

Scott Summers often thought about the genetic quirks that had made the X-Men what they were.

Almost as amazing as the powers they wielded was the fact that those powers varied so from individual to individual. Warren could do what Man had dreamed about since he watched his first bird wheeling in the sky. Jean could pull and push the physical world with the power of her mind. And Bobby, who was standing outside at the moment serving as their lookout, could create an icy version of anything his imagination could devise.

Hank, of course, had been blessed with incredible strength and even more incredible agility, and was able to absorb an extraordinary amount of punishment. However, from Scott's point of view, those were hardly his friend's most imposing talents.

It was Hank McCoy's mind that had always most impressed the leader of the X-Men—a mind that grappled with the most complex and arcane concepts as if they were nothing more challenging than grocery lists.

Was Hank's elevated level of intelligence a mutant ability, linked to a rogue gene like his more obvious powers? Or would he have been born a genius even if his genetic makeup was basically normal?

Even Professor Xavier hadn't been able to answer that question with any certainty. And in the long run, of course, it had no practical significance. But that didn't keep Scott from wondering.

Especially at times like these, when Hank applied his remarkable intellect to a task so complicated and so alien that Scott wouldn't even have known how to approach it.

Back at the professor's estate, the furry, blue X-Man had embraced the technological gifts of the otherworldly Sh'iar with the eagerness of a child on Christmas morning. He had adapted Sh'iar technology to every possible use—including an analysis of the star it had come from.

And now, confronted with what was an equally alien and no doubt equally intricate scientific system, Hank seemed more than happy to sit cross-legged on the floor amid a landscape of exotic components and create what men would once have called impossible . . .

A doorway between dimensions.

To be fair, the professor had mapped out the basic approach he wanted Hank to take. But trapped as he was in another man's body, Xavier couldn't be very precise in his instructions. His student was forced to fill in what were necessarily a great many blanks.

In an attempt to accomplish that, Hank had dismantled not only the lamp-like fixture—obviously, a key piece of the puzzle—but also a large portion of the conduit-laden wall behind it. As Scott, Jean, Warren and Jeffrey stood by and watched, their friend pondered one strange-looking Quistalian gizmo after another, scratching his furry jaw with his claw-like nails and muttering incessantly to himself.

Suddenly, he slapped himself in the forehead with the palm of his left hand. "Of course," he said. "Why didn't I see it before?"

See what? Jean wondered, her voice whispering in her husband's mind.

Scott shook his head. *I don't think Man was meant to know.*

Without warning, Hank launched himself into a flurry of single-minded activity, rummaging among the alien parts he had piled on the floor around him and fitting them together in new combinations. In a matter of minutes, he had created one of the most bizarre, sinister-looking devices Scott had ever seen—and he had seen some doozies in his day.

The machine was Hank's height and roughly hourglass-shaped, festooned with dark tubing and amber nodes that had until recently graced other surfaces. Some of its cables were still connected to an alien energy source the X-Men had located deep within the walls.

The only component of the apparatus that remained

from its earlier version was the part that looked like a heat lamp. Apparently, that was still needed to focus certain energies on its subject.

His work completed, Hank cast a self-conscious glance at his teammates. "It took a little longer than I anticipated," he said with a hint of embarrassment in his voice.

"Several minutes, at least," Scott noted wryly.

Warren smiled. "Whoever said Rome couldn't be built in a day never met the likes of Hank McCoy."

Jean approached the transdimensional transport device and gave it the once-over. "At the risk of wishing I'd never asked," she said, "just how does this contraption work?"

Hank shrugged his massive shoulders. "Quantum theory predicts a multiplicity of universes or dimensions, each as valid as any of the others. What we wish to do is open a door from one dimension into another—and only briefly.

"In order to accomplish that, we're going to draw on the differential in quantum energy states between our frame of reference and the Nameless Dimension. Then we—or rather this machine—will utilize that differential to create an area in which there is no differential, the scope of which is determined by the machine."

Warren looked confused. "You lost me at the bakery," he said.

But Scott had followed his friend's line of thinking. At least, he *believed* he had.

"But if it's creating an area of no differential," he began tentatively, "doesn't that affect the overall energy differential that's powering the machine in the first place?"

Hank's eyes lit up as he warmed to the topic. "A good question, *mon capitan.* However, the area of zero differential is so small, its effect on the total dimensional differential is negligible. What's more, time is passing at a different rate in the area of zero differential, so its effects aren't felt for some time in either dimension."

Jean looked at Scott. "And that," she said, "is why I shouldn't even have broached the subject."

But Jeffrey didn't seem to feel that way. To Scott, it seemed seemed Jeffrey was hanging on Hank's every word. Of course, it was actually the professor who was intent on his protégé's explanation—and for good reason. Xavier wanted to make certain Hank knew what he was doing before he subjected himself to his X-Man's creation.

Hank indicated the apparatus with a sweep of his powerful arm. "It's ready when you are, sir."

Jeffrey nodded. But for all its simplicity, the gesture spoke eloquently of Professor X's gratitude.

Scott was glad they had been able to come through for the man. After all, Xavier had sheltered them from a cruel and often dangerous world and given their lives a positive focus. If they had repaid the favor even a little bit, it was well worth the risks they had taken.

Hank moved to the side of the device and flipped one of the several toggles he had built into it. The apparatus came to life, humming merrily with power. He moved to a second toggle and was about to flip that too . . .

Until a cry came from outside the enclosure. It was thinned by distance and muddled by a host of tinny echoes, but there was no mistaking its urgency—or its source.

"Bobby!" Jean declared.

Warren was the first one out of the room, his body flying parallel to the ground and his great wings beating furiously. Hank was next, propelled by his mighty arm and leg muscles. Scott and Jean came last of all.

At least, that was what the leader of the X-Men initially

believed. Then he noticed that Jeffrey was close on their heels.

Sprinting across the outer chamber and back down the corridor, Scott was blinded by the afternoon sunlight even before he emerged into it. Still, he could see well enough to understand that his team was under attack.

Their assailants *looked* like normal human beings—the kind of people one might run into at a pancake house, a church social or a bowling alley. But normal human beings wouldn't have been firing sizzling white beams out of their fingertips or finding traction on a steep, ice-coated slope.

Or glowering at the planet's premier mutant fighting force with wild, silver flames in their eyes.

"They were on top of me before I knew it!" Bobby yelped, hurling a hastily-made ice ball at one of the interlopers—only to see his target backhand the missile aside.

It was pretty clear who had gathered and empowered these anonymous individuals—twelve of them, by Scott's estimate—and sent them trudging up a remote mountainside. Lucifer, from his vantage point in the Nameless Dimension, had obviously observed what the X-Men had done and was making a bid to seize Hanks' machine.

Opening his visor a crack, Scott projected a seething, red optical blast at the nearest intruder. It didn't send him hurtling down the slope the way it should have, but it did knock him senseless.

More importantly, it gave Scott an idea of how much punishment Lucifer's troops could take. It was knowledge all five X-Men could use as they went toe to toe with their ionic-energy-powered adversaries.

"Hit 'em hard!" Scott bellowed.

His comrades did exactly as he told them. Jean propelled one assailant headfirst into a tree. Hank leaped through the air and dropkicked another one. And Bobby whipped up a storm of diamond-hard ice pellets, bringing a couple more of the enemy to their knees.

To Scott's chagrin, he couldn't find Warren right away. Then he saw his winged teammate come zipping through the trees, little more than a blue and white blur.

Naturally, Scott thought Warren would use his momentum to take out an opponent as quickly as possible. But to the surprise of the team's leader, the winged man overlooked a couple of logical targets and headed straight for the spot Bobby was defending.

At that point, Scott figured his friend had a less obvious tactic in mind—one that might take some heat off his beleaguered comrade. But instead, Warren headed for Bobby himself, looking as if he meant to rip the X-Man's head off his frozen shoulders.

At the last possible moment, Bobby seemed to sense what was coming and threw himself to the ground. But even then, Warren missed him by only the narrowest of margins.

"Hey, watch where you're going!" Bobby told him, shooting his teammate a pained look as he flew by.

But before he knew it, Warren had turned and was buzzing him a second time. And though he saw the winged man coming, Bobby could barely move quickly enough to get out of the way.

"Are you out of your mind?" he demanded, watching Warren loop around again. "I'm not one of Lucifer's zombies!"

"No," shouted Scott, as the truth hit him with the force of one of his own optical blasts, "*you're* not, Bobby." He tracked Warren's flying figure with his pointing finger. "But *he* is!"

And Scott drove his friend off with a short, fiery optical burst. Barely managing to escape it, Warren wheeled, hovered and fixed his team's leader with a shockingly malevolent gaze.

Bobby's expression said he didn't understand. "What's going on?" he demanded of Scott.

Yes, what? Jean wondered, transmitting her thought faster than she could have given voice to it.

Warren's mouth twisted and a single word came out. "Halt."

As if they were telepathically linked to the winged man, Lucifer's energy-powered raiders paused in their advance up the slope. With the suspension of hostilities, the mountainside grew serene enough to hear a breeze rustling the pine trees.

"My god," said Hank, as he came to the same conclusion as Scott. "It seems the Xavier doppelganger wasn't the only one planted among us."

Bobby's jaw fell. "You mean—?"

"That's right," Scott told Bobby grimly. "Our friend Warren is an ionic-energy construct *too.*"

CHAPTER SEVENTEEN

"Congratulations," Warren responded, his voice thick with malice. "How exquisitely perceptive of you."

Except it *wasn't* Warren, Scott reminded himself. It was an ionic-energy-powered duplicate of his friend, not unlike the copy of Professor Xavier back in Salem Center.

"The real Archangel," Warren explained, "was incapacitated by the Quistalian security system he encountered in Antarctica. I am what you rescued instead—leaving your friend to freeze to death."

Bobby's icy features twisted with fury. "You no-good sonuva—" he began—but never finished his exclamation. Instead, he let his powers do his talking for him.

A moment later, a mallet-shaped hunk of super-dense ice went hurtling in the winged man's direction. Had it hit him, it would surely have battered him unconscious, ionic energy or no ionic energy.

But the Warren-doppelganger was as lightning-quick as his namesake. Twisting out of the way before the ice-mallet could strike him, he executed a tight loop and came back at

Bobby with a vengeance. And with that, the battle was rejoined.

Instantly, Scott staggered one of Lucifer's puppets with a bright red optical blast. But before he could finish the job, another adversary released an energy bolt in his direction.

Scott threw himself to one side in an attempt to elude it. Unfortunately, he couldn't avoid the bolt entirely. It slammed into his right arm, spinning him halfway around.

His side numb with the impact, the mutant told himself he had to move. Otherwise, he would be hammered with another energy assault, and that one might take him out for good. Whirling as quickly as he could, he faced his enemy again.

But before either of them could strike, something blue bounded into the fray and sent Lucifer's henchman sailing toward a solid-looking tree trunk. The man slammed into it with skull-rattling force, then spilled down the slope and lay still.

As the blue "something" paused for a moment, Scott recognized it as his friend Hank. Of course, he couldn't look directly in his teammate's direction—not while his visor was open.

Capitalizing on the help Hank had given him, Scott squeezed the mechanism closed again and looked for Jean. He found her beyond some close-growing trees, spinning an enemy in the air like a majorette's baton—a tactic she had perfected years earlier. As long as the man couldn't get his bearings, he couldn't fire off an ion-bolt at her.

But one of Lucifer's other lackeys could—and in fact, one of them was about to do just that. Opening his visor again, Scott planted a beam in the center of the man's chest, sending him skidding head over heels down Bobby's icy surface.

A moment later, Jean's adversary slid down after him,

albeit a little faster and with a bit more torque. They hit a tree one after the other and lost consciousness.

As Scott paused to reassess the odds against them, he caught a glimpse of something. Whirling to face it, he saw that it was Bobby—a look of surprise on the mutant's crystalline face as Warren's duplicate propelled him headfirst in Scott's direction.

Had Bobby been anything but an ally, Scott could have neutralized him with an optical blast. And had Scott not been his teammate, Bobby could have protected himself from the collision at his target's expense.

However, neither was equipped to cushion the impact for both of them—which was, no doubt, why Lucifer's agent had made a battering ram of Bobby in the first place.

Scott threw his arms up to try to soften the blow. However, it was too late. Bobby hit him full in the face with piledriver force, driving the X-Men's leader to the ground.

Scott had the eerie sense that he was rolling down the slope, sunlight and carpets of pine needles spinning by too fast for him to follow. Then he felt a second impact and darkness descended.

Through the eyes of Jeffrey Saunders, Professor Xavier had witnessed the entire startling battle on the mountainside.

Xavier's heart sank as he watched his protégé go down under the force of the energy duplicate's assault. After all, Scott was the first mutant the professor had recruited to his school, and not coincidentally the one on whom he depended more than any other.

Bobby was somewhat less stunned than his friend, but the Warren entity rectified that problem instantly. Without slowing down one iota, he slammed the icy X-Man headfirst into a tree trunk.

Bobby slumped to the ground, unconscious. And a moment later, one of Lucifer's soldiers blasted Scott with an ion stream, making sure he was out for the count as well.

Without Scott and Bobby to keep Lucifer's troops off balance, the other X-Men would be at a severe disadvantage. In fact, they would be fortunate not to fall victim to Warren's doppelganger themselves.

As Xavier thought that, he saw the winged man rocket into the sky. It seemed to the professor that he was gathering momentum for a rush at Hank or Jean. But instead of plummeting into the thick of the battle, Warren's duplicate swooped toward the doorway in the side of the mountain.

And Xavier understood why. The apparatus intended to free him from the Nameless Dimension was fully assembled and ready to effect a transport . . . and the mountain doorway led right to it.

There was no possibility of Jean or Hank trying to stop the doppelganger. They were too busy battling Lucifer's other pawns. And both Scott and Bobby were lying on the ground, unconscious.

That left only one person who could intervene—one individual who could stand between the imprisoned alien and his hunger to conquer Earth in the name of the Arcane.

And that person shared a body with Xavier's consciousness.

The professor spoke urgently to his host. *We must stop him, Jeffrey. We must keep him from using Hank's machine.*

Jeffrey didn't hesitate. He clambered back up the slope and scampered inside the doorway. Then he pelted down the corridor, which the Warren entity had already left behind, the echoes of his footfalls resounding all around him.

When he reached the large outer chamber, Jeffrey saw that it was empty and began to bolt across it. But Xavier, spurred by a hunch, compelled his host to glance back over his shoulder.

Seeing a flash of white wings, Jeffrey dove for the floor—and felt the too-close wash of air from their enemy's passage. Then he watched as the Warren duplicate alighted effortlessly in front of him, a cruel grin on his handsome face.

"You know your servant well," Lucifer observed through the medium of his energy construct.

Warren was Xavier's student, not his servant—his ally, not his slave. However, the professor couldn't question his adversary's choice of words—not when his host lacked the ability to speak.

"I know him well now too," said the winged man, though the sentiment was still the Quistalian's. "I know his strengths and his weaknesses. And therefore, I know you do not possess a way to defeat him."

It was true, Xavier was forced to admit. It wasn't even remotely possible for Jeffrey to stop Warren. But the thing facing them wasn't the *true* Warren. It had the mutant's memories and abilities, but not his determination, his courage or his penchant for innovation.

And that changed the equation entirely.

"Cower there like the beaten primitive you are," said the imposter, widening his cruel smile. "Or come after me in your fragile human shell. It makes no difference. In the end, Lucifer will prevail."

And with a last, confident glance at Jeffrey, the winged one turned and headed for the semicircular portal.

The professor had his host follow, albeit at a cautious distance. He didn't want the Warren entity to feel threatened or challenged. He just wanted to be in striking distance when his chance came.

Stopping short of the threshold, he watched the winged figure walk around the smaller enclosure and inspect Hank's handiwork from all sides. After a moment or two, it nodded its head with satisfaction. Obviously, it was pleased with what it saw.

Kneeling, the doppelganger took hold of the second toggle on the side of the already active machine. It seemed to listen for a moment. Then, acting with Lucifer's knowledge of Quistalian technology, it flipped the toggle up alongside the first one.

The machine didn't hum any louder. However, Xavier knew what had happened by the blinking of the amber nodes embedded in its side.

The Warren duplicate had created the zero differential region of which Hank had spoken. He had established a tenuous middle ground between Earth and the bizarre reality of the Nameless Dimension.

There was only one more switch left on the alien device— the one that would open a temporary passage leading through the area of zero differential, permitting someone like Lucifer or the professor to transit from one frame of reference to the other.

The winged man flipped it up.

Instantly, the component that resembled a heat lamp began to burn with terrible intensity, casting a lurid, crimson radiance over the seamless floor of the enclosure.

There was no time to waste. Before the Warren entity realized that Jeffrey might try something, before he even had an inkling of it, Xavier used Jeffrey's speed and quickness to his advantage.

Jeffrey took two long, powerful steps and shot across the enclosure like a cannonball, shoving the winged imposter into the energy cone cast by the gateway machine.

For a fraction of a second, nothing happened. Xavier had the sinking feeling that he had miscalculated somehow—and therefore placed his host in peril of his life.

Then the doppelganger began to shrivel in the glare of the alien projector, its seemingly human form twitching and dissipating like smoke in a strong wind. It opened its mouth, either to accuse its tormentor, call for help or simply bemoan its fate, but the only sound that emerged from it was thin and pitiful and impossible for the professor to understand.

Despite that, Xavier knew exactly what was going on. The Warren entity's ionic energy bonds, carefully crafted in the moment of its conception, couldn't retain their integrity—not when they were exposed to the unusual physical forces that prevailed in the zero differential zone.

As he looked on through Jeffrey's eyes, Xavier saw the doppelganger waver wildly like a scrambled picture on a television set. Its hands curled into fists, evidence of its futile resolve to survive. Then, still crying its silent cry, it faded from view entirely.

The professor gazed longingly at the crimson energy projected by the alien apparatus. And why not? It represented his highway home, his escape from the awful limbo of the Nameless Dimension.

There was just one problem.

The gateway's terminus in the Nameless Dimension had opened some distance from Xavier's true body. He could sense the disturbance it made, even feel its throbbing presence in the thick, fluid atmosphere. But it would take several minutes for the professor to reach it.

And for all he knew, Lucifer would reach it first.

From his vantage point in the Nameless Dimension, Lucifer had seen his energy construct open the critical passage between realities—only to be destroyed a few moments later by Xavier's human host.

The Quistalian didn't mourn the imposter's passing for even a second. It was, after all, just an agglomeration of ionic energy, a thing to be used and discarded as the mood struck him.

All he cared about was that an escape route had been opened for him. In his eyes, Earth was beckoning like an impatient lover, inviting him to execute his long-delayed plan of conquest.

And all Lucifer had to do was reach the transdimensional gateway before his captive did.

It sounded so easy—ridiculously so. Unfortunately, though the Quistalian had an inkling of Xavier's location, he couldn't tell with any certainty which of them was closer to the exit.

And if the mutant reached it first, he wouldn't oblige Lucifer by leaving the doorway open. He would close it by any means necessary.

Gritting his teeth, the Quistalian took off in the direction of the transdimensional gate, his purple cape undulating behind him. He had waited too long to be turned away now, he told himself.

One way or the other, he would have his heart's desire.

Professor X knew exactly what he had to do. He had to shut down the machine and eliminate the link between dimensions.

Then he had to destroy the apparatus that his student had worked so hard to put together.

If Xavier did this, he would likely be giving up his only chance to return to his rightful reality. After all, as far as he knew, the gold and scarlet cylinders his X-Men had acquired were the only ones that existed on Earth. And without them, there was no way to build a second machine.

However, he couldn't take the chance that Lucifer would beat him to the gate and gain access to Earth again. It was far too dangerous a possibility to even contemplate.

A pity, the professor thought, feeling the pang of lost opportunity. He had come so heartbreakingly close . . .

He reached for the third toggle switch with Jeffrey's hand, intending to collapse the transdimensional passage . . . when he met with an unexpected layer of resistance.

At first, Xavier feared it was Lucifer, exerting some sinister kind of influence over Jeffrey. Then he realized it wasn't the Quistalian's doing at all.

It was Jeffrey's.

The realization took the professor by surprise. Since the moment he had convinced his host to bolt from the police car at the outskirts of Salem Center, Jeffrey had gone along with Xavier's every wish.

Why would the young man wish to depart from that policy of compliance? And why *now?*

The professor had barely posed the questions when the answers swam up to him out of Jeffrey's consciousness. *You have to go home*, Jeffrey told him, more in feelings than in words. *I can help.*

No, Xavier replied. *The risk is too great. If Lucifer should reach the gate before I do. . . .*

The professor expected Jeffrey to react in one of two ways—either by continuing to plead his case, futile as it was, or by depressing the toggle and cutting the transdimensional link. As it turned out, his young host did neither of those things.

Please, said Xavier, *I cannot do this without you.*

Then he felt something—not through Jeffrey's body or

Jeffrey's senses, but through his own faculties back in the Nameless Dimension. A fire was sweeping through his blood, invading even the tiniest capillary.

But it wasn't a fire of agony. It was a fire of awakening, of inspiration, eliminating all traces of fatigue and imparting to the professor a vigor he hadn't known for years.

You have to go home, Jeffrey iterated.

And this time, Xavier understood. His host wasn't just encouraging him to take advantage of his opportunity to escape. He was giving the professor the tools he needed to do it.

Xavier didn't know how Jeffrey had learned to do such a thing—how he had acquired the ability to channel his youthful vitality back along what had till then been a one-way link.

But somehow, he *had* learned. And now the mutant had become the beneficiary of that vitality.

Still, the professor thought, he didn't dare race Lucifer to the gate. Not when he had only a vague idea of the Quistalian's location. Not when so much was at stake.

Suddenly, as if in response to his concern, he heard a voice in his head—and this time, it wasn't Jeffrey's voice. It was Lucifer's, colder than any ice Bobby had ever conjured.

Give up, the voice advised him. *I have already won, Earthling.*

The message was clearly meant to demoralize Xavier, to panic him. And as the professor used it to home in on the alien's location, he saw that Lucifer was indeed closer to the gate than he was.

But not by all that much.

If Xavier swam as hard as he could, drawing on the youthful strength Jeffrey was making available to him, he might be able to reach his goal ahead of Lucifer. He might be able to regain his freedom without allowing the Quistalian to do the same.

Left to his own devices, he would never have made the attempt. But under the circumstances, he would have to. His host wasn't going to allow the toggle to be depressed otherwise.

But if it's clear I'm not going to make it, the professor insisted, *we must shut down the passageway.*

Jeffrey's answer to his demand was instantaneous. *We'll shut it down,* he agreed. *Just hurry.*

Having made the best bargain he could, Xavier struck out for the gate.

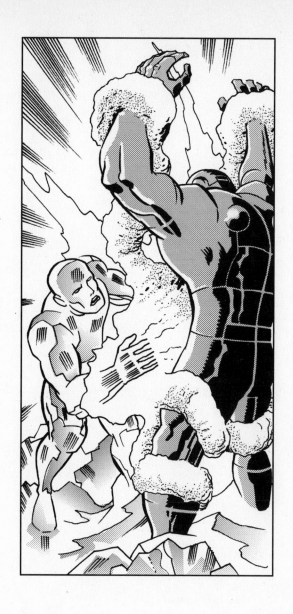

CHAPTER EIGHTEEN

In the days before Lucifer robbed him of his ability to walk, Charles Xavier had been a decent athlete. He had even won a medal in the hundred yard dash as a teenager.

Then his legs and spine had been crushed beneath a ponderous block of stone in a Tibetan mountain village.

Some human beings, faced with the prospect of a lifetime of paralysis, might have decided to embrace sedentary pursuits. They might have stopped making any real demands on their bodies.

But not Charles Xavier.

He hadn't discontinued his physical training. In fact, he had put more effort into it than before. He had honed those parts of him that still worked, knowing that the rigors of his personal crusade would require him to use every last tool at his disposal.

The professor was glad he had been so foresighted as he swam for the transdimensional gate with all the strength at his disposal. Off to one side, he could see the scarlet and purple figure of Lucifer plowing through the Nameless

Dimension with the power of his mind alone, his path lying at an oblique angle to that of his adversary.

The Quistalian was still noticeably closer to their common goal, a series of concentric ripples that resembled the disturbance a stone made when it was dropped into a still pool. But there was no doubt in Xavier's mind that he was moving faster than Lucifer, slowly but surely closing the gap.

After all, Lucifer's progress was powered by one mind, one heart. The professor's was powered by two. And if his means of propulsion was more prosaic, it didn't mean it was any less effective.

What's more, the Quistalian knew it. Xavier could tell by the way he kept glancing in the mutant's direction, as if he were concerned about the outcome of their race.

Extending his purple-gloved hand, Lucifer sent a bolt of ionic energy sizzling at Xavier. However, the professor had plenty of time to see it coming and slither out of its way. The alien unleashed a second bolt, but it too failed to hit its mark.

You must be desperate, thought Xavier, *to fritter away your energy on futile attacks.*

Lucifer's response was tinged with fury. *We will see who is desperate when I beat you to the gate.*

The muscles in the professor's arms felt as if they were burning up, but he continued to stroke for all he was worth. *You mean* if *you beat me to the gate,* he rejoined.

Xavier wasn't normally inclined to trade taunts with an opponent. But then, this wasn't just a race for survival anymore, was it? It was the last event in a death match the alien had begun many years earlier, in a remote, walled village in Tibet.

Lucifer had crushed his spine without a second thought, as if the mutant were nothing more than an insect underfoot. He had condemned Xavier to a life of pain and pity and limitation, and the professor would be damned if he was going to let the Quistalian get the last laugh.

The pattern of ripples was getting closer to Xavier. It was taking on added definition with each urgent stroke.

You cannot beat me, Lucifer insisted, his thought ragged and full of anger. *You never could beat me.*

I beg to differ, the professor thought back at him.

The gate loomed ahead, visible now within its expanding web of ripples. It looked like a hole in the dark fabric of the Nameless Dimension, roughly circular but changing with each pounding heartbeat . . . and he could see a crimson light burning inside it.

The same light he had seen before Lucifer dispatched him to this reality in the first place.

Xavier took into account their relative positions, knowing how much depended on his decision. He did his best to gauge their respective distances from the gate. And he came to the conclusion that if nothing went wrong, he would reach the passageway first.

I'll destroy you yet! the Quistalian roared in his brain.

Again, he fired a series of ionic energy bolts. They were harder to avoid at this closer range, but the professor managed it. Lucifer fired a third time, his mouth twisted in a curse beneath his helmet—and Xavier wriggled out of the way as he had before.

At that point, the gate wasn't much further ahead of him—a dozen meters at most. Smelling victory, the professor arrowed through the thick, liquid atmosphere with the last of his borrowed energy reserves, pulling with arms that had gone all but numb . . .

And plunged through the shifting, seething egress mere seconds ahead of his frantic adversary.

Impaled on the point of crimson light, Xavier felt the same terrible sensations he had experienced in his last passage through the gate. His arm and leg muscles cramped painfully, his skin blistered and cracked, and it seemed as if a fiery poker were turning his insides to jelly.

But through it all, he clung to one thought, one responsibility that had yet to be carried out.

Close the gate! he demanded of Jeffrey. *Close it now!*

Then the professor felt something hard beneath him and opened his eyes, and saw that he was lying in a fetal position on the floor of the Quistalian facility back on Earth. The bizarre machine that Hank had constructed was towering above him, its single projector glowering down at him like a monstrous, baleful eye.

Jeffrey was standing there too, his hand poised over the toggle switch. He looked drop-jaw amazed that their gambit had worked.

"The gate!" Xavier rasped—out loud this time, no longer a voice in Jeffrey's head.

Assured that his grandfather's friend was safe, Jeffrey flipped the switch—but not before the professor saw a purple-gloved hand materialize in the cone of energy projected by the apparatus. Its fingers outstretched, it seemed to be reaching for freedom, refusing to be denied after all its long years of imprisonment.

But it would be denied once again—because with Jeffrey's flip of the toggle, the passageway between dimensions slammed shut. The hand in the purple glove twitched once, then constricted into a painful-looking claw and receded into the nothingness from which it had come.

Xavier heard a scream in his brain—a long, heartfelt cry of anguish and despair that cut across the dimensions like a knife. Then even that last vestige of his enemy was gone.

The professor looked up at Jeffrey. "Thank you," he said, his voice hoarse from all he had been through.

His former host didn't say anything. He just stood there gazing wonderingly at Charles Xavier—trying to cope with the unexpected feeling of loneliness in his head.

The professor, too, felt as if he had suffered a loss. After sharing a consciousness with someone for a considerable length of time, it was difficult to exist on one's own again.

But somehow, they would manage.

When Jean Grey saw her husband fall victim to Warren's energy duplicate, she felt as if her heart had fallen out through her ribs.

Scott was her anchor, her rock, her reason for living. And for all the gentleness he showed her when they were out of uniform, he was one of the most powerful human beings she knew.

But Jean wasn't just any woman. She was a member of the X-Men, someone who had sworn to defend her world from its enemies at any price. And even with her husband and her friend Bobby lying senseless on the ground, she still had a duty to discharge.

She might not have liked it, but that was the way it had to be.

All this passed through Jean's mind in the space of a pounding heartbeat, as a ragged-looking man with a tangled, gray beard hurled a blinding white blast of energy at her. Ducking the ionic stream, she jerked the man into a tree with her telekinetic power.

Then she looked around. *Get a handle on the situation,* she thought. That's what Scott would have done.

It seemed to her that half of Lucifer's assault force had been knocked for a loop already. So far, so good. But that left the other half still standing, still scratching and clawing their way up the mountain.

And then there's the counterfeit Warren, Jean reminded herself with a flare of anger. *We can't forget him.*

Just as the mutant thought that, she saw a red and white streak plummet from the sky. *The imposter,* she told herself, *coming back to take a shot at me and Hank.*

But a moment later, she saw that she had guessed wrong. The doppelganger wasn't rejoining the fray at all. He was bypassing it, heading up the steep, wooded side of the mountain.

Then Jean realized what "Warren" was up to. The Quistalian facility they had discovered . . . it was open, unguarded. And Hank had already turned on the transdimensional transport machine.

If the imposter got his hands on it, he might be able to pull Lucifer out of the Nameless Dimension—bringing the Quistalian's machinations to fruition after all. And if that happened, the professor might be trapped in that alternative reality forever.

Jean couldn't let that happen.

However, before she could make a move to stop it, she saw an energy bolt whiz by her face and strike a tree, cracking its trunk in half. Knowing she had to respond to the attack or suffer another one, she raised a swarm of pine needles and cast it in her antagonist's face.

Then Jean started up the slope. But before she could get very far, another ionic energy beam sliced past her, cracking some branches off a pine. Half a second later, a third one speared the ground beside her foot.

Lucifer's troops weren't very good shots, she mused, but they were getting closer with each attempt. And with their ionic-energy-fueled strength, they could climb a lot more quickly than she could.

At the moment, it seemed, there were two of them after her. *I can handle two,* she assured herself.

Lashing out telekinetically, Jean sent one of her attackers tumbling down the incline. She was turning her attention to the other one when something smashed her on the bone of her ankle—hard enough to make her cry out in pain and lose her footing.

As she fell, she worked hard to maintain her focus. One of Lucifer's soldiers felt the result of that as she harried him with dirt and loose branches. But another beam came out of nowhere and punched her in the shoulder, leaving her arm numb down to her fingertips.

Jean had been in tough spots before and had gotten past them. She would do it again, she promised herself.

Blocking the pain of the shots she had taken, she took hold of one adversary and spun him into a second one. Then she lifted another one and sent him hurtling over an out-cropping.

But it wasn't enough. Jean knew that even as she applied the force of her mind again and again. Lucifer's pawns were coming back at her faster than she could bat them away.

As she buffeted a balding man in a red flannel shirt, a skinny one in a white shirt and pants toppled a tree in her direction. She managed to ward it off before it could fall on top of her—but the distraction allowed a third man to blast her square in the chest.

Suddenly Jean was lying flat on her back, gasping for breath, striving hard to keep the shadows on the edges of her vision from overwhelming her. *Breathe,* she insisted. *Don't let Lucifer beat you.*

Catching sight of one opponent, she clenched her jaw and cast him away from her. A second one came at her and she did the same. But she never saw the one who had out-flanked her until it was too late.

His energy beam dealt Jean a glancing blow in the temple, but it was enough to make her world shiver and go dark. As her head lolled, only one thought went through her mind . . .

Forgive me, professor. Please forgive me. . . .

Hank McCoy had a feeling he was battling alone.

It began when he saw Warren's duplicate use Bobby as a battering ram, knocking both Scott and his icy ally for a loop. And it grew worse when Hank failed to find any sign of Jean.

Then he noticed that there were at least three of Lucifer's puppets stalking him at any given time, no matter how many he knocked down. At that point, he was reasonably certain of it—of all his teammates, he was the only one still fighting the good fight.

What's more, Hank told himself, the counterfeit Warren was lurking somewhere, getting ready to finish what Lucifer's other pawns had started. So as the furry X-Man dodged energy blast after sizzling energy blast, he had to keep one eye open for a winged assailant.

It wasn't at all his idea of a good time.

Catching sight of an adversary down the hill and to the right, Hank leaped for the trunk of the nearest tree and swung around it twice, gaining centrifugal force with each revolution. Then he let go at just the right moment and slingshotted himself at Lucifer's pawn.

The energy zombie released a blast of ionic force from his fingertips, but it barely came close enough to singe Hank's fur. Then the mutant bowled the man over with enough force to knock him out.

One down and an indeterminate number to go, the X-Man thought wryly, wishing he were as devil-may-care as he pretended.

Suddenly, the woods around him began sizzling with silver energy beams, each one coming from a distinctly different direction. Hank was forced to vault one way and then another, bouncing around on hands and feet in order to elude the web of destruction.

Obviously, he thought, he had maneuvered himself into a carefully laid snare—one that Lucifer himself must have masterminded. The trick for Hank was to find a way out of it.

To his credit, he had logged extra time eluding multiple energy blasts in Xavier's danger room in Salem Center. The mutant put that investment to good use now, managing to stay half a step ahead of his opponents.

However, Lucifer's foot soldiers were gradually closing in on him, narrowing Hank's already narrow margin of error with each whizzing energy bolt they cast at him. The mutant had to bob and weave with increasing urgency just to keep from getting hit.

And though it sometimes seemed to others that Hank's energy was boundless, that was hardly the case. Already, fatigue was laying its claim to the X-Man's powerful muscles. If he was going to make his move, he would have to do it in the next couple of seconds—or not at all.

Here we go, he thought.

The one clear edge Hank had over Lucifer's puppets was his ability to climb. Capitalizing on that advantage, he chose a sturdy-looking fir tree and swung his way to its highest branches.

Then, as his adversaries sliced through the greenery with one blistering silver bolt after another, the mutant abandoned the fir and launched himself at one of its neighbors. But he didn't stay there for long either. Instead, he took flight and found purchase in a third tree.

Little by little, Hank began to put some distance between himself and his tormentors. He began to enjoy some breathing room. And he used that buffer to think about going on the offensive again.

Then his luck changed, suddenly and irretrievably.

As Hank vaulted from one tree to another, a series of rotten branches collapsed precipitously beneath his weight. The effect was to sabotage his leap, leaving him short of his destination.

Of course, he wasn't called the Beast for nothing. It would be simplicity himself for him to get his feet beneath him and land unhurt—that is, if there weren't a pack of human hounds dogging his trail.

Even before Hank reached the ground, he felt an energy beam singe the air in front of his face. He had barely landed when another one kicked him in the ribs like an angry stallion, knocking the wind out of his lungs.

Fighting for air, he tried his best to scamper away. But instead of running *from* his enemies, he ran right *into* one.

The fellow was overweight, with a baby face and greasy blond hair. And his eyes were blazing with a terrible splendor as he drove his white-knuckled fist into the mutant's face.

The monstrous impact sent Hank flying into the base of a tree. As he fought to clear his head, he saw the blond man advance on him again, eager to land another blow for his alien master.

And this time, he wasn't alone. There were four other men with him, each of them spilling light from their eye sockets as they approached, regarding the X-Man as if he were a pestilence that had to be stamped out.

"Don't worry about me . . ." Hank gasped, ever the comedian. "I'll be fine, really . . . just give me a moment . . . to catch my breath. . . ."

His opponents didn't seem to appreciate his attempt at humor. They kept on coming, their hands balled and ready to bludgeon, their faces all set in the same grim, twisted way.

Hank recognized the expression, though it had been years since he saw it last. *Lucifer,* he thought, with a twinge of revulsion.

Gathering what was left of his strength, he did the last thing his enemies would have expected of him—he launched himself into their midst and hit them with everything he had, hands and feet lashing and striking. Unfortunately, it wasn't enough.

The Quistalian's puppets unleashed a storm of cold, silent fury on him, landing blow after bone-rattling blow. Hank endured it for as long as he could. Then he began to feel consciousness slip away like water draining through a sieve.

"You know," he muttered through the haze of his pain, "I'm beginning to think . . . you don't like me . . ."

And just like that, the beating stopped.

Hank looked up through the battered flesh around his eyes, scarcely daring to believe Lucifer's soldiers might be done with him. Then he saw why the energy pawns had discontinued their bombardment.

They had their hands full with something else at the moment—something that had them clutching their heads and swearing as if a pack of demons had taken residence in their skulls.

Hank had seen people do that before . . . under the impact of a massive psionic assault. And to his knowledge, there was only one being capable of executing such an assault, in this dimension or any other.

Professor Xavier.

But the professor was in the Nameless Dimension, incapable of lending a helping hand—or so Hank had believed. Now he wondered . . . what if one of his teammates had activated the Quistalian apparatus and enabled Xavier to escape his dimensional prison?

With an effort, Hank rolled over onto all fours and tried to catch a glimpse of his mentor. And he was rewarded with a sight he had feared he might never see again.

That of a single-minded Charles Xavier dragging himself onto the crest of an overhanging rock, hurling bolt after psionic bolt at Lucifer's henchmen like an avenging angel.

But Lucifer's puppets weren't ready to fall just yet.

Fortified by the ionic energy that allowed them to topple trees and X-Men alike, they withstood the professor's mental barrage. Then, grimacing with the pain it must have cost them, they fired back at Xavier with the same formidable level of intensity.

The professor was shaken by the first blinding bolt that hit him, but he managed to remain upright nevertheless. The second bolt had more impact, doubling him over. But it was the third blast, from the fingertips of the baby-faced blond man, that laid Xavier out like a dead man.

No! Hank cried in the recesses of his mind.

And in those same recesses, he felt the touch of a familiar, comforting presence, silently assuring him that what was real and what he had seen were two very different things.

Of course, the X-Man thought. *If I hadn't been so groggy, I would have figured it out for myself.*

Xavier hadn't fallen at all. Hank knew that now. It was

just an illusion forged in the professor's mind, designed to encourage Lucifer's soldiers to drop their defenses.

As the baby-faced man climbed the rock to inspect his victim's inert form, the real Xavier peeked out from behind a tree. However, neither the babyfaced man nor any of the Quistalian's other lackeys seemed to catch sight of him— another result of the professor's ability to create believable illusions.

Hank sent out a thought in the hope that his mentor would pick it up. *I can help, sir.*

No need, came the reply.

And indeed, there wasn't any. As Hank looked on, Lucifer's pawns twitched as if a charge of electricity had suddenly ravaged their nervous systems. Then they crumpled to the ground, and the mutant got the impression that they wouldn't be getting up anytime soon.

A moment later, the illusory professor faded from view. That left only one Xavier on the mountainside—the genuine article.

Hank grinned at him as he ascended to Xavier's level. "Welcome back, Professor."

Xavier didn't return the grin, but his features softened a bit. "Thank you," he said softly. "It is good to *be* back."

I'm sure it is, Hank thought.

Ignoring his exquisite collection of bumps and bruises, he picked the professor up in his arms and went looking for the rest of team.

Floating in the air, Charles Xavier considered the dark, oily-looking apparatus that had freed him from the endless tedium of the Nameless Dimension.

The professor felt an irrational pang of gratitude to the device, which had already been disconnected from its

Quistalian power source. But it wasn't so overwhelming a pang that it prevented Xavier from giving the command he needed to give.

"Destroy it," he said.

Scott, who still had a bad bruise and a headache to show for his collision with Bobby, didn't hesitate for even a moment. He opened his visor and released a blood-red optical blast at the device, bathing himself and his teammates in the beam's reflected glare.

For a moment, the machine held together, even under the considerable force of Scott's assault—evidence of the care and skill with which Hank had put it together. Then it shattered into what seemed like a thousand individual components, ruined beyond any hope of repair.

And with it went Lucifer's hopes of escaping his exile.

"Good riddance," said Bobby, as Scott closed his visor again. "To tell you the truth, that thing gave me the creeps."

"Though it performed its purpose," Hank reminded him.

"It did at that," said Jean. She glanced at the professor who was held aloft by her power. "I don't imagine Lucifer was very happy about losing his shot at freedom."

Xavier recalled the gloved hand that had forced its way up through the transdimensional gateway, only to be sucked back into it at the last possible moment. "Probably not," he replied dryly.

"Or with what the professor did to his henchmen," Scott added.

Xavier shrugged. "I merely took advantage of the fact that they were human beings at their core—and not the sort of pure-energy agents with which Lucifer had recently plagued us."

It was true. If the Quistalian's lackeys had been made entirely of ionic energy, like the doppelgangers or the pair who had accosted the professor and Bobby on the road, he might not have been able to stop them.

But Lucifer's assault force had been made up of everyday people—people imbued with immense power, to be sure, but people nonetheless. And because they were biological entities with brains and nervous systems, they had been vulnerable to the professor's potent mental bolts.

"And, speaking of Lucifer's agents . . ." Xavier said, allowing his voice to trail off meaningfully.

All twelve of them were still lying outside on the mountain, blissfully unconscious. The professor had cut them off from the Quistalian's influence and power when he assaulted their brains, so they no longer posed any kind of threat in that regard.

However, they had seen Xavier in action and learned the location of the alien facility. Something had to be done about that. And in the professor's opinion, he was just the man to do it.

He looked at Jeffrey, who was standing apart from the mutants, near the doorway that led from the smaller chamber into the larger one. The young man looked very much out of place in the alien chamber, with its dark, serpentine patterns and its eerie lighting.

"Come," Xavier told him, all too familiar with Jeffrey's understandable insecurities. "We still have some work to do."

With that, Jean took Jeffrey's hand and gently led him out of the room. Xavier followed, still buoyed by the power of Jean's mind, and the rest of his X-Men came after him.

Outside the confines of the corridor, in the open, pine-scented air, dark clouds had begun to gather in the east. There was a smell of ozone in the air, presaging rain.

Using a stud on the side of the key that Scott had gotten from the doppelganger, the X-Men resurrected the metal slab that separated the facility from the rest of the world. Then Hank covered the spot with an ample supply of pine needles to keep hikers from stumbling on it.

The professor considered Lucifer's energy-fueled pawns, scattered in various, awkward poses among the trees. His brief contact with their minds had revealed that each of them had done something heinous in his life—something that had given the Quistalian access to their psyches in a way Xavier didn't quite understand.

The professor wished he could erase whatever it was in these individuals that had caused them to do these things. He wished he could cleanse them, transform them, redeem them. But he wasn't God. It wasn't his place to remake men in his own image.

On the other hand, Lucifer had already changed them—and Xavier felt eminently justified in undoing what the Quistalian had already done. Besides, he needed to make sure these twelve posed no further threat.

So he entered their minds again, one by one, and relieved them of all their most recent memories. He scoured out all knowledge of Lucifer, the power they had wielded and the alien facility they had stormed. And he made them forget they had ever seen the X-Men or a Professor Charles Xavier, much less battled them on a mountainside.

Next, Xavier roused them from their slumber, brought them to their feet and opened their eyes—though he didn't yet restore their ability to interpret what they saw. Then he sent them on their way, making them look like simple sleepwalkers as they descended the slope.

They would continue that way, unseeing and unknowing, until they reached the road that had brought them to the mountain. Only then would the professor truly awaken them and leave them to their own devices.

"I don't get it," said Bobby. "Why didn't Lucifer send some of his ionic-energy constructs after us instead?"

"No doubt," Xavier told his protege, "because his ability to generate and direct such entities was not unlimited. Lucifer must have believed that twelve amplified human beings would be more effective against you than two or three pure-energy warriors."

"They *were* effective," Jean noted. She turned to the professor. "Until you made it back to Earth."

"Indeed," said Xavier, "that altered the equation. Had my participation in the conflict been a consideration from the beginning, Lucifer's strategy might have been different. But I was in the Nameless Dimension, where he didn't think I would become a factor."

"Good thing for us," said Bobby, "that you *did* become a factor."

"There is only one more task ahead of us," the professor noted.

Hank nodded. "Let's go get Warren."

Unfortunately, they no longer had the winged energy duplicate to transport them across the valley to the Blackbird. However, they still had Bobby Drake's Ice Express.

As Bobby created a narrow ice slide for them—one that would melt long before anyone noticed it and had reason to become curious about it—Xavier hoped fervently that Warren was all right. He hoped that the winged man had survived, despite Lucifer's predictions to the contrary.

Judging from the solemn expressions on the faces of his X-Men, the professor was hardly alone in that regard.

CHAPTER NINETEEN

As a mutant, Warren Worthington was capable of withstanding the wind-whipped cold of high altitudes. Otherwise, he would have frozen to death a long time ago.

Shivering in the feathered wings he had folded around himself, he gazed across the Quistalian chamber at the mouth of the corridor on the other side. It was packed with silver spheres—the same spheres that had overtaken Warren, suffocated him until he lost his grip on his gold and scarlet cylinder, and gradually forced him back from the facility's exit.

But even with his escape route blocked, the mutant hadn't given up. He had searched every inch of the towering chamber, especially its lofty ceiling, attempting to find an egress that wouldn't lead him into the hostile embrace of the silver globules.

And he had failed.

The one benefit Warren had realized from all his activity was a temporary increase in his body heat. But without food or water, there was no way he could have kept it up.

Little by little, he had been forced to slow down, then to stop flying altogether. And that was when the cold began to seep into his bones, reminding him that he was in a sub-zero environment.

Warren knew he was in desperate need of heat—even a little. If there were active machines in the facility, he reasoned, they had to have a power source. And even the most efficient power source was liable to give off a little thermal radiation.

With that logic in mind, he had examined the floor and walls of the chamber, hoping to find a warm spot. And after a long, painstaking hunt, he had found one—directly in front of the cylinder array.

It wasn't exactly balmy there, but it was an improvement over the surface around it. Hunkering down, Warren had tucked his hands into his armpits and brought his wings in close and tried to conserve what little remained of his body heat.

For a while, as he sat there on his haunches, he had nurtured the hope that his teammates would find a way to rescue him. But as seconds had stretched into minutes and minutes into hours, that hope had dwindled.

Worse, Warren had come to wonder if his comrades might have perished—because nothing short of death would have prevented them from finding a way to free him. And that thought, more than his own dim prospects for survival, had been the most difficult burden for him of all.

Suddenly, there was a thought in his brain: *Warren?*

He looked around, his muscles painfully stiff, his mind thick and sluggish from what he had been forced to endure. *Who . . . ?*

And then he answered his own question. *Professor*

Xavier. Who else? But . . . wasn't he imprisoned in the Nameless Dimension? And if he was, how was he communicating with Warren?

Unless it wasn't the professor at all, the mutant thought. Maybe he was getting hypothermic and suffering delusions. Or even worse, maybe it was Lucifer in his head, only pretending to be Professor Xavier.

It's not Lucifer, the voice assured him. *It's me. And I'm no longer imprisoned in the Nameless Dimension.*

It couldn't hurt to play along, Warren told himself, his arms and legs beginning to cramp. It wasn't as if his situation could get any worse.

"All right," he said out loud, his voice echoing madly in the chamber. "It's you. What you want from me?"

A moment later, he saw something happen to the air in front of him. It seemed to coalesce, to take on a filmy, gray substance. Warren had seen its like before. It was an astral projection.

And sure enough, the face that seemed to float near the top of the ghostly image was that of Professor Xavier. But that didn't mean much to the winged mutant at the moment. As far as he knew, Lucifer was capable of pulling the same trick.

The projection looked around. Then it turned back to Warren. *I don't want anything at all from you. Just hang on as best you can.* It paused for a full second. *I think I know now what to do.*

And with that, it seemed to fall through the floor until it had faded entirely from view.

Warren frowned, trying to figure out what Lucifer might have hoped to gain from such a trick. Was he raising the X-Man's hopes, only to dash them a few moments later? Was he torturing his last, remaining victim while he still had the chance?

Or, the mutant wondered as his shivering got worse, was it possible he had received a visit from the *real* Professor X?

Warren just hoped he would live long enough to find out.

Scott Summers, who was waiting with his teammates on the brink of the frozen crevasse, hadn't expected Professor Xavier to take any more than thirty seconds to investigate Warren's situation. As it turned out, Xavier took less than twenty-five.

"I have a plan," the professor announced suddenly, the light returning to his eyes as he leaned forward in his golden antigrav unit.

Scott listened closely, eager to hear anything that would help them free their teammate.

"Apparently," Xavier continued, "Warren was able to identify a warm spot on the floor—the result of thermal radiation from the facility's power source. It has been a boon to his survival. But it may also prove to be the key to our rescue attempt."

"How so?" asked Hank.

"Taking advantage of my immateriality," said the professor, "I dropped below the level of the floor and took a look at the power generator. Unfortunately, it is buried rather deeply. As a result, it would be difficult to reach and disable in the short period of time Warren has left.

"However," Xavier went on, "the power source's connections to the mechanisms that deploy and guide the globules are significantly more accessible. If we could sever them, it would render the spheres inert. At that point, they would be so much debris."

"But we still need to get into the place to sever the connections," Bobby pointed out.

"True," Xavier conceded. "However, it seems to me that getting *in* should not be quite as difficult a task as getting *out*. Warren, after all, was simply shunted back into the main chamber. I believe that would happen to anyone trapped by the globules."

Jean nodded. "So all we have to do is crack open Bobby's ice seal and the globules will bring us inside."

"And once we're there," said Hank, "we can clear the way for what should be a blissfully uncontested exit."

"Or we could find out there's a backup system and get trapped in there along with Warren," Bobby noted.

The professor looked at him. "I believe that is a risk we must take if we're to have a chance of recovering Warren."

"Then what are we waiting for?" Hank asked, showing his long, sharp teeth. "Let's go crack Bobby's seal."

He had already begun to move toward Bobby's slide when Xavier stopped him with a word. "No," the professor said suddenly.

"No?" asked Scott.

Xavier frowned, as if he were mulling something over. "On second thought," he said, "I believe Bobby has a point."

Bobby looked incredulous. "I do?"

"Indeed," the professor told him. "If the entire team goes in and it turns out that I have miscalculated, we may all be trapped inside. But if only one of you enters the facility, we will still have additional options if something goes wrong."

"And who would that be?" asked Jean.

Scott believed his wife already knew the answer to her question. Certainly, *he* did.

"That would be me," he said, just to make it official.

"That is what I was thinking," Xavier admitted. "Scott is clearly the one best equipped to gain access to the globule mechanisms and to destroy their links to the power source."

"I wouldn't mind riding shotgun with him," Hank suggested.

"Me either," Bobby chimed in.

But the professor shook his head. "No. It would be more prudent for Scott to go alone."

When Xavier put it that way, Scott reflected, none of his students were likely to argue with him.

"I will be in contact with you the entire time," the professor told him. "Good luck."

"Thanks," said Scott.

He glanced at his wife, reminding her of how much he loved her . . . just in case things didn't work out the way they planned. Then he lowered himself onto the beginning of Bobby's slide and pushed off.

The descent into the crevasse made Scott's head spin as he negotiated curve after curve. But as he approached the bottom, the angle of descent gradually flattened out and he slowed down accordingly. By the time he reached the end of the ice slide, he had decelerated enough to be able to leap off without hurting himself.

That left him standing in front of the ice-encrusted pile of silver spheres blocking the way into the alien facility. The pile looked dormant, harmless . . . but Scott wasn't fooled for a second. He knew from experience how formidable the globules could be.

Nonetheless, he took up a position not six feet from the pile, opened his visor and unleashed an intense crimson blast. Bobby's ice began to crack under the assault, exposing the silver spheres.

At first, they broke free one at a time, shuddering with long-restrained energy. Then it was like a dam breaking, as the entire pent-up swarm of them burst from the narrow exit and surrounded Scott on all sides.

Quickly, he closed his visor, willingly giving up his only means of defense. If he was going to yield to the spheres, he was going to have to do so utterly and completely.

Unfortunately, Scott was unprepared for the enormous pressure the globules exerted on him. They clustered around him, squeezing him, crushing the breath from him. He felt as if he were drowning in a sea of shining rubber.

And yet, this was the outcome the mutant had hoped for. This was the result he had invited. And for better or worse, this was the fate he would have to live with.

There were too many of the globules for Scott to see past them, so he didn't know for certain if the professor's plan was working. But he had the impression, right or wrong, that they were squeezing him back down the corridor toward the main chamber.

He did his utmost to remain conscious, to find air in the relentless press of gelatinous surfaces. It wasn't easy, however. More than once, he found himself gasping for breath without success, darkness starting to close in all around him.

But somehow, Scott hung on. It was only a matter of time, he told himself, before the spheres released him. Only a matter of time before he reached the end of his journey.

And suddenly, his prediction came true.

The globules spit him out like a watermelon seed, spilling him onto something hard and cold. As the X-Man greedily pulled breath into his starving lungs, he opened his eyes and looked around.

And saw that he wasn't alone.

"Warren?" he rasped, his voice echoing in whispers.

The feathered mound on the other side of the chamber

stirred at the sound. Then one of its wings lifted a bit and revealed the huddled, shivering form of Scott's teammate.

"S-Scott . . . ?" the winged man croaked back at him.

"It's me," Scott confirmed, getting up and crossing the immense chamber to join his friend.

En route, he couldn't help glancing at the entrance to the corridor. It was packed with quivering, eager-looking globules. They looked as if they couldn't wait for Scott to try to make it through them.

But that wasn't why he had come. He had bigger fish to fry.

When Scott reached his teammate, he knelt down beside him. Warren was shivering so hard it hurt to look at him.

"So . . . it *was* . . . the professor . . . ?" the winged man got out.

It took Scott a moment to understand. Then he nodded. "It was him, all right. Hang in there a little longer, buddy. We've got a plan to get us both out of here."

Warren managed a smile. "You're just . . . trying to make up . . . for the time you . . . shot me in the back . . ."

Scott remembered it well. In fact, it had come up in the Blackbird on their way to Columbia.

He had felt guilty at the time. Even if he was only doing what the professor demanded of him, even if it was for Warren's own good, it had gone against his grain to turn his beams on a fellow X-Man.

"Quiet," Scott told his friend. "I've got work to do."

Right on cue, Xavier made his presence known. *I'm here, Scott. Start by moving Warren and breaking up the floor where he's been sitting.*

Scott did as he was told. He helped his friend up and moved him to another part of the chamber. Then he opened his visor and trained his beams on the place where Warren had been huddling.

The Quistalian material that comprised the floor was tough, but Scott's optical blasts were tougher. Before long, the smooth, dark surface began to buckle, to groan—to exhibit stress fractures which gradually grew into much larger stress fractures.

Finally, with a shriek like that of twisting metal, the floor gave way—revealing the complicated maze of dark conduits and alien mechanisms that lurked underneath it.

Closing his visor for a moment, Scott approached the ragged hole he had created. He could feel the warmth emanating from it—waves of thermal radiation generated by the Quistalians' lusty power source. However, he couldn't actually see the thing. It was buried too deeply beneath the viper's nest of alien components.

Professor? he thought.

He had expected to hear Xavier's voice in his head. Instead, he saw a pale blue line superimpose itself over the Quistalian machinery—as if someone were drawing it in the air.

Scrutinizing the line, the mutant saw that it corresponded exactly with one of the narrower, more straightforward conduits. Unfortunately, the thing was occluded by a great many other conduits. Only an inch or so of it was exposed at any given point.

But it wasn't the first time Scott had been called upon to exercise pinpoint accuracy. Far from it.

That day in the Balkans, for instance, when he and Professor Xavier had shimmied their way to the top of Lucifer's bomb and peered down an almost unnoticable seam to find its fuse . . . that, he had to say, had been an even greater challenge.

Do you see it? asked Xavier, the author of the pale blue line.

I do, Scott assured him.

Be careful, the professor cautioned him. *If you damage one of the other conduits, you may cause an explosion.*

Despite the severity of the situation, Scott had to smile. *I'll try to keep that in mind, sir.*

Kneeling at the edge of the hole, he scanned the high-lighted conduit from end to end. It took him a few seconds to identify the easiest part of it. Then he took a breath, let it out . . .

And opened his visor the slightest crack.

Instantly, his optical beams leaped out and speared the conduit he had been aiming for, slicing it in two with surgical precision. And before the beams could carve any deeper into the tangle of alien technology, the mutant shut his visor again.

It's done, he told the professor.

And? asked Xavier.

Scott turned and gazed at the mouth of the corridor. It was still jammed tight with an accumulation of silver glob-ules. However, they didn't look as if they were so eager to go into action anymore.

To be sure, he opened his visor and blasted one of the spheres for just a second. The thing flattened a little under the impact, then came bounding in the mutant's direction like a big rubber ball.

But Scott could tell immediately that it didn't have any propulsion behind it. It was just reacting to his optical barrage the way anything of its shape and consistency might react.

In other words, the sphere was dead—and so was the defense system that had driven it.

Before Scott could celebrate, he heard a hacking cough come from elsewhere in the chamber. Turning, he saw that

Warren had slumped over on his side. Obviously, his friends had to get him someplace warm, and fast.

Well? the professor prompted.

The spheres are inoperative, Scott reported. *But Warren's in a bad way. I'll start digging us out from this side.*

And we'll do the same from our side, Xavier assured him.

Acknowledged, Scott replied.

Then he went to Warren's side, put his arm around his friend, and opened his visor to pound at the globules in earnest.

When Warren Worthington III opened his eyes, he had no idea where he was at first. Then he saw the face of Jeffrey Saunders looming over him, looking as worried as Warren had ever seen him.

The mutant smiled.

"It's okay," he told Jeffrey, his voice weak but stronger than it had been in the chamber. "I'm not dead."

In fact, Warren felt pretty good, considering how perilously close he had come to freezing to death. It occurred to him that Professor Xavier had had something to do with his miraculous recovery. After all, the man was an expert on everything that concerned mutants—including how to bring one back from the depths of hypothermia.

He sat up a little and looked around. Apparently, he was in the Blackbird's rear cabin—and he had more company than just Jeffrey.

"Looks like sleeping beauty is awake," remarked Hank, sliding onto the seat beside Jeffrey.

"You know something," Warren whispered to his teammate, "right now, even *you* look good."

"Careful," said Bobby from the front of the cabin. "You'll give our pal Hank a swelled head."

"The one deformity I don't have already," Hank noted, displaying his long, lower teeth in a broad grin.

"Scott?" Warren asked them.

"In the forward cabin," said Bobby, "along with Jean and the professor. For some reason, he thinks he can fly this tub better than I can."

Warren chuckled. "For some reason, so do I."

"I'm wounded," Bobby told him.

"And I've got organs that are still thawing," Warren returned. "Welcome to the club."

He glanced at the door that led to the forward cabin. When he got a chance, he would have to thank Scott for saving his life. His teammate really *had* made up for blasting him in the back that time.

Not that Warren wouldn't have done the same for Scott a thousand times over. That was, after all, what friends were for.

Hank put his big, furry hand on Jeffrey's. "It's all right," the mutant said. "He's the *real* Warren."

The winged man didn't get it. "As opposed to . . . ?"

Bobby laughed. "Hoo boy. Have we got a story to tell *you.*"

"Indeed," Hank agreed. "You know how Lucifer replaced the professor with an energy-based lookalike?"

Warren nodded. "So?"

Hank shrugged his shaggy shoulders. "He did the same thing to you."

Bobby fashioned a cigar out of ice. "And outside of the improvement," he quipped, "we couldn't tell the difference."

"You do a lousy Groucho Marx impression," Hank observed clinically.

"Says the tribble with the high IQ," Bobby shot back.

While his teammates exchanged friendly barbs, Warren absorbed what Hank had told him. A doppelganger . . . that looked like *him?* He began to see why it had taken so long for his comrades to rescue him.

"What happened to him?" he asked Hank. "My duplicate, I mean."

The furry X-Man jerked a big, blue thumb at Jeffrey. "Our friend here took him out. Otherwise, he would have freed Lucifer and trapped Professor Xavier in the Nameless Dimension."

"At which point," Bobby added sourly, "freezing to death would have looked like a pretty good option."

As pleased as he was surprised, Warren smiled at Jeffrey. "Hey, pardner," he said, "way to go."

For the very first time, he saw Jeffrey smile back at him.

Professor Xavier hovered in his anti-grav unit in front of the large titanium cube and peered through one of its windows.

The cube was empty, devoid of the energy entity that the professor and his X-Men had left inside it. What's more, he wasn't the least bit surprised at this turn of events.

"Lucifer opted to withdraw him from our frame of reference," Xavier concluded.

"Why bother?" asked Bobby.

He and his teammates had accompanied the professor to the underground room. Jeffrey was with them as well, looking a little daunted. But then, he was peering at the cube on his own this time.

Hank shrugged. "An incarcerated doppelganger was of no use to Lucifer," he said, answering Bobby's question.

The professor nodded. "True. And it probably nettled him

to see his creation hopelessly imprisoned here—much as he himself was imprisoned in the Nameless Dimension."

"So that's that?" Warren asked skeptically, his voice still a little weak from his experience in the Antarctic.

Scott smiled. "You don't sound confident."

"How can we be?" Jean added. "Lucifer has proven he can strike anytime, anywhere. We've all got to be on our guards."

Hank chuckled. "And when has it ever been any different?"

"Comes with the territory," Bobby pointed out.

It *did* come with the territory, Xavier reflected. Danger was a fact of their lives, a reality his students had accepted since the first time they put on their original black and gold uniforms.

However, a triumph was a triumph—and this one was more impressive than most. They had beaten back the darkness for one more day, proving yet again that no force in this or any other universe could prevail against a determined band of X-Men.

"At least we can relax for a *little* while," Bobby declared hopefully. "Say, long enough to watch the *Lethal Weapon* trilogy."

Hank sighed. "Once a heathen, always a heathen."

"Actually," said the professor, "we still have some work to do. For instance, my energy duplicate installed a Quistalian surveillance system in my study. And—"

Hank held his furry blue hand up. "And we need to *unin*-stall it. It's as good as done, sir."

Xavier inclined his head slightly. "Thank you, Hank."

The X-Man smiled. "You're welcome, Professor."

Xavier turned to Jeffrey. "We will also need to return our friend here to Westminster House. Judging from the calls we've received from the police, people there are worried about him."

"I'm not surprised," said Jean, smiling at Jeffrey.

"I'll go with you," Warren volunteered. "I could use some fresh air that's not thirty degrees below zero."

"Me too," said Bobby. "Especially if it means I don't have to help with that Quistalian surveillance system."

The professor turned to Hank.

"I can handle it on my own," the furry X-Man assured him. "In fact, it will probably go faster that way."

"Very well," said Xavier. He turned to Scott and Jean. "And you?"

Scott put his arm around his wife. "There's a breeze blowing, sir. I think we might attempt another overnight on the boat."

"That is," Jean added dutifully, "if there's nothing to keep us here."

"Go," the professor told her, sending her off with a flip of his hand. "If I need you, I know where to reach you."

Jean's brow furrowed. "You—?"

"I'll explain some other time," Xavier assured her.

And he would, of course. The professor was good at keeping secrets—but not from his X-Men.

In the Nameless Dimension, the being called Lucifer watched his enemies revel in their triumph.

How right the mutants were when they observed that he could strike at any time. How perceptive of them to underline the importance of their being on their guards.

Someday, Lucifer would find a way to escape his imprisonment. And when he did, he would crush the X-Men under his boot like the annoying insects they were—especially their cursed leader.

It might take time, but he would return to Quistalium in

triumph, once more the conquering hero. He would receive medals and praise and gifts of property from the Supreme One. He would see throngs cheer him again, their cries echoing wildly in the synthetic canyons of the capital.

"My time will come!" Lucifer spat at the nothingness, his mouth twisting cruelly beneath the forward edge of his helmet, flecks of spittle finding purchase in the severe, dark brush of his beard.

It would happen. Someday. . . .

CHAPTER TWENTY

P rofessor Charles Xavier caught sight of Westminster House as his van negotiated a shoulder of pine-covered woodland. The red brick structure seemed to rise out of the hills around it, exuding the kind of quiet confidence many modern buildings lacked.

Though Xavier had seen the place ever so recently, it had been through the obscuring filter of an interdimensional barrier. As he gazed at Westminster now, without that impediment, it looked like a sturdy old friend—a good choice of institution for Jeremiah Saunders' grandson.

The professor turned in his seat to glance at Jeffrey. The young man was craning his neck to get a look at the grounds, his expression clearly one of eagerness. Apparently, he had come to feel comfortable there despite the briefness of his stay.

The leader of the X-Men was happy about that. He couldn't have departed Westminster knowing Jeffrey felt unsettled—especially after all the fellow had been through of late. The least Jeffrey deserved was a chance to rest, to gather himself.

"Nice area," Bobby observed thoughtfully from the driver's seat of their rented vehicle.

"Very nice," Warren agreed from the seat beside Jeffrey's. His blue skin was covered up by his image inducer he wore whenever he went out in public. "I'll bet it's even prettier in the spring."

"Maybe we ought to come back then," said Bobby. He turned to Xavier. "You know, just to check it out."

The professor was pleased by his companion's suggestion. "I see no reason why we shouldn't."

The road wound its way through the autumn hills a while longer. Then it brought them to the institution's rounded brick gatehouse. As they approached it, a security guard in a blue uniform came out and asked them the reason for their visit.

Bobby rolled down his window and poked his head out. "We're bringing back one of your clients," he explained.

Making a face, the guard peered into the van through a window. "Which one is he?"

Warren smiled and patted Jeffrey on the shoulder. "My friend here," he said. "His name's Jeffrey Saunders."

The guard's eyes opened wide. "Saunders? Holy . . . that's the kid who got away from the police, isn't it?" He took another look at Jeffrey. "Hard to believe he could do that."

Bobby smiled at him. "I guess you never know about someone just from looking at them. For all I know, you could be one of those mutants everybody's talking about."

The guard grunted good naturedly. "Yeah, right. Anyway, you can keep going. Mrs. Stoyanovich told me to expect you."

"Thanks," said Bobby.

Then he rolled up his window and drove the van up to the main building, where they found a small parking lot and slipped into an empty space. The guard must have phoned ahead, because Mrs. Stoyanovich was coming down the institution's front steps as they started to disembark.

Unfortunately, Xavier couldn't just levitate himself out of the vehicle. He had to wait patiently until Bobby went around to the back of the van and got his wheelchair for him, then helped him slide into it.

At the same time, Warren opened Jeffrey's door. Jeffrey got out and looked around wonderingly.

"Jeffrey, Jeffrey, Jeffrey," Mrs. Stoyanovich said, obviously relieved to see her charge again. She took his hands in hers with undisguised affection. "Whatever possessed you to take off like that?" she asked plaintively. "Don't you like it here?"

Bobby and Warren looked at the professor. He nodded, silently assuring them that he would take care of a response.

"It seems," Xavier told the red-haired woman, "that Jeffrey likes this place very much, if his expression a moment ago was any indication. I believe he just needs some time to adjust."

Mrs. Stoyanovich smiled understandingly at Jeffrey. "Most of our clients need that time," she said, "but they take it on the premises." She turned to the professor. "It just amazes me that he was able to travel twenty-some-odd miles to find your school. Obviously, he remembered the route from the last time he was there."

To the professor's knowledge, Jeffrey had never been to Salem Center before in his life. However, he didn't feel it was either prudent or necessary to tender the woman an explanation.

"Obviously," he replied.

Mrs. Stoyanovich shook Xavier's hand. "I can't thank you enough for all your help, Professor. However, it would probably be best if you and your friends didn't linger too long. We would like to try and get Jeffrey acclimated as quickly as possible."

"I understand completely," Xavier said. "However, I would like to give Jeffrey something to make him feel more at home here. I promise it won't take more than a few minutes."

The woman considered the request for a moment, then nodded. "I think we can spare that," she replied.

The professor glanced at Warren. "If you don't mind . . . ?"

"Not in the least," said the winged man.

He went back to the van and pulled out a box about a foot square. It was covered with red, white and blue wrapping paper with the name Salem Sporting Goods emblazoned on it.

Mrs. Stoyanovich was obviously curious about the box. However, she didn't press Xavier about its contents.

"You mentioned that you had a basketball court on the grounds," the professor recalled. "Could you show it to me?"

Of course, he already knew where it was. But Xavier couldn't have said that without revealing more than he wanted to.

"Of course," Mrs. Stoyanovich told him.

Then she escorted them all around the side of the main building. Beyond it, there was an asphalt basketball court. It was in excellent condition—even better than the professor remembered.

Jeffrey's eyes lit up when he caught sight of the court. He left the company of his friends and Mrs. Stoyanovich and jogged over to it with unbridled eagerness. Eyeing the nearer of the two baskets, he went through a pantomime of dribbling and shooting.

Warren glanced at Xavier. When the professor nodded, he walked over to Jeffrey and gave him the box he was carrying.

Jeffrey looked at it, then at Warren, then at Xavier. It was clear that he didn't know what he was supposed to do with it.

The professor shot him a mental image of his hands removing the wrapping paper and opening the box. Jeffrey frowned a little and took the gift. Then he began doing as the image suggested. When he got a glimpse of what was in the box, his frown turned into a grin.

Ripping the cardboard open the rest of the way, he took out a brand new basketball—one that would last for years, according to the clerk at the sporting goods store. As the wind pushed the wrapping paper and the empty box off the court, Jeffrey bounced the ball on the asphalt surface—one, twice, three times.

Then, without warning, he whirled and dribbled toward the nearer basket. When he got within a few feet of it, he launched himself off the ground, his feet appearing to climb an invisible stair.

Finally, when he reached the apex of his ascent, he tomahawked the ball into the basket. Man and ball reached the ground at about the same time. Grabbing the basketball, Jeffrey turned to Xavier.

The young man was grinning—and not just with happiness. He was grinning with gratitude as well.

No, the professor told him telepathically. *It is we who are grateful to you, Jeffrey. And I am the most grateful of all.*

Jeffrey seemed to absorb Xavier's thought for a moment. Then he turned around and dribbled in the direction of the basket again. His second dunk, which involved a half-spin in mid-air, was even more spectacular than the first.

"Wow," breathed Bobby, genuine awe in his voice. "They can use a guy like that on the Knicks."

"And you'd be his agent, I suppose?" Warren responded.

"I could do worse," Bobby told his teammate.

Mrs. Stoyanovich chuckled. "I see now why it was so important that we have a basketball court, Professor."

"Yes," said Xavier.

Jeffrey dunked the ball a few more times. Then, still grinning, he sat down on the court and tapped out a rhythm on it. It seemed to the professor that the young man would be all right here.

Goodbye, he told Jeffrey telepathically. *I will come back to visit with you from time to time.*

Jeffrey stared at him for a moment. Then, getting to his feet, he tucked his ball under his arm and came over to Xavier.

Before the professor had an inkling of what Jeffrey intended, the younger man bent over and wrapped his free arm around Xavier. Then he hugged him as hard as he could.

The mutant wasn't often inclined to display his emotions—especially in public. However, he made an exception this time. Embracing Jeffrey's broad, muscular shoulders, he hugged Jeffrey back.

After a second or two, Jeffrey stood up again and Xavier let him go. Then the professor turned to Mrs. Stoyanovich. "We'll be leaving now," he announced evenly. "Please keep me informed as to Jeffrey's progress."

"I will," the woman promised him.

Taking Jeffrey's arm, she guided him back toward the main building. Xavier watched them go for a moment, Jeffrey still clutching his new basketball. Then he turned to Bobby.

"If you please," he said.

"Of course," his protégé responded, knowing exactly what he meant. Taking hold of the professor's wheelchair, Bobby pushed him back in the direction of their van.

Warren fell in beside them. "There goes a special individual," he observed, pumping a thumb over his shoulder.

Bobby glanced back at Jeffrey. "Very special," he agreed.

"I just hope he realizes how valuable he was," said Warren. "I hope he has some idea of what a great job he did."

Bobby turned to their mentor. "What do you think, sir?"

Without swiveling in his chair, Xavier plumbed Jeffrey's mind for a second. Then he nodded in response. "Yes, Bobby, I believe he does."

When they reached the van, Bobby wheeled the professor over to the passenger's side door and opened it. Only then did Xavier allow himself a look back at Jeffrey.

He felt a pang as he saw Mrs. Stoyanovich gently guide Jeffrey up the steps of Westminster House. After all, the professor had enjoyed a special link with the fellow. As a result, the professor knew him better than anyone else in the world.

He wasn't able to interpret all of Jeffrey's thoughts, tangled and incomplete as they were. But it was clear to him that the young man felt better about himself now than at any other time in his life.

Xavier was pleased. If anyone had earned the right to feel proud of what he had accomplished over the last few days, it was Jeffrey Saunders.

But Jeffrey wasn't the only one who had come away from the experience with a new perspective. The professor had been forcibly reminded of something he was sometimes inclined to forget . . .

"How little a handicap means when one's spirit refuses to be vanquished," he said out loud.

His X-Men looked at him and smiled.

"Amen to that," said Bobby.

Yes, thought Xavier. *Amen indeed.*